THE DAIRY OF ANNE FRANK

AND

MORE WISH FULFILLMENT IN THE NOUGHTIES

(THREE NOVELLAS)

ANDREW TONKOVICH

ISBN 978-0-9971257-3-3
Library of Congress Control Number:2019907488

Author photo: Yasser Marte

BLUE JAY INK

Published in the United States by
Blue Jay Ink
451 A East Ojai Ave.
Ojai, California 93023
bluejayink.com

THE DAIRY OF ANNE FRANK

AND

MORE WISH FULFILLMENT IN THE NOUGHTIES

(THREE NOVELLAS)

THE DAIRY OF ANNE FRANK

OR

SHOW BIZ IS MY LIFE!

(A PEDAGOGICAL FANTASIA)

AFTER PHILIP ROTH

"Do any human beings ever realize life while they live it--
every, every minute?" No. The saints and poets, maybe –
they do some."
— Thorton Wilder, *Our Town*

Everyone, real or invented, deserves the open destiny of life."
— Grace Paley, *A Conversation With My Father*

"Our time presents a unique opportunity for learning
by means of humor – a perceptive or incisive joke can be
more meaningful than platitudes lying between two covers."
— Marshall McLuhan,
The Medium is the Massage: An Inventory of Effects

BEFORE THE ACCIDENT I'd worked for weeks pretty much alone on the staging of my new play – admittedly, my first and only play to that point — an elaborate and unshy morality tale based on one of my Composition student's persistent typos, a kind of revenge story meets revisionist fairy tale posing as good clean family fun, if your family was up for that kind of fun. If perhaps your family was a good, clean family. Mine wasn't, not particularly, as it turned out. We were hygienic and plenty fun, but it was possible that we were not good, or at least not good enough, if by "family" and "we" you meant mostly me, part-time writing teacher, wife and mother and ex-daughter, newbie playwright, which actually sounds like a lot of people now that I count myself up like that, lucky me.

Nonetheless, as I am fond of saying these days. That's all: just "Nonetheless." What a great word! It has everything, and nothing, too. And, yes, even "less."

It's my mantra, lately. My womantra, ha ha, suggesting confidence, wry humor and sarcasm about my unlikely embrace of, yes, confidence, humor and sarcasm, if absent any evidence to actually support confidence about anything at all in the face of tragedy, not even the comic and cruel kind so often offered up in second-rate dramas - "dramadies," they are called lately, annoyingly - which cannot make up their minds, finally, if they are serious or funny, allegorical or realistic. Where so much urgent and necessary information, the assumptions upon which so much might depend — the main character turning out to be, yes, blind, dead, or perhaps a talking dog! — is deliberately withheld from the audience or reader until it is most cruel not to any longer — woof! — and where that singular important and vital and urgent detail is then meant to be a revelation somehow, instead of just sadism, duplicity or condescension. Or, worse, loaded with plenty of atonal smart-ass ambivalence and hip, self-conscious overwriting and implied off-stage commentary and long, difficult pauses in between, and close-ups, actors staring off into space, with too many opportunities (if you ask me and, no, you didn't but still) for the more clever or angry members of the audience to stop and reconsider, at last, the puzzling imagery of, yes, that defining "face of tragedy" metaphor itself and its logical unavoidable, unattractive relations: the nose of tragedy, receding hairline of tragedy, lower intestine of tragedy, sagging bosom or other worn and shriveling body parts of tragedy, please, please, please do not make me go on!

Nota bene, I find it hard, you will observe, to complete a sentence for all the interruptions, distractions, digressions, the obligation to complete my modest project of singlehandedly re-deeming drama, wresting it from the hands of the always-calling-attention to itself crowd instead of just maybe paying attention, please. Even now, after what turned out to be my big impossible success. And what does real, genuine tragedy or comedy look like anyway and, more to the point, when?

Or to finish a thought either. Or a lecture, joke or sto-ry. Or, yes, as it happened, a play. Things happened so quickly, and yet even then were somehow still interrupted, interruptible. Somebody's cell phone went off in class, and loud. I asked whose, and would they please turn it off. Female students checked their purses, the men and boys their pockets and backpacks. I continued, reminding us all of Wittgenstein's observation that the limits of our language are the limits of our worlds and then it turned out, embarrassingly, that it was, yes, my own phone, left on, because I barely know how to use it much less turn it off. My credibility was certainly damaged, not that anybody noticed, and not enough to matter, not enough to undermine my so-called teacherly authority in the classroom. It was, of course, a wrong number. I answered and hung up and apologized big-time and put the device in my briefcase, but also felt something like the personification, right there, of the human exception who proved the rule, so awkward was I, so unaware of my own power, so unfamiliar was I with my own ringtone, so unused was my cell. I liked the attention. From then on I kept the machine on purposely just about all of the time, turned the volume up as high as it would go and hoped and hoped that somebody, anybody, would call again between 8 AM and 9:50 in the morning so that I could make another useless point at my own expense, offer a genuine "teaching moment" and perhaps a learning moment, too.

*   *   *

Thank goodness, then, for ellipses, those short rows of connecting dots in between so much on the page. My own lines, spoken and written and thought, quietly and loudly, seemed to me at the time all either too short or too long, and then, with those three tiny, sadistic dots in a row, ironically even that much longer. As a beginning playwright, I was the Goldilocks of syntax, conversation and contemporary amateur dramatic writing for the stage. I seemed to locate discomfort, then something slightly better, or worse, then lose it, or find it again, and off we'd go, cold porridge...broken chair...breaking into and entering a home full of vacationing bears, with those three helpful punctuation marks left in between, to taunt and call attention, little stepping stones. Of course I overused them, my script looking like it had been overly perforated by some crazy, reckless dot-making machine and missing only the helpful instruction to "tear here."

Yes, perhaps I was once — even, okay, honestly, only a few short weeks ago — unhappy, frustrated, bitter and disappointed with the whole construct itself, of writing anything at all, quietly angry as only a long-time if also part-time English teacher can be, certainly more than fed up with the expectations of the basic indented all-American paragraph, topic sentence and thesis statement, all of which I was supposed to be teaching, not to mention (which people say when they actually do mention it) the supposedly democratic give and take of the parts of speech organized in a straight horizontal line, on a page, double-spaced, in a personal or analytic essay, which lately had not seemed to me to express, reflect or resemble anything like real life (or at least my life) in terms of word choice, punctuation, cell phones, bears, and where a sentence felt to me more like a judgment, a verdict or punishment. And where the verdict was guilty or, at best, a hung jury, a mistrial, a juror removed or the judge refusing to come out of his quarters, crazy or drunk or incompetent, at any rate a miscarriage of justice with me having to reread the student drafts over and over and over, only to encounter the very same mistake each time.

This weariness, confusion and ambivalence generally made for too-long monologues (as above and, alas, below...so get used to it!), mostly delivered to myself, my favorite if increasingly weary audience, and all ending up in the same way, in my angrily whispered one-word catechisms of only moderately useful affirmation or surrender, depending. But frequently with those meaningful and yet otherwise useless three tiny dots in between, the letter "S," as it happens, as constructed in Morse Code, that most familiar feature of the universally recognized call of distress, mayday, mayday, a cry for help, the dot-dot-dot before the dash-dash-dash, dot-dot-dot.

Meanwhile and still and, yes, none...the...less, I had found at about this time, immediately before the accident — if that's what it even was — and the staging of my terrific new play that "nonetheless" had the added benefit or detriment (you choose) of being one of those mysterious and dangerous words which confused and disoriented a person (me, at least) if you heard it too often, stared at it too long, said it too frequently, took it apart, perhaps began to consider its actual meaning, the mathematics of it, by way of how it actually appeared in print and sounded wrong or odd if you spoke it too slowly, if you suddenly noticed what was not there in it, or spotted the frightening n-e-t spells "net" in the middle and, disoriented and overwhelmed, fell right in.

You never knew where one of these traps might be hidden, and needed to quickly take evasive action. I found that reading very fast helped. Then again, so did reading very slowly. Or even reading at only moderate speed. And out loud, to others, if they were available or willing, though my natural audience was mostly not. My lovely young only-child daughter Sasha was off at middle school or lacrosse or chorus, and my tenured professor husband was busy at work, teaching literature instead of, like me, teaching remedial and compulsory and endlessly re-introductory introduction to academic essay-writing classes. Or, best of all, just not reading those student essays at all, only thinking about reading them and, honestly, trying hard not to think of them at all either, not even, which was not as easy as it sounds. Easier. Making coffee instead of reading them, checking my email messages, getting up to stretch or do laundry, or playing with the cat.

The cat, c-a-t, was short enough, thankfully, small enough, fat enough to be always and only a cat. It just lay there in a comfortable and cat-sized sheath of warm sunlight on the cluttered kitchen table, or taunted me by resting its fat furry head on the tall stack marked "Essay # 2 – Tues/Thurs 8 AM."

Helpfully, there is only and comfortingly just an "at" in cat by way of other, smaller, complicating and distracting words. We have exactly one c-a-t at our house. It is a fat cat at that so, yes, fun to say!

The animal is healthy, large but not quite in its prime, though it is numerically certainly finite. Arithmetically, this particular cat can be divided only by one and by itself, "at" being a subset of cat. We do not own a d-o-g. Same deal though. There is "do," which is kind of right for dogs, whereas cats are less active, more existential, as in "at." (Gee whiz, you can certainly learn a lot about almost everything by mostly ignoring your responsibilities, procrastinating, thinking hard, playing with your house pet, and not doing your job.)

Our own big, fat nimble unambiguous big-boy tabby is, thankfully, just exactly what he seems to be, and he seemed to me to be there to help me, or at least pretend to, purring and acting exactly as he should have, accepting just the right amount of interest or attention or affection as he could endure from me, and then standing up, turning, and disappearing.

As it happened, I was actually, briefly, tempted to document this phenomenon, to dramatize it, to give the animal, or at least the short, perfect word for the animal, a small part herself in my potentially terrific revisionist stage play about the Holocaust, of all things — a brief cat cameo, a walk-on, a prance-on, by my own terrific pet himself or the representation of my pet, an actor in a cat costume with whiskers and tail and ears or, perhaps somebody only holding a small sign with just the word "cat" written on it — but I was running out of time as it was, even before the genuinely but still comically tragicomic development which led to my husband's injury and short or perhaps long-term or even permanent memory loss, and another, more famous cat's starring role. The show was on, after all, in only a week and a half. Designing and sewing a fat cat suit on top of all the other costumes was just not going to happen, nor was I likely to recruit at the last minute a child or very tiny round person to fit into one, and so art would have to imitate life in some other equally unlikely production, perhaps a second original and similarly impossible play about justice and epistemology and proofreading, that one set in an animal shelter maybe, a P.D. Eastman-esque tale with rhyming couplets and fanatical members of PETA and the search for a missing parent or pet, a la *Are You My Mother?* and *Go, Dog, Go.*

.

*   *   *

My twelve-year-old daughter Sasha, a "pre-teen," as she likes to call herself, mockingly, of the whole artificially constructed and commercially commodified life-cycle paradigm, often finished my sentences for me as kids will, occasionally coming to my rescue in fact. No, she did not do it so much to help me out but to just move things along for both of us, Mom, showing her befuddled old mother both pity and affection, as well as her impatience, all in a kind of easy telepathy.

Either way, I appreciated it, mostly. She was certainly handy to have around, my precocious and beautiful girl, and seemed to relish the authority and utility of bringing some end to my otherwise endless un-declarative sentences, digressions, self-interruptions, neologisms, my failure to locate my reading glasses and my amateur linguisto-philosophical musings.

My husband Jake was distracted plenty because of his extra administrative work at the college, the result of chairing the English Department this busy academic year, "observing" teachers in their classrooms, sitting on hiring committees, disciplining faculty, mediating squabbles, writing letters of recommendation, producing curriculum and establishing Student Learning Outcomes (SLO's, referred to, instructively, ominously, awkwardly — you choose — as "slows") and also by the busy near-end of the fall semester, Halloween, Veterans' Day and then Thanksgiving, too, but distracted mostly by his own personal stalker. More on her, much more, later. As a result, and understandably, he wasn't listening much to me either.

*　　*　　*

Which is all to say, long-windedly, that reading anything at all could therefore (and, yes, nonetheless!) become paralyzing and disorienting for me, especially when it came to very small words that were not, unfortunately, easy or reliable descriptors of domesticated animals (cat, dog, bird, fish) or, okay, very big words also, all familiar enough, but which looked so worryingly foreign and unfamiliar, inspiring something like that panic of momentarily not recalling your own phone number, PIN, account password or Social Security number, or waking up from a deep mid-day nap and not knowing where you were or even who.

No doubt this affliction, syndrome, compulsion, hobby was the result of reading and commenting on the dozens, by now hundreds of earlier drafts of those same mostly lousy community college student essays whose final versions I had let pile up in Week Twelve of an interminable sixteen-week semester, all written on the topic of the famous journal kept by a Jewish-Austrian girl hiding in an attic in Amsterdam seventy-five years ago, each offering their bloodless, if mostly sincere thesis that it was certainly very wrong (!) that she'd had to hide up there, that the students hoped that *they* wouldn't have to hide in any nasty "random" attic themselves but that it was kind of "awesome" and *exiting*, meaning exciting, that she was such a good *writter*, meaning writer, and so on, disappointingly, but all of them taking their baby steps, I still hoped, stubbornly, toward context, proofreading, critical thinking, historical analysis, civic literacy, political engagement and strong complete sentences, not to mention — was this really too ambitious a hope? — absolute and unequivocal and unshy positions on the Nazi occupation of other people's countries meaning, yes, being strongly *against* it.

★   ★   ★

So possibly, yes, I used "nonetheless" in self-defense, sending out that strange word's invisible paralyzing syntax-scrambling anti-brain-ray while allowing people to think that I, Hope Mary-Anne Watterson (nee Kaminski) of Las Palmas, California, USA, itself a nearly fictional locale in its exemplary ordinariness and prosaic typicality, was all about insisting on affirmation or personal grit in the face of unacknowledged struggles and unstartlingly predictable challenges, which of course I was also, sort of, when I tried to, if not completely by choice, maybe out of need for just more choices, finally, than only the frustration or loneliness which comes from being around so darn many good, wholesome, well-meaning teachers and students, so many patient and enduring and nice people, unstubborn and sympathetic and clean and good and willing to suffer, no, perhaps even enjoy, finally, every kind of foolishness, uncare, sloppy-silly misapprehension and cruelty to history, the written word, Jews and Gentiles and believers and nonbelievers, it did not seem to matter.

"Hope," I said, to myself, loudly, "Yes, you!" when I had

gotten tired of the other, when there seemed nobody else around to explain, to listen, to affirm or contradict me or to interrupt my good talking-to of myself, the windows of my living room wide open to engage a warm Indian summer in late fall, the sprinklers out front automatically on if, as usual, at somehow the exact wrong time of day, essays stacked up or spread out or arranged alphabetically, but in every way otherwise still completely untouched.

Because, sure, it's mostly nice having a name like mine to call out, with its affirmation or encouragement, like perhaps Grace or Charity or Joy, that big girl-family of weirdly Puritan-sounding proper nouns-as-proper adjectives, their first name somehow modifying their last. Or even, perhaps Nice. Of course, nobody I know is named Nice, or Kind or Despair. Not yet, anyway. Stick around. The entire world's a stage, and we are all, well, you know, writing plays about it, and looking for backers, inviting an audience of our family and neighbors and friends, and casting actors who often very much resemble ourselves, clumsy if talented stand-ins for other real people, whose soliloquies turn out to sound so much like those looped mini-sermons and pep talks, private addresses, angry rants and digressive political observations we have tried our best — which was not really very good — to quiet but, happily, unhappily, have failed to, and nonetheless.

*　　*　　*

Or maybe I'd stop to utter my own full and complete given name, to sing it with the explicit hyphenation in-between the Mary and the Ann because, as my own parents explained, endlessly, two nouns together preceding another noun required that short, trim horizontal ambassador of adjectival joining. My good, dear folks, once both high school English teachers who loved each other, they really put the fun in hyphen.

I missed them lately, especially, lost at sea on a doomed luxury cruise in a raging storm somewhere in the hypotenuse of the Bermuda triangle or, if you wanted to know what really happened (and you don't, believe me), both in fact killed too-slowly by Alzheimer's, almost simultaneously, expiring in adjoining beds at the same local geriatric care facility, lost to each other and not even knowing it, or maybe knowing but unable to do, or think, anything about it. Timing was everything, and believe me it was just too much or, as so many say, way much.

Or maybe, just for more laughs on such a weekday afternoon, I'd embrace the useless honorific, "Professor," because I was of course absolutely not a professor (despite my inclination to profess, as you see, all over the place). I am actually an "adjunct part-time instructor," contingent faculty, temporary, non-Senate faculty, freeway flyer, no tenure, no health benefits, no officially guaranteed work next year, no office of my own at the community college but married, luckily, to a handsome, wonderful, smart man who has himself rehired me each year and on whose health and dental and vision insurance his whole family — our family — depended. This was not really so much to laugh about but it was somehow esteeming, or distracting — both, and each together that clever strategy of flattery by which so many part-timers were tricked into working under these conditions —

and just plain fun, with me pretending sometimes, right there in my own living room, to be both roles, that of the student, hand raised or not, and the professor too. I loved calling on myself, and then responding or, better yet, not calling on myself and lecturing on and on and on about whatever I wanted, no interruption.

Yes, sometimes, class, it is such a burden being not only a person but a concept too, and a lousy concept at that. An adjunct instructor, indeed a "part-timer" is what they called me, even my own husband, though mostly in his emails. "Adjunctivitis" is the self-deriding name-ailment-syndrome constructed by our multi-campus cadre of super-ironic part-time pedagogues who occasionally find each other in the halls or restrooms or between classes, pink eye-contagious in their shared helplessness, political estrangement, mutual un-aid and self-disregard.

Luckily, I have a nickname too, which helps me in moments requiring more of a sense of personal self-worth, the more the merrier. Sometimes I used that, whimsically. Part-timily, you might say, by way of an incantation on a weekday afternoon.

"Hopey," I might say to myself and to the cat, too. "Hopefully!" Then, laughing, "Nonetheless!" and "Nonetheless, kitty-mitty! Nonetheless, extremely cat-like pet!" I might say further, elaborating on a theme. Or as an interrogative: "Nonetheless?" I might pretend to grab my invisible fencing foil, put on my invisible hat and invisible big nose and, red ball-point in hand, like Cyrano, advance then on that big stack of student essays, sneak up on them, holler *En garde!* including at that particular one on top with the deeply wounding if amusing and instructive (!) title which inspired so much, and then, knees bent, scooting in graceful steps, move forward, then retreat, then deliver a fast, precise, deadly swish of the air just above it, painlessly, humanely, of course, if uselessly.

The deed done, I would offer in my best very worst French accent, "Nun-zuh-less!" I hold my imaginary foil to my forehead, and bow with a flourish. Some fun, that.

*   *   *

Notes, sketches, other people's scripts, my own working copy of the play, books marked full of post-its, a *New York Times* article print-out or two or ten, photographs of my famous historical subject, a clipboard. All lay scattered on the massive oak table in our family room, stacks and more stacks of unread, un-marked, ungraded student papers, in manila folders, loose-leaf binders, most of it secured by favorite old bricks and lovely smooth stones gathered from the backyard, a horseshoe, a rusted pot-metal weathervane of a now tragically tail-less sperm whale (wind damage) but cardinal points still intact around him in a flimsy halo, a polished purple and white geode, objects heavy and solid, and suggesting both utility and commitment and yet more whimsy, always, and of imagination and control of the imagination, not to mention protection from it, none of any of this flotsam able to get away from me were, inexplicably, a big if welcome wind to blow through or somebody try to mess with it, whoever that might be.

Well, nobody and nothing there on the table fought back

from the dining room table or in its vicinity or answered, thank goodness, except me, and yet this further contrivance, this disorientation became inspiration for me in itself, matching nicely the small, manageable tumult of everyday life which you dealt with, didn't you, especially if your tenured full-time faculty husband had for months been dealing with a crazy girl student stalker, poor guy? I often didn't know where he even was — physically, I mean — because he and the school and school security wanted "her" not to know, and the rest of us were frequently just helpful human camouflage, blinds, and decoys on his personal security safari. Jake moved around a lot, to stay away from her, one step or room or hall ahead. It was, he confessed, difficult to keep track of where he wasn't, so much was he on the move, so briefly ubiquitous, then not, a purposely moving target, and for him to still let me know his actual whereabouts or was-abouts, all to avoid her. Which meant that often I didn't know when he really wanted me or anybody to know either, might even be telling me some innocuous untruth about his whereabouts. It was confusing, if purposely, and alienating and stressful. We would have noticed or lamented that we were coming apart as a couple, except that we didn't really have the time to lament, and it was so obvious anyway as to make noticing redundant and useless.

Sometimes I almost didn't recognize him, which was also the point of course. My sweet, handsome hubby had for weeks now left the house in the mornings wearing a funny hat, dark glasses, and a fright-wig. This actually made him more noticeable in a tight-knit neighborhood and small town as ours, with a vigorous Neighborhood Watch, some of whom were not yet clued in. Sample call to 9-1-1: "There's a circus clown in front of my next door neighbor's house. He looks dangerous." So who else could it be, watchers of neighborhood, but Jake?

He felt he had to do something, anything, and that being more noticeable might indeed attract more notice, and therefore safety, despite him being unrecognizable as himself, and to himself and maybe, somehow, to his victimizer. This was a crime-fighting syllogism so perverse as to be impossible to argue with, and which our avuncular old Las Palmas Chief of Police Bob Myers, a gentle widower nearing retirement, had recommended as good for keeping her at bay. She appeared and disappeared, attended classes only irregularly now, did not check in with anybody, and might strike anytime, anywhere. So that almost everyone in town knew where he was, by which I mean had just been, was going to, could arrive next, an oddly dressed fellow who couldn't really be anybody else other than himself, whose amateur role-playing at pretend anonymity spoke to the confusion that would ensue — spoiler alert!, and big-time — around identity and responsibility and throw so much into doubt, which turns out to be a difficult if productive place to inhabit, if on a nice street next-door to expectation, adjacent dreams, down the block from belief and disbelief, a nice duplex whose respective embrace of and suspension we are meant, alternately to exercise, as if picking which neighbor to visit, rob, ignore, share a casserole with or deliver misdelivered mail.

*   *   *.

She, our anti-heroine, was less easy to find, to notice, and might also perhaps be in disguise, who knew? We locked the doors at night, set the security alarm, turned on the outdoor spots, closed the shades and then, tucked safely in bed, struggled to get to dreamland and, of course, could not.

The doctor prescribed a nifty drug, his and hers, a bottle for each of us. Doxepin, it was called, an anti-seizure medicine, he told us. You will sleep, soundly, with a rich dream life, he said, and wake up extremely drowsy but well-rested and reconciled with man and beast. He was a real poet. I pointed out that we didn't, either of us, actually have seizures. "You don't have appendicitis either, Hope," he said. Everybody laughed. He was also pretty funny for a doctor. "Could I have some of that for her?" I had asked, meaning the kooky psycho-babe husband-stalker. Everybody laughed again. They thought I was kidding. I guess I was pretty funny, too, especially considering that I was being completely serious.

*   *   *

Weeks and weeks of trying to describe, to accommodate, to acknowledge and also to ignore the future defendant had changed the way we thought, slept, ate, spoke. "Her" and "she." These were the pronouns we'd lately used more and more around the house for Crazy Chinese Stalker-Girl, weirdly, integrating her into conversation exactly the way Jake and I once had for our own dear baby daughter fetus, when she had transitioned from a gesture, an idea, a concept to our softly uttered ambiguous little "it" to becoming an entity, to becoming a female personal pronoun all her own, especially after we were shown the ultrasound in the doctor's office.

Jake, who in happier times rode his ancient three-speed red Schwinn to campus, with a basket and old-timey bell, now drove to work with colleagues, or joined the vanpool, or borrowed a car and parked down the street, and walked back to our place with a chaperone, adorned in his silly disguise, with neighbors up and down our street waving and greeting him along the way, somehow both happily defeating the very purpose — a cheerfully awkward phrase, "very purpose," if ever there was one, as in "That was very purpose of you, him, her — of his feint and fulfilling it too, and perhaps pointing me in that direction, of multiplicity and confusion, toward writing my famous play in the first place.

I often heard them exclaiming. "Hi, Jake. Hi, Prof," they said. "Look, everybody, it's Jake Watterson." The fourth wall, they call it in theater, was easily broken, cover blown. The whole block was acting, and it was pretty bad acting. It was *The Truman Show* or *The Hunger Games* or perhaps only everybody going along with what they call in Sociology "the social construction of reality," a term or concept unfamiliar to so many of my students, and to which many were actively hostile, resistant when I insisted on its verity by way of explaining human behavior, expectations, language, jokes, even human empathy. It was a concept I felt I had some responsibility to defend, especially lately. But many of my students insisted that reality was entirely individual, subjective, discretionary, perhaps even optional, as if it were only another app on their phones, available but not perhaps actually a requirement of the class, their major or of life, something that came included with the tiny portable machine and why, Mrs. Watterson, had I even brought it up, why was I so off-topic, they asked, and would any of this be on the test?

But who else could it — he, Jake — be, dressed like every stranger in town you never met, every visitor who had never walked that street or visited our neighborhood except somebody who was pretending to, or not to? This was a proud and tightly knit community, after all, its big blue sign with the civic eyeball announcing an official welcome or, more practically and honestly, a default "Please go away, now" requested situated at the entrance to our tract. Either way, it promised that we, neighbors united, reported "unusual activities," which of course nobody actually did. Or usual activities, either, for that matter. It was, of course, difficult to distinguish among so many activities, circumstances, accidents, situations, even events that were less than activities.

Jake played along, a good sport. He liked to tip his hat or stroke his fake moustache or adjust his clumsy wig a la Dick Van Dyke. We were all trying to have something like fun with it. Except that no, things were not what they seemed. Or they were, unfortunately, exactly as they seemed. We were scared, unnerved, or should have been. Embracing dramatic writing, however allegorical and punny and clumsily didactic, with overdrawn characters and singing, talking, dancing farm animals might not exactly have been inevitable here but it certainly did not hurt. It was there, and I took it, as William Mulholland famously advised about the water he and the schemers of Los Angeles stole from up north and then built a long pipeline to put it in, the famous aqueduct which runs right past our town today as it happens (so much happens, has happened!) and on its way to Southern California, before the pumps famously broke, a dam collapsed, innocent people died, people called Mulholland a big crook and, out of grief or guilt, as many people may not know, he pulled out all of his own teeth with a pair of simple pliers. Why his teeth, I always wondered. Poor William Mulholland. And, seriously, I really do need to reset the clock-timer on the automatic sprinkler system, another semi-autonomous machine whose power I have ignored, underestimated, perhaps envied. There's a drought on, after all.

But I digress which, yes, I admit I did a lot, both in class, at home, in composing the play about Anne Frank and especially, mostly, in my mind. In some of those places it mattered; in others, not so much. I was never sure which, or to whom, but I had the sense all along that this distinction was important to somebody, if impossible, finally, to determine who. Whom. Maybe to me. Soon. I give something like credit to poor old toothless Bill M., after all. Pulling out teeth was new, meant something different than hair, or eyes or, toe nails or whatever self-crippling procedure might to that point have been available on the menu of masochistic punishment, redemption or penance for human grief and guilt. You had to give credit to the engineer-genius for coming up with the dental self-extraction angle.

*　　*　　*

Jake often entered our house through the garage. He hollered that he was home, Honey, and slammed the door behind him, hard. I'd first hear the click of the lock, and the turn of the deadbolt. He took alternate routes from work to home, sometimes waited for his official school-appointed, school-sanctioned chaperones including the campus cops, the community college vice-president and the Chemistry teacher, a small timid-seeming man who assured us that he did martial arts, as if he were going to use karate or jujitsu or something against the skinny-kooky girl student. There had been a lot of people around, all the time, each of them looking out for Jake or, more accurately, looking out for her as in "Look out!," but you can see the confusion about victim and victimizer, looking and looking for and looking out and looking out for, target and targetter, both having the small, important, perhaps instructive word "get" in them. Nonetheless. Nonetheless!

Jake coordinated his movements, or thought he did, or pretended to, to avoid any real chance of running into the mildly insane young woman international student about whom nobody could officially really do anything, they assured us — not the school, not the police — and to most especially not find himself alone with her for fear that she would again behave inappropriately, which was, ironically, the go-to descriptor of his own behavior thus far, though her doing an unsolicited strip-tease for him in office hours is what had gotten everybody using that phrase — "inappropriate behavior" — in the first place.

*   *   *

Crazy Girl's real name was, like her, something thin and beautiful and Chinese, but almost nobody west of Taipei, Taiwan, ROC, could pronounce it so she went by, you guessed it, Tiffany. That super-popular nom de nutty was, at least, the English-language name which was written, finally, on the restraining order, on the class roster, on the essays she (or somebody) had written for my husband's class until she dropped, and on the personalized California vanity license plate on her brand-new Beemer, "TIFFNEE," the custom pink, white and black Hello Kitty-themed custom luxury convertible which I'd first noticed parked at midnight across the street from us early in the semester, after she'd suddenly declared her love for my husband Jake in only her expensive bra and panties, before the episode in the backyard, the scary-weird handwritten letters and emails written to our Sasha, telephone calls at 3 AM and, of course, most damagingly, the successful attack from above.

*   *   *

Our own sane and good and clean little girl-woman "pre-teen" daughter was at a friend's house on the Thursday afternoon of the accident, which is what the insurance called it, or the incident, which is what the police called it, or the occurrence, which is what Tiffany's lawyer, who struck me as a kind of mystic in his sharkskin suit and silk scarves, Italian shoes and his fingers closed in some kind of bespoke mudra, later called it.

I was working at home. As each moment when I wasn't sleeping and dreaming or still not sleeping or not dreaming or teaching or not teaching or reading or not reading and therefore also not commenting on and therefore, yes, not grading at all the stack of almost-end-of-semester student draft essays on *The Diary of a Young Girl*, I was sewing costumes for the show — my show! — working out the projections, recording or editing music and voice-overs and sound effects, painting pieces of the set or searching our local thrift stores in person or on online at Craig's List or E-Bay for props (pails, red-checked shirts, a cow costume or two or three, if I was lucky, and I usually was) often doing all of these at once.

The play was titled, yes, no kidding, *The Dairy of Anne Frank*, challenging both credulity and good taste or maybe it was called *The Dairy (sic) of Anne Frank*, just to make sure, *sic erat scriptum*. Thus it was written, or rewritten. The theater manager and I were still unsure, debating about whether to include the Latin in the actual title, on the printed program or up on the marquee, or whether to include it anywhere at all. That decision was just one more item on the long to-do list I'd kept on my clipboard, of questions, notes, reminders and last-minute possible script changes, staging or lighting problems, and advice and direction for my actors.

Writing the play had begun early in the term as an escape, and, clumsily obvious I see now, an exercise in both cheerful indignation and the absolutely required if suspect professional generosity, however twisted, of a long-time writing teacher, both typical of my line of work, the remediation of our world and its young readers and writers on Tuesday and Thursday mornings via the discipline and example and cooperation of open-hearted democratic public education. It had become been my effort to teach somebody and, yes, to teach somebody a lesson, too, and I believed that the play succeeded and failed — satisfyingly —- on both counts in a way in which real life had not, which seemed right, though I was content to leave that big critical and popular judgment up to the audience, and the reviewers (assuming there would even be any) and to go for the time being mostly for provocation, easy humor, the juxtaposition of dreaming as against the fulfillment of dreams, the evocation of a long-forgotten memory, all of it and more (!) an amateur fabulist's dare to have somebody call me on it all, to stand up and say that, no, Hope Watterson, none of this could happen, not ever, had not happened, might not happen, or even should not happen.

But then, when the play was done, I would stand up, yes, or arrive from behind the curtain on the stage where it would have be read or performed, and I would sweep my hand in the direction of the set to acknowledge that it had indeed, waving at the props and actors as if to say too late, people, there is, or might be, wish fulfillment fulfilled, sweet revenge achieved, emotional compensation made good, righteous indignation celebrated and here, just now, in this very theater (as in "That is very theater of you!") in my tribute to the late, great malopropistarianist-comic Norm Crosby, my hero and mentor and perspiration lately, all of it at once.

And then I would spread my arms so very wide in acknowledgment, take a deep bow, accept the applause of my colleagues, students, friends and neighbors and call out the play's unlikely star and its inspiration, trepidation, constipation for appreciation too, because I owed it all to him, didn't I?

And if the show closed after only just that one night or even if it was well-enough received, either way I would have reconciled at least temporarily with my own native tongue, sometimes called a mother tongue, made peace or armistice with the war on words, of words, for words, against words that was my struggle, which if you translate it back into the original German is a plenty troubling phrase in these circumstances, or any circumstance, not that anybody would likely notice or care, not unless you called attention to it, which was of course my real job, a second job — calling attention. I worked at that occupation, preoccupation, if only for myself, was my own boss, self-employed and could afford to lose it because, first, it was (so far) unpaid, and it was more than part-time anyway, meaning that I was doing it when I was supposed to be doing what I was supposed to be doing and getting poorly paid for, which was grading those drafts, or sleeping soundly, two things which, actually, I was not doing.

And besides, I had the other part-time job as an adjunct teacher to fall back on, the one where I was supposed to ignore what was most obvious and pretend, where I was supposed to accept, compromise, accommodate, sit still for, be insulted, taken for granted and otherwise surrender (and still be nice about it), something almost nobody is required to do except teachers.

*   *   *

The exemplary student, the subject of this clumsy object lesson gone mad, the putative potential dramatic star of my cautionary tale of a remedial Composition writer and his-our-your moral obligation to be ethical and intelligent too (to credit Lionel Trilling, among others), that otherwise harmless young and hirsute Arab boy-man, had, naturally, other problems beyond just being enrolled in my Composition class, poor devil, and his all-around illiteracy. First was pronunciation, which is of course different than prounouniation, which is itself just a very funny non-word to mispronounce or — why not? — mispronunce. In some misguided attempt at cheerful public relations, political negotiation or reconciliation on behalf of Middle East diplomatic relations, he insisted on calling himself "ally" instead of the way you'd expect to hear a presumably Arabic name, his, Ali, like the greatest heavyweight boxer ever and every other "Ali" you'd ever known or imagined was hijacking and/or blowing up the airplane you were on.

Still, I admired the gesture, Ali offering to be everybody's friend like that, ambassador of goodwill, though I had corrected his other misspellings and word choices over and over and over again for weeks, recommended spell and grammar check, offered the standard editing mark right next to the circled word, written "sp" on the board for him and the whole class to see and talk about together, brought in a dictionary and finally taken in my reading of his subsequent drafts to underlining, circling, and offering, yes, "sic" in brackets, as if and thusly.

And, yes, of course, I had sent "Ally" to free tutoring and to the campus Writing Center for help, where he did who knows what. Still, he would not, after five drafts, miles of lines and ar-rows and circles and ever-lengthening rows of question marks drawn in red, blue, black ink, a happy face just that one time (for encouragement, god help me) and even a sad face (for another kind of message and some levity, too), change that one mistake, or even acknowledge it.

For my part, I would not, absolutely, violate my policy: I would not, I swore, tell anybody the answer outright. Or out-wrong. I would not correct their work for them, damn it. That was not my job. This was of course a stupid and delusional and arrogant policy, and I see now that I was in writing my original play trying to change it in that parallel world which I'd created, imagined and written about for the stage, in front of a differ-ent audience, larger. Or to revisit perhaps that similar moment, hazy in memory, lost in shame, disappeared in misunderstand-ing, miscataloged in recollection, something of an itch on my conscience, or perhaps more severe. More on that later. I did not see it clearly at the time and had all kinds of reasons not to, and not to look for it, which is something of an important detail that I just plain forgot but which now, as it happens, may indeed account for so much.

Nonetheless, you should, it turns out, always, always, al-ways tell everybody the answer, even unasked, for free, no strings attached, and to anybody who will listen and especially most of all those who will not. In fact, you should, teacher or not, wander the hills and valleys and the hallways, wide boulevards and nar-row alleyways, highways and byways of our land, pushing your shopping cart through the Buy-Way or the Sav-Rite or while driving your U-Haul or waiting in line to pay your overdue gas bill, telling the answers for free, shouting them when necessary, whispering loudly or using your hands as a bullhorn, all as a matter of course, of course.

There will always be other problems and questions, after all, which you and I have not even anticipated, other opportunities or choices to consider and reconsider, to revise your policy, to change the course syllabus, to assign a quiz (yes, an open-book quiz, please), to write something else up on the white-board in American English or Latin, to ask, to draw a cartoon, a Venn diagram, a big question mark, you'd be surprised. And this may indeed be a good thing, something about the difficult perspective of learning, and of the stubbornness of democracy and the late composer and poet John Cage's observation that however awful they might appear we must understand that things (situations, circumstances, moments) are indeed generally getting better, just so very slowly, people, that it is impossible to notice, not from where he or you or I are standing. Especially, it seems, if you are standing up in the front of a classroom and are forced to confront the same remedial composition essays year after year, with the same errors and clichés and misunderstandings, no, class, our text is a memoir, nonfiction, not all books are novels, etc, (which is not pronounced "ex cetera").

*   *   *

So, naturally, when I finally failed the first draft of his first crack at the paper in week four, Ali wondered why, the poor dumb kid with two elderly parents from Egypt who loved him (he told me proudly), asking me sincerely why I didn't "like" his paper, how he could do better, Mrs. Watterson, excuse me Ms. Watterson, what was wrong anyways, he had worked so hard on the paper, how he could please get an "A" (of all things), and so I asked Ali, right there, in front of the class, what the title of the famous book — nonfiction, a memoir, an autobiography — was that we'd read together, and of the play on which it was based, and of the movie, and what kind of text, document, book, object exactly it was that Anne Frank had in fact written. And then without waiting for an answer I asked him, cruelly, yes, sadistically, how to spell it and then to take a look at the title, please, one more time, of his final essay draft and of every draft he'd produced before that and then, finally, Ali the ally of us all smiled weakly at last and said that, indeed, he had sort of wondered now that I mentioned it why I'd kept underlining, circling, crossing out the title of his paper like that.

I suggested that wondering was just fine, wasn't it, a good thing in life, Ali but that I wondered myself about why he hadn't asked me or another student or a tutor or a librarian or even a stranger, or raised his hand in class or looked up the unfamiliar three-letter Latin word in the dictionary, something, anything. Of course, I admit that it was not so much a real question as perhaps a mean one, and so instead of complaining more or apologizing, entertaining regrets or feeling bad, I began writing the early scenes and dialog of a play about it as soon as I got home, which is how complications ensued, how my troubles began, how now brown cow and how say you now?

*   *   *

And so I wrote and wrote and wrote, somewhat giddily, as recompense or charity or perhaps even more low-stakes easy sadism — as a rule hard to tell with public education teachers — and I also took the liberty of casting Ali himself in the actual play too, all of it feeling less actual still than hypothetical, especially after making someone exactly like him the main character in it, the lead, the star, art seeming to be an acceptable expression of something like justice or reconciliation for me just then, though you will see that as pedagogical strategy "not so much," as the kids say. I couldn't pay the cast, so I sent him an email, offering Ali extra credit, which I have found means something to students, though of course it means absolutely nothing at all, not to teachers, not to anybody. In real life there is barely credit for anything, much less extra.

"How much extra credit?" Ali asked me, brightly, hopefully, cluelessly, nonetheless and exactly as anticipated when I finally showed him the script in person, after class a week later, printed out, bound with brads and a photo of Anne Frank on the cover, his lines highlighted in yellow. "Oh, lots," I said. "Double extra," I promised, "two scoops, with sprinkles and whip cream, and a cherry on top," reciting some long-forgotten measure of exaggerated and sarcastic reward from my own childhood, completely lost on him, for all kinds of reasons, but at least consistent with the strong milk-products theme of the work itself.

And he asked sincerely if I thought that all that superduper extra credit might be enough for him to at least pass the class, and I responded that I thought that, yes, it might indeed, sure, why not? But did he have any acting experience, I asked. He did not. "Good," I said, "perfect," and smiling. "That's the best. Just be yourself," I said, and I truly meant it because he was being himself anyway and I did not want or need any more than that, and so was I, being myself, or so I imagined at the time, if soon would not be.

And then? Almost overnight, show biz! As I now had secured my star, the one-act one-woman rant I'd originally conceived of, as we (more correctly, they) say in theater, just me and a half-dozen puppets and music and clip-art slides, something more like a lecture or performance art, found a booster in the Theater Arts instructor at the college, who admired my project, he said.

It quickly developed into a complete three-act drama with a cast of two, then three, then ten, the result of the welcome arrival, a complete surprise to me, to anybody, really, of first one unlikely backer of the play, then another, most of them friends of Professor Dan, the theater guy. All were unsolicited if welcome gestures of civic boosterism, some predictable and some completely anonymous: the mayor (for whom I had once knocked on doors), the couple who owned the café where I sometimes went to drink dark roast Italian coffee and (pretend to) grade papers, the manager at the lumberyard where I now bought plywood and hardware and other set materials, a half-dozen friends and colleagues of Jake's and mine from the college, some of them just trying to make points with the department chair, but still...

*   *   *

Or maybe people in our small town were hungry for gritty dramatic presentations of life, with startling meta-fictional elements, historical reverberations, contrived pastoral themes, anthropomorphized representations of domesticated animals, idealized depictions of communal farm life and it didn't hurt that now, on top of all of that, the weird lady playwright's husband was lying in a hospital bed, though I am once again getting ahead of myself, or at least some version of me. It has indeed been hard to keep track of those, of part-time teacher, wife, mother, faculty wife, humiliater of students, nascent playwright, object of criminal harassment, parser of sentences, ICU habitué, overly self-conscious story narrator, each and all of them racing toward something like a finish line, though that also seems likely to be subject to change, redrawing on the pavement, rearranging the deck chairs on the R.M.S. *Carpathia* always on its way, too late, to rescue R.M.S. *Titanic*, teaching a new dog old tricks, that big, thick white line itself impossible to distinguish among all the other lines, chalk marks in a downpour, and so on.

*   *   *

The play's opening scheduled for the first Saturday night in December had already been moved from its original location in our big backyard to a small if nice-enough performance room at the college, a perhaps too-big, too-quick step up in my authorial journey from total obscurity, but which paralleled nicely my new impulse or compulsion to expropriate wildly from actual true-life incidents, and then, most recently, to complete and total snow-balling into a "world premiere" at the five-hundred seat auditorium at our tiny if solid downtown Las Palmas Civic Center Arts Complex, complete with local advertising and a modest production budget, not to mention a real tractor, pitchfork and hay, donated by the tack and feed store out in the canyons, and refreshments provided by the natural foods co-op, where the manager — a nice enough if now totally boring guy from high school nearly thirty years ago — was in love with me still, having once been the beneficiary of some reckless affection on our single, spontaneous date behind, I am embarrassed to say, the stadium bleachers. Cliché, I know. Discovering him there, still here, when we ended up back in Las Palmas fifteen years ago, still living in my own home town and his, where Jake got a job (of all places) and my parents were, it turned out, dying, was by turns humbling, instructive, if sometimes annoying, as if Derek were always and forever there to remind me of something, though I was never sure of what, a human placeholder or a greeter or a weird fairy god-person assigned to me.

He treated me now with exactly the right mixture of professional regard due a grown, married woman and also healthy if mostly nostalgia-driven lingering middle-aged carnal interest. I admit that I liked it. Ole' Derek was always smiling erotically, big white square teeth and sexy wrinkles at his mouth and eyes, and asking me how "the kids" were doing these days, just like that, "How are the kids doin' these days?" by which he seemed to be trying to combine his recollection of me at age seventeen lying on my back with a pretend interest in public education and an embarrassed need to acknowledge that neither of us were today who we once were, however disappointing that was always going to be from now on, but which was still a pretty big turn-on for him I guess, and why not?

He stood tall at his customer service counter behind the peanut butter grinder and next to a red plastic "Take a Number" dispenser with no numbers left in it, and wearing an apron reading "Go Vegan." Behind him was displayed a framed photograph with his wife Cherie, the two of them surrounded by their six tall and handsome boys, each dressed in a Boy Scout uniform so that the parents looked like terrified civilians in a ransom picture, two middle-aged tourists being held hostage by a small if unarmed militia of extremely well-groomed adolescent forest rangers.

I thanked him for the donation of apple juice, lemonade, cookies (including vegan and gluten-free), popcorn and healthy sodas and promised that he and the co-op would be acknowledged in the program, gave him four comp tickets and then told him that "the kids" were doing just fine, just fine being the pleasant fantasy-world in which most citizen-parent (voter-or-not)-taxpayers chose to, needed to, live as regards public education. I told him that I was fine too. Not to brag, but I was a quietly brilliant, still attractive, still promising, still not-quite middle-aged onetime hometown beauty, academic standout, had stayed in above-average physical shape, indoctrinated teenagers and young adults in logic and reasoning skills for a living, had accommodated reasonable changes and disappointment mostly (until now), resisted change too, when necessary, loved dearly her handsome husband and precocious daughter, had gone off to college once, then grad school, come back to take care of her old parents, inherit their house when they lived and died and still had made something of herself and then — just like that — written, out of nowhere, a full-length play about the victims of the Third Reich and the related scourge of sloppy writing that was being produced for the stage, and yet was still a woman reasonably, sexily available for at least conversation and flirtation.

(If also a liar, unbrave, reluctant in real life to complain or critique or elaborate, not about my failure, my procrastination, the obvious substitution of dramaturgy for paper-grading and commenting, for writing "comma splice" or "Where is your thesis?", a question which I could not ask Derek, could not ask a lot of citizens, and clearly was stymied over myself, autobiographically, and in the construction of the play...)

Still, mostly, I liked to think I had contributed in my small way to the larger civic good, having thus far done everything short of being elected to public office. I mention that here because, first, I also liked to think, occasionally what my life looked like once, before, earlier and because, second and also third, all of it would change momentarily, and I would be rewarded for my unseemly self-esteeming, vanity and high school eroticism by becoming the near-widow or perhaps even the tragically abandoned or betrayed wife, a woman whose husband had suffered a serious injury as the result of an aerial attack and who had fallen, as was soon reported on the front page of our local small-town newspaper by Friday afternoon, I kid you not — wait for it, or don't, it certainly did not wait for me — "into a comma."

*   *   *

I know, I have gotten ahead of myself again, a familiar race, in which I am both winning and losing, simultaneously, as well as watching, perhaps from those very bleachers under which I was cavorting with Derek the future vegan and father. I had done that a lot lately, allowing one of me to take the lead, pacing my other self toward coming up from behind. I got the telephone call that late Thursday afternoon, a week before the show's scheduled Saturday night, eight o'clock sharp, opening, while putting what I thought were the last touches on props and costumes in preparation for our first real, complete full-cast dress rehearsal later that night. Krista, a guidance counselor at the college said as calmly as she could but still sounding completely insane, that my Jake ("Your Jake," she said, as if there were others, as if the day's victims were all Jakes, as if the E.R. would be overwhelmed with injured boys and men named Jake) was on his way to the hospital, knocked out cold after Crazy Chinese Tiffany fell or leapt or pounced from the stoutest, highest branch of the big magnolia tree out in front of the administration building as he walked under it on the brick walkway on his way out to the parking lot, she ("her") clutching her tiny, expensive binoculars, pink Hello Kitty cell phone and in a cosmically perfect inside joke for English majors everywhere, a paperback copy of *A Separate Peace,* breaking her own ankle it turned out, and putting him in a short-term punctuation mark, according to the crack writers and editors at the *Las Palmas Press-Telegram Gazette and Weekly Coastal Foothills Advertiser,* name long, circulation huge, readership less so, judging from all the free copies left on the stand all week until the arrival of the next edition. But plenty of ads, especially lately for medical marijuana and the neon-and-skin showing gentlemen's clubs east of here, over the county line, beyond city limits.

"On his way" was the phrase Krista used, but it was not only his way. There were others. Indeed, an ambulance arrived on campus and the attendant paramedics and driver, lacking knowledge of the criminal history of her case, unsuspecting, or trying to save everybody time and money, loaded Tiffany in back with the object fixation of her affections, reasoning later in that contrived retrospect of authority in which we all sometimes live (and in which I seem to write) that Jake perhaps wouldn't have minded (or noticed) since he was unconscious anyway.

So much for the restraining order, not that it mattered now. She was close to him at last, lucky her, kooky girl, with the two of them lying together in proximal violation of the court order and school policy, Las Palmas F.D. rescue policy and good taste, not to mention credulity or realistic storytelling, yet cooperating somehow with every bad dramatic trope you'd want to avoid in, say, a stage play or real life, whichever came first and, sure, why not, who knows, and, yes, nonetheless? And, as if answering that need for a special twist or clincher detail, it is called, as if hundreds if not thousands of previous trips had not been completed, successful deliveries of patients to the hospital not executed, a previously spotless record not maintained, it was on this one fateful trip, with the unconsciousness man and the broken girl inside that the ambulance driver lost control, swerved, bumping up the curb, hitting exactly one of the two massive long-standing, long-bending palms which stood guard on each side of the "Welcome to Las Palmas" sign to indicate the official and aesthetic if not actual boundaries of our town, and challenging instantaneously the verity of our collective self-naming, one lone palm suggesting a whole other place, experience, not to mention contradicting our literal, geographical, cartographical and perhaps existential verity. One palm, not two. It was a joke, yes, and nobody was further hurt by it beyond the two patients already strapped into their gurneys in the back of the ambulance, but it was a joke which arrived nonetheless with the demand for action, I thought, requiring that we as a community either locate and plant another tree to replace the smashed one, of exactly the same height, toward meeting and matching expectations, symmetry, wholeness, or failing that and more radically, that we rename the whole city, and change the sign to read, more accurately, "Welcome to La Palma," singular.

The show's opening was, by the way, now only ten days away.

*   *   *

Tiffany, aka Qing, pronounced "Ching," was now an injured if happy and yet elegantly emaciated twenty-year-old girl-woman still obsessed with, one, my husband and, two, all things Hello Kitty, this unlikely mental illness or compulsion or extreme hobby (you choose) accommodated and encouraged by way of being, it was understood, a wealthy heiress from Taiwan with, clearly, a nice allowance and an eating disorder. There was no three; that was it. Her interests were singular except doubly so, connected, tag-teamed in some kind of private narrative through-line which made sense to nobody except maybe to her, storing a hopeful kitty-creature to somebody else's hubby. She was living and studying in this country, a bulimiac visitor-guest of our welcoming pay-as-you-go Republic, attending our completely unremarkable community college (and paying serious out-of-state, out-of-country fees) to please or appease or perhaps escape her distant family (in both senses of distant, and in no real sense of family), to meet and perhaps wed a nice all-American man, achieve citizenship, not eat much that anybody could see, and evangelize for Hello Kittydom.

Qing's cadaverous beauty — she weighing in at maybe 100 pounds — and her see-through pale white skin, dark eyes, sleek black hair, allowed her all kinds of permissions, rule breaking, and social access normally unavailable to a student of healthy weight and only average if opaque looks. She appeared as if she might fall down in a strong wind. She was the obvious "international student," as we did not get many, the weird, pretty girl and/or the pretty weird girl, with the startling blue veins and capillaries, the deep crazy coal-black peepers, the big broken smile of beautiful, small crooked white teeth except for the sexy small incisors.

Miss Qing Yuan was the perkiest, shiniest goldfish in

the bowl, if also the one you suspected was eating the other fishies at night, when nobody was around to count. And everybody at school knew it, though were mostly too polite to point that out, tell anyone in charge. Except to whom would you even go with such obviousness, in a world with so many competing obviousnesses?

*   *   *

She'd actually been enrolled in my own composition class early in the semester, "Intermediate College Writing A-1," just like the famous steak sauce, but stopped attending after the first week. She was so very delightful to be in the class, she told me on Day Two, standing up and sharing this as if we were introducing ourselves (we weren't) or at an AA meeting, maybe a Hello Kitty fan club get-together, it was hard to guess except that she was clearly in charge, or imagined she was. Instead of just sitting in her chair or getting up to address us, Tiffany walked to the front of the class, standing right next to me. She pointed out to her instructor and the other students that the name of Anne's imaginary diary friend (as in "Dearest Kitty") was the same as that of her own ubiquitous pink and white Japanese bobtail cat totem-obsession.

"See?" she offered, holding the book open to the first page, as if she were about to read to a group of preschoolers. I noticed her thin hands, which were nearly transparent. I saw them, and I saw right through them. I thought of that old line about somebody so thin that if they stood sideways you couldn't see them, and I sincerely wished she would stand that way now. I also saw the two of us standing there, just a few feet apart, in front of the class, as if this were a scene out of a play — yes, a play, very much of the wicked, absurd tone and mean spirit of exactly the one I would begin to write, as it happens! — or of court testimony, a flashback or a bad dream but of course I didn't see anything at all, not really, and certainly not what I should have seen.

"See? Mister Frank Anne likes Hello Kitty, too," she exclaimed. "Now see?" She pointed and smiled, and, once again, I just did not know where to start. She just kept asking me to see. I saw just fine. I nodded, too, understanding nonetheless how pointless would be my objection, explanation, whatever, and so I only nodded and smiled, hoping she would just sit back down and shut up. The rest of the class seemed indifferent, as always, though perhaps in new and in different indifferent ways. They snickered, said nothing, stared at their desks or watched, blankly.

I tried to consider her perspective. I didn't try too hard, but still. That the image which appeared on Tiffany's purses, garments, socks, shoes, backpack, fanny pack, cell phone, and of course upon Tiffany herself (two delicate HK tattoos, one on each shoulder) had also sixty years earlier somehow delighted the martyred little Jewish Dutch girl living in a secret upstairs room in Amsterdam, Holland might have been just about the very best news any student of remedial writing and revisionist Kitty-history could have gotten. And my pointing out her mistake, her confusion, to Qing-Tiffany (or Tiffany-Qing?) was probably pretty bad, even cruel and unnecessarily sadistic, or perhaps, who knows, necessarily so. Yes, I should have known better. Perhaps I did. I might have considered her feelings, or instead divined that this situation was well, well beyond only a spelling error, the gratifying, even thrilling transposition of two letters to form a completely different word, a new history of the Second World War, and a completely perfect world, which is just what I did. I knew better, and I knew worse, and they turned out to be the same thing, really.

Her stubborn confusion became, as things turned out, not so much an obstacle to Qing-Tiffany's reconciling of luck and reality as more of a challenge, a gambit to prove me wrong, her attempt to lose me my job and steal my husband and frighten my daughter, all choreographed to take revenge on the only person, I am thinking now, to ever have contradicted her until just then, and so unflinchingly.

*　*　*

Because, yes, I did that one terrible, reckless thing which you are never, ever supposed to do, that single and singular no-no of humane progressive modern pedagogical practice and praxis and good instructor social hygiene and teaching manners, and I offered her the one response that is not ever, never allowed, never permitted, out of fear that it might discourage students, hurt their self-esteem or otherwise make them feel bad about themselves, about learning, also about teachers. I violated that big rule taught by every mentor teacher and Vice Principal in every School of Education university or college class in our happy-faced clown confederacy, affirmed in teacher orientations every day in America and in weekly staff meetings over lousy coffee and creamer (never any real cream, or at least half-and-half) and lame parent-teacher conferences.

No, I did not find a gentle, generous way to "reframe" her nutty question. I did not suggest an alternative route to locating a more reasonable one. I did not "break it down" or ask if she could think of a different way of asking. In short, I just said "No." Just like that, and pretty loud, too. I told the Tiffster outright, no hesitation, no apology or warm-up that, no, Anne Frank, murdered in 1945 in Bergen-Belsen, was not a fan, was never a fan of "Hello Kitty" the doll or the franchise or cult or hobby or whatever it was, and that neither she nor anyone could or should connect the cute little pink cat through space and time and across the centuries, generations and oceans, like that, to Amsterdam, June, 1942 or to our classroom here in California. It was sarcastic, sure, but only as much as I felt it clearly needed to be, and it needed to be, or perhaps could not avoid being. A few students grinned, even laughed, at this point, for which I was grateful I guess if confused about why the others did not do a thing in the face, or whatever anatomical metaphor, of this confrontation.

*   *   *

She never came back to my class, for which I was relieved, and I chose to chalk that up (or, rather low-odor dry erase marker it up) to a kind of lost-in-translation moment, a cultural barrier unreconciled, extreme ESL misapprehension on her part, immaturity, something that would work itself out eventually, hopefully with other teachers and students and tutors and librarians and counselors — not me or, why not, perhaps me? — become something we'd all laugh about later and which would in retrospect perhaps make sense to her, too, to both of us, but the two Kitties became, it turned out, only a serendipitous and too-available vehicle toward more affirmation for her, a connection, a synchronicity which you could not have made up, except that she did, and so was embarked right there on her nutty mission. In retrospect, which is lately hard to distinguish from introspect, or inspect or speculation — from the present and the dramatic and the future and point of view or any number of tense problems — I surely might have handled the situation better, to paraphrase the reports and memos offered later in the professional assessments of the ombudsman, administration, union rep, campus police, my husband, colleagues and the college president. I get that now, believe me.

My rejection became only a challenge to her, though why, I wonder now, did my ridicule — if that's what it was — or denial or reproach even matter? I didn't wonder for long. All kinds of people told me. Answer: Yes, I "enabled" her, psycho-babblically speaking. I rolled out a long plush red-velvet carpet and I asked her to walk it. I placed a juicy green apple upon my head and stood there waiting for her to string her bow and shoot it, and miss, and hit me in the face. I poured wet cement and she stepped in it, in high heels. I took a Polaroid and invited her to draw all over it with her tiny finger while the print was still wet, and she did that, too.

I was the perfectly impossible yet irresistible way, path, toll road, to beautiful, urgent meaning for a moderately to, it turned out, dangerously mentally ill person, high functioning, with enough money and eccentricity to never, ever be challenged about her fetish, her weirdo worldview, her privilege and distance.

Reminding her, insisting, that Anne Frank had lived and died many, many years before the arrival of the iconic cartoon cat caused her to turn on me right there. Against me. And so, just like that, abracadabra, okey-dokey, quid pro quo, ipso-facto, Bob's-your-uncle, she transferred her interest, repurposed her resentment and confusion to increasingly uncomfortable, inappropriate, potentially dangerous insertion into my Jake's daily comings and goings, waiting outside his office or, worse, inside his office, ambushing him on campus, following him home, standing at our backyard gate watching Sasha jump and flip and somersault on her mini-trampoline with bright nylon net cage and waving at us at sunset, and then sunrise too, tottering on her high heels and short skirt, and shouting hollow and loud compliments which sounded only like threats when she spoke them: "You house so beautiful. You baby girl so beautiful. You so beautiful," and asking, politely, eagerly, while undressing to her Hello Kitty-themed panties and training bra right there on the sidewalk, "I marry husband you okay yes? I marry Professor Mister Jake?"

*   *   *

That first time she showed up I brought Sasha indoors, fast, and locked the doors. I photographed Qing from the upstairs guest bedroom, noting the Kitty-centric license plate on her remarkable colorful-ugly BMW. I called the city police and the college, too, and I notified our mostly useless Neighborhood Watch. Once again, nobody paid attention, though they did — not watch — all together, helpfully. And when they did notice, they assured me there was nothing I or anybody could do. "She needs help," they said.

"I need help," I said, for at least the second time, and again they thought I was joking which, once again, I was not.

It happened again a few days later. And so I did this all over, calling everybody in town, with two wannabe cop volunteers — two seniors, an old man and old woman, identically dressed, each holding a walkie talkie, Community Patrol Reservists (yes, "CPR") according to the patches on their fake uniforms — finally arriving to ask her to leave, with lots of cheerful eye-rolling and jolly head-shaking and the elderly if spry woman fake-officer asking if she could use our restroom while the nice old dude staggered over to gently interrogate but ultimately be completely charmed by flirty, half-naked Qing-a-ling, put her in her luxury automobile and send her home, free as a weird bird.

And again she appeared, a third and a fourth and a tenth time, Jake trapped in the house or sneaking out the back or the side while Sasha and I distracted her. I finally took the garden hose to her myself one late October morning. It was kind of sad, and cold out. She looked like a drowned mole, or gopher but, unlike real pests, she at least stayed out of the yard after that.

******* * * *

Jake woke up the first time after a two full nights and days in the ICU, Saturday afternoon, with a bad headache and a severe plot twist, not just a strain, but all credulity badly injured: no recollection, not of the accident or of me or Sasha or his life before Qing, after whose health and well-being he immediately inquired.

"How's Tiffany?" he asked.

Alas, not a joke, no, despite my attempt to produce a wry smile or summon some easy hardy-har-har, stop kidding around, how's Tiffany indeed, imagine that. (Insert smiley face icon here.) He was otherwise "stable," the docs said, not critical. But before I or anybody could respond much at all Jake closed his eyes again, before I could tell him that Tiffany was recovering nicely, in fact handcuffed to her own personal hospital bed down the hall and wearing a cast on her broken left leg, and before he disappeared, again, back into his eye-fluttering twilight.

It happens, the doctors assured Sasha and I. The world required further reorganizing by his brain, into which he'd retreated for now. Let's allow it to do its healing work, they said. Let him rest, they said. He'll be just fine. Really, they said.

Jake was otherwise completely healthy, they promised, and soon enough he had his own bright, sunlight-filled private hospital room to lie in, if often unconsciously, moved out of intensive care by Monday night. Not that he had any idea, but the machines hooked up to my man appeared to be working, producing their comforting mechanical murmurings and occasional alarms. I did not know what to do. I embraced the Socratic Method, as modeled in the classroom. I asked questions, as I'd so often encouraged my students to do. I wondered out loud about the intermittent alarms going off, most of which nobody on the hospital staff responded to. That part, the audio track, seemed less convincing than the rest of the scene happening up on the third floor, the adjustable bed and the saline drip bag and the bandage wrapped around his head as if in a cartoon or a movie or play about a wounded man. The nurses and doctors had, generally, no strong opinions either way. I found this discouraging. It was as if the electronic alarms going off were phone calls coming from my husband's body, unanswered, and so automatically going to message. Still, he actually seemed okay with it, lying there doing, I wanted to, liked to, needed to believe, his healing work, as was expected of him.

In this small, bright world of suspended animation, yet another medical expert was always on his or her way, slowly, presumably, perhaps only potentially, then another expert, specialist, technician, or visiting doctor. "You must be his wife," they said to me, when they acknowledged me at all. After a while I heard it as an accusation.

"No," I said to a young handsome Indian man. "I want to be his wife. I choose to be."

None of the medical professionals acknowledged the others, even when he or she, mostly a he, were standing right there in the room. It was as if they had not studied the same human brain or lobe or cortex, suddenly were no longer perhaps even doctors at all, maybe not even science majors or even minors or college graduates, just random pedestrians who happened to arrive upon the scene of a man, lying not on a sidewalk but, conveniently, already in a hospital bed.

"You must be the doctor," I started insisting to anybody wearing a white smock.

I wanted to pull in a stranger, the janitor or somebody else's relative, a woman or man or child visiting down the hall as a witness, to confirm what was happening in the room, which was, I thought, not really very much at all.

I stayed in Jake's room myself of course, missing most of the dress rehearsals that weekend, letting my Assistant Director and best friend Amy take over, unsure whether to postpone the show's opening or cancel it altogether now, or assume the best, a quick recovery, if it wasn't already too late to actually be quick. Sasha came and went, chaperoned to and from the hospital and back to a girlfriend's house, just like in family movies where exactly this kind of thing happens, funny yet tragic and yes, neighbors who had apparently also seen these movies prepared us all kinds of food, some delivering it to the hospital, some leaving it on our front porch where, helpfully, local dogs or raccoons or coyotes did their predictable damage to already inedible cheese-covered noodle casseroles and zucchini-bacon quiches and colorful jellos with marshmallows and macaroni salads too, lucky animal scavengers. We did not ever eat like that, and especially when we didn't even want to eat in the first place, thanks anyway.

The staff rolled in a matching hospital bed for me, this after I'd spent so many hours sitting and napping and being uncomfortable in a chair next to Jake's nifty adjustable bed. I worked on my laptop, or so it turned out later, checking email and messing with the script, notes, to do lists for the show. My fingers moved on their own, like a medium with her cups or operating an Ouija board. I did not know at first that I was composing, editing, revising, catching up to events and themes as they happened, and spontaneously integrating these into my play. It felt more like transcribing. But I seemed to have been adding lines, including for more parts, updating the story with events right out of what passed for real life, details and descriptions and new characters quickly finding their way into my edits. It seemed like a good use of my time, the doctors having assured us that Jake would be himself soon, now that he was occasionally awake and even ambulatory, or asleep again, and them not. His failure to commit fully, as it were, to total consciousness and recovery was disappointing, but everybody still hoped for the best. I guess it was something less than a coma now, the way it came and went, arbitrary and subjective, the way some people used a comma. A usage problem.

I had a difficult time with their assurances, and so these problems of mine involving impatience, skepticism, my trust issues, also found their way into the play, as it turned out. First, they did not really know my hubbie personally, so "being himself" was largely speculation on their part, wasn't it, and I wondered how they would even know, how they would recognize him short of asking me, or him. Second, I should have heard in their voices the ominous possibility that Jake could, would, perhaps also not ever really "be himself" at all, that he would be someone else or, worse, nobody else.

They spoke in easy conversational variables suggesting an uneasy relationship between expertise and expectation, sometimes only a passing familiarity, and their word choices mattered to me more than I cared to admit. I would have enjoyed it had my husband been the subject, or direct object, or indirect object. And so I kept reworking the script each night, Monday, Tuesday, Wednesday, weirdly inspired, all bets off, anything possible, the details of real life entering those of the play, as if in a rush to affect the outcomes of both, simultaneously, as in a dream where through the effort of the conscious you, the dreamer, might influence the subconscious, escaping the pursuer or avoiding the fall or landing softly or, yes, just waking up.

Friends and colleagues visited. Neighbors came by. Colleagues took my classes for me, giving the class a break from their regular teacher and helpfully providing me more long-term cover for my previous failure to return work to students, those draft essays lying on the dining room table still. Lying, still. Like Jake. He woke up once in a while, then more often. At these times, my husband seemed just fine to everybody, just shaken up, they all said. Jake's mother arrived from Cleveland on Tuesday morning, to help out, she said. She checked into our guest room and did not help out, not particularly, but everybody agreed that it was good that she was there. Except me, silently. Jake smiled and accepted her hugs and kisses. She pulled a chair close to him upon her arrival. They had never been close in the first place and it was obvious to me that he was only pretending to know her.

Per the neurologist's instructions, everybody wore helpful name tags, "Hello! My name is _____," provided by our case worker, so that the staff could use our names, Jake would relearn them, and that this bit of dramaturgy would encourage his busted synapses to open up a special lane to speed these messages on their way back to his old self.

My mother-in-law's tag read "Margaret-Mom," so when Jake smiled too-broadly and said, "Hi, Margaret-Mom," everyone was discouraged if also amused. He and she briefly spent time alone together in his room, the rest of us outside in the hall, waiting for a psychic breakthrough in his frozen brain-sea or at least her somehow valuable motherly diagnosis. When we all reconnoitered in the waiting room after their private time, Margaret and Sasha and Jake's nurse and I, his mother reported confidently that he also seemed "just fine" to her, but then, as if misunderstanding completely the nature of the problem here, turned to me and asked who Tiffany was and if Tiffany was a fellow teacher, maybe, or one of Sasha's "little friends," and she wondered if Tiffany had already come by to visit and could I remind her please, again, who our good, dear friend Tiffany was again?

*　　*　　*

Tiffany was in fact herself, and being herself, just down the hall, asking for Jake we were told, looking to get out of bed to search for him despite the cast, and marry him but mostly looking at the back of the head of a hospital security guard posted (at my request or, rather, insistence) outside her door, and also looking at a couple of days of further observation, a psych eval, physical therapy and a court date for a couple of misdemeanors, not to mention, finally, suspension from Las Palmas Community College, big fucking deal that. She lay there confined in stout wrist restraints, surrounded by flowers — who sends flowers to the perpetrator, I wondered? — the rumor out on the floor being that her parents were on their way from the ROC, possibly flying in on their own private jet, eager to take her back home.

Meanwhile and despite and nonetheless, Jake kept asking for her, and yet still declined to acknowledge our own sweet daughter, when he was not slipping back into his Sleepyland. Me, he dismissed or accepted or ignored, depending on how you viewed these things, as alternatively a good friend, a high school buddy, a professional caretaker of some sort, maybe a relative or variety of interpreter or health advocate or counselor, some kind of job with the hospital or the County, an inexplicably devoted administrator. An old girlfriend maybe, on a very good or especially hypothetical day.

He seemed to want me around, but only as a familiar prop in a scene which was, like so many, becoming a clumsily, obviously instructive bit of discouraging dramatic elaboration on what was happening over in real life, as against what I hoped for in something more than real life, something like a better life, something like genuinely convincing drama.

Yes, heartbreaking if useless moments surely did abound, were welcome even, if you required this sort of badly and poorly realized dramatic narrative, which I guess I did, to say the least, or to say it even desperately. I kept taking my notes, my transcriptions, listening for some instruction perhaps, some direction as they say in the theater, not that I really knew what they said in the theater. I could not help believe that my long-lived procrastination, while inspiring so much pent-up sudden creativity, was now catching up even with me, and so very quickly, and perhaps leaving me behind. My anger or disappointment had been nearly, if not quite constructively well-organized to this point, manageable you could say, but with the universe now meting out its proportionally perverse and cruel retribution for what I had done, not done, failed to anticipate, left incomplete, set aside, stacked up, sorted and ignored. Yet I told myself I could still make some sense of it, by paying attention, and closely, by locating those stand-out dramatic moments of real life most easily adaptable, co-optable, believable, if you will.

Meanwhile, I had to endure some genuine grief, with my eyes and ears wide open, my heart in my mouth, my pencil in hand or behind my ear. I sat at Jake's bedside like I was taking dictation. A writer, some famous writer once said, is somebody on whom nothing is lost, which is a funny phrase if you hear it or read just right, or wrong. On whom would nothing be found, gained, saved or used? Who needed more of nothing?

My groggy husband referred to me once, mid-week, as a teaching colleague, accurate I guess if disappointing, and for which the doctor suggested I should have been grateful except that I hoped (as you would), for so much more than a professional relationship with your life's true love and the father of your child, a very good man who I wondered how I would love and live with if he didn't, couldn't love me back. Not that I wouldn't, but how, exactly. Roommates? Office mates? Two nice enough people who shared a house, the now unneeded old costumes and disguises packed up in a box in the garage next to my wedding dress and Sasha's baby clothes and our hiking and camping gear, perhaps offering the only clues to this mildly mysterious relationship?

*   *   *

Hospital, then home to shower and feed the cat, and then back again, checking in at the theater. After a few days and nights all sense of place and setting disappeared, so that I was certainly not living at home anymore, if not yet actually living in a hospital, if you call that living. So there would, of course, be a hospital room in the newly revised play now, an injured spouse, a missing palm tree and, I hoped, a miraculous or just ordinary coming-to scene, with total and complete recovery and no brain damage, who knew?

Like everybody up on the third floor, I felt myself over-illuminated and garishly backlit and also front-lit by the ubiquitous if totally unconvincing fluorescent hospital lights, of which there were always plenty, and always too bright, the expression of a kind of agreed-upon institutional dishonesty about the quality and meaning and purpose of light itself. Rushing from the theater, where I hollered and screamed, here I used my quiet hospital voice, and went around switching lights off when I could. I thought hospital thoughts, and then tried not to. I started thinking about what I'd said and done since arriving here, and what I had written about what I'd said and done, and what we had rehearsed so far in the play, choreographed into an approximation of events which I could now not separate one from the other — wasn't even going to try — and it is possible that I wondered, and perhaps even wondered aloud, how anybody could tell the difference between one drama and another, distinguish between badly staged imagined scenes and real-life ones, also badly staged, all the while hoping that this one would end, would stop being so darn instructive, so rich, and that the sense of poorly-realized control — but control, nonetheless — which I had found in the writing and rewriting of my play to begin with would return instead of be usurped by the presence of the one important player I had failed to cast, to understand had been there, waiting all along, the opposite of an understudy, and overstudy, a human handgun which I had not seen hung there by somebody (maybe herself) on the wall like in Chekhov, but which went off not in the third act but before the curtain had even gone up, before I had even thought of a curtain.

So there were increasingly more opportunities for edits and rewrites, the coercion or cooptation of my creative process by real time, by waiting room and lobby time, by the promise that time, of all things, would somehow heal my husband's wounds after what was now nearly a full week. And so in real life Jake woke up again and again and again, each time asking about the well-being of his assailant instead of asking about his wife, his family, his cat. I probably had some responsibility to answer him honestly. But I was a playwright now, or pretending to be one, had tricked some people into believing I was one, if having based my only dramatic premise thus far on correcting a spelling or word choice mistake (or, remarkably, both!) and on the reliable misapprehension of history by innocent and illiterate young people. Cheap move, too easy, perhaps, and for it I had, it now seemed, been punished.

This was the mindset I was in at least, sitting after not sleeping a whole lot myself, at the edge of my husband's adjustable bed, staring at the needle in his arm, the dark rings permanently occupying his eyes (nicely mirroring my own), wearing the neck brace which we'd all signed, in a perverse effort at whimsy or bravado.

Yes, if ever there was an alternative universe, I was in it, as I had perhaps even somehow created it. And now, at last, I had my big line, my big scene, my answer when he asked about his assailant once again.

"She's fine," I considered saying about Ms. Death-From-Above. Or, "Why do you ask, honey?"

"She's dead," is what I should have said, murdering her and the idea of her in the little theater-in-the-round that was his damaged head. Instead, I hesitated, searching in his eyes, as people do at these moments, and yet still not yet particularly seeing my husband.

But then, before I could answer him for real, before I could turn the story around, he fell asleep again, as so often, and I wondered both why I had waited, and also how many times one person could pass out and ever come to again, and I was not eager to find out, also impatient and scared so, no, trying not to wonder at all.

And then, as if to answer my question, my provocation, Jake was back, sort of, maybe for reals, late Friday morning, after a full week, seven days and nights in the hospital now, in what seemed like, this time, awakeness and presence and consciousness for good. He sat up, looked around, considered his surroundings once more, knew better it seemed than to ask about her again, ate a hearty hospital breakfast, then a second, and promised to stay awake, as if he had some power to do that finally. I read him the article about him, and us, the copy still lying there on his night table, with the impressive and high-larious typo. We both got a good laugh, as they say, as opposed to a bad laugh. I was in a funny place where, trying to find him, I considered carefully each and all of his behaviors, including the sound of his laughter, which now seemed more robust, high-quality and perhaps deceptively reassuring.

Eventually, he fell back asleep, laughing gently to himself. We'd been told repeatedly for so long that he was absolutely not to do that, laughing or not. Still, I let him this time, deciding on my own that this was just a nap and not ultimate brain death. That was selfish, and weak of me, but I had quietly cried to myself for days, not slept a lot, drunk too much coffee and been denied that big scene I wanted. And trusted my diagnosis by this time as much as anybody else's in the place. My own color was probably not so good either, and I'd so enjoyed Jake's hearty, exaggerated perfect laughter, and so the sight of him lying there with a smile on his face was something like control or even revenge.

*   *   *

Of course, I was otherwise careful, responsible, if persistent. For days I had whispered to Jake that I loved him. I sang
songs. I told him stories. I just would not shut up about us.
Us! We. Him and me, he and I, Jake and Hope, and Hope and
Jake. Proper nouns, pronouns, coordinating and subordinating
conjunctions. I'd brought in more photo albums, my old jour-
nals, Sasha's drawings, holiday cards, the screen capture of the
ultrasound, of her growing in my tummy, of our house and our
fat tomcat. Other people liked it all, my performance art piece
in the room, or pretended to, the otherwise easily unimpressed
nurses and doctors and specialists and techs, even the security
guard who guarded Tiffany's room. He walked over during his
break, looking happily conspiratorial and stood next to me and
whispered.

"She ordered them herself," he said softly. At first I
didn't know what he meant. "The flowers, the big bouquet," he
said. "The patient had them delivered. I asked the gift shop
downstairs."

He stuck around, pleased to have helped out. I'd already
told that young guard, Jake, everybody in the room, the story
of our life together, nearly twenty-five years, waiting for some
glimmer of recognition from my husband, wanting even a tiny
flash that might suggest that the clichéd but so coveted glimmer
was peeking through, me trying to summon it to light up a little
stadium in his head which would shock my injured hubby into
the big recognition, reboot his hard drive, from our meeting in
college American Literature Part I Survey class to the birth of

Sasha and moving here (of all places) and burying my folks and inheriting our house and him getting tenure and me writing the play, with his encouragement and, he'd said, pride in me.

Of all of it, Jake was indeed most interested in the show, and encouraged me to tell him and everybody in the room — nurse, friends, his mom and the Security guy — about it, how it was going.

So I explained the premise again, the dramatic situation to Jake, the story about characters he might recognize, and the developing parallel story of the first-time playwright, the wife of this man I knew, we all knew, a beloved father and professor who'd been injured, that she needed to rehearse, to finish the set, to work hard to get to her big opening night but that she, I, the playwright, was torn because she could not feel secure leaving her man, the patient, for long because when she came back she, I, me, this character, all of them, felt so worried that leaving him would cause him to forget her even more completely.

"Who?" he asked.

"Her," I said. "The wife. Me." I admit it was confusing, possibly even if a small Chinese girl-woman had not fallen on your head.

"Well," he said, seeming to think aloud, "If you were the wife — if you were her — you, she, should still by all means do the play. It sounds great. And the husband will be fine, I think," he said. He paused. "He'll be fine. I promise."

And that was enough, in fact the very best I'd gotten thus far before he closed his eyes once again. And his little smile for me, if it really was for me, and if it was from him, well, that seemed enough too. The show would, as they say, go on, this one and that one and the other one, too.

*   *   *

That mock-dramatic reading I had performed from the newspaper had seemed to amuse or distract him, me offering the sentence with the misplaced coma in various inflections of irony or amusement or mock outrage, and then laughing for both of us, too hard. And I thought briefly that he might be there, here, back with me for good, or tried to. I attempted sincerity the next day, back the following morning, showing him the full-page ad for the play's opening on Saturday night, now only a day away, featuring Anne Frank herself wearing bib overalls and a wide-brimmed straw hat, with a pasture, a barn, a cow, the diary in one hand and a pitchfork in the other, a looming dark swastika in the background. And then I tried to crawl into bed beside Jake, lie under the thin hospital sheets with my Jake, who only lay there stiffly, still apparently wondering who I was if not really seeming to object to a cute middle-aged stranger-woman. I held him, resting my hand on his chest and fitting the top of my head in between his collarbone and neck brace and I said, once again, "It's me, Jake. It's me."

He allowed this for a minute or two but then reached up and pressed the "Summon Nurse" button and, pretending not to be hurt I held him just a moment longer and asked my wounded hubby if he needed something, could I help him with anything but I did not wait, could not wait there, not to risk hearing him ask about her again — her! — and not me — me! — and so I got up and walked out, to wait out in the hall, with its white noise and white light and white walls and white silence, interrupted only by squeaky (white) shoe soles and the irritating echo-symphony of beeping life-supporting machines further interrupting what little there was left to interrupt.

Naturally, no nurse arrived. Instead, a new doctor or intern showed up to make, I assumed, an announcement or offer a report or update to whoever happened to be there, and so I followed him back in, dutifully, if shamed, to hear yet another diagnosis, one similar to the one offered before, again pretending I was not hurt or disappointed. I was afraid of what he meant to say, to report, and wondered if Jake understood the doctor to have arrived as the result of actually calling for a nurse, if his tumbled synapses could apprehend the irony or humor or tragedy of this cause and un-effect.

Jake's swelling was way down, explained this particular new and totally unfamiliar doctor. Jake's color was assessed as good. He dutifully affirmed his own full name and the name of the president, and the vice president, too, which is better than a lot of healthy people. "Ask him his congressman," I suggested, "our asshole Republican," but the doctor ignored me. It was eleven o'clock in the morning, and all of that seemed useless and obvious, and not any different than before. Still, it was welcome news, some kind of diagnosis.

"We'll continue to observe him," the doctor said to nobody, as if observing meant something other than just letting him lie there in bed, that passive observing at which they seemed not even to particularly excel. He pointed once again a tiny flashlight in my husband's eyes and asked him to rotate his neck, this despite or because of the recently removed brace, which seemed wrong to me. I almost said something. Jake obliged before I could intervene, actually moving it, perhaps because he had forgotten that it had been hurt. I was impressed, and wondered if the hospital room itself, my own cocoon of unlikely cosmic-theatrical convergence was perhaps the source of all this reconnoitering. It was the kind of reaching speculation to which I'd become victim or beneficiary of. Yet instead of exclaiming or noting what seemed obvious, even dramatic improvement the doctor only nodded and asked, "And how are you feeling today, sir?" but did not wait for an answer, not particularly, and left.

The rest of the day (Day Eight) was pretty much like this. Nobody seemed willing to commit or affirm. They were being cautious, and cautiously optimistic. "Well, yes, his color is certainly good," offered one expert specialist technician after another. "He's responsive and his vitals are fine, Mrs. Watterson." And, finally, "I think we'll want to transfer him, downstairs, take him off supports and plan on cutting him loose real soon."

Jake seemed okay with all of it. He certainly wasn't responsive to me. I tried to recall what color exactly he had been before. I was sure it had been a good, healthy color, a human flesh-colored color, husband-colored as I recalled, as the photographs of him and the rest of us taped all over the room showed. I didn't get too close to him again, worried he might be spooked, or hate or ignore me or that, yes, his neck might go stiff again, paralyzed by his wifey-pooh's smothering love therapy, and call the nurse again, not that one would come, though who knew what variety of useless or unimpressed medical professional might.

*   *   *

Anne Frank was, you will remember, very big just then, popular, the whole concept of her, the idea of her, a narrator-character of a short epoch, with short stories and novels and revisionist biographies, even a musical or two dramatizing in song the enduring life-and-death and everlasting life-death and survival story of the most famous young dead, murdered, disappeared, immortal girl-woman in history.

And milk was big, always, and yogurt and Greek yogurt and low-fat yogurt and cottage cheese and cream cheese and ice cream, gourmet ice cream sandwiches lately, too, and especially beneficial dairy-based probiotics, all with calcium and vitamin D. Organic, one percent, two percent, non-fat! And people liked cows, always. So the premise of the play was kind of perfect, zeitgeist-wise, unless you were lactose intolerant or maybe a Nazi, which sort of worked also, because even those very unusual and difficult people probably wanted high-quality community theater, smart, funny, challenging original work with room for interpretation and some kind of new, different take-away, and not yet another lame production of *Guys and Dolls* or *The Sound of Music.*

The once-vibrant baby boomer nostalgia for the heroically martyred, celebrated young Jewish girl, a superstar once of post-war popular culture and literature, was being revived it seemed, with the additional new, accurate details, sobering and even sadistic, of her death in Bergen-Belsen, of her frank (ha, ha) sexuality, normal teen girl antagonisms toward her mother, and her devoted or perhaps guilty-feeling father's literary construction of a juggernaut bestseller industry manufactured out of her lost, skeletal, fetishized young body, and, yes, of her own genuine and undeniable prowess as a young writer, a diarist.

I am, as you will have guessed by now nearly fifty, white, nominally Protestant, a product of solid democratic liberal public education, a reader who has always kept an ancient dusty mass-market paperback copy of the diary on her shelf, along with Salinger, Tom Robbins, *The Bell Jar* and poems by Neruda and Langston Hughes. Yes, young people used to carry these books around with them once, imagine that, as if they were prizes, gifts, totemic objects, holy universal translators of experience, passports to civic and cultural and political literacy, and for protection perhaps, announcing their allegiances to curiosity, liberation, and to each other.

As so many kids, I'd written a report on Anne Frank in the sixth grade, and seen the play on stage, the movie with sexy Shelley Winters, and as a young adult had made the pilgrimage made by so many, with Jake, my Jake, my husband, when we'd been not much older than our Sasha was now, ruck-sacking and Eurailing and hostelling our way all over Western Europe, to Amsterdam as you did, or should have, in the Eighties, to climb up to her attic house museum, to see up close the secret life lived in the famous "Achterhuis."

Surely Anne Frank had stirred not only the generation just before mine, those self-involved 60's types, but my own peers too, raised on the cultural remnants of World War II and the Holocaust, landmines of memory — think *Combat* on Channel 34 every Saturday morning, *Hogan's Heroes* for god's sake, Elie Wiesel's *Night*, assigned in tenth grade along with *Farewell to Manzanar*. Perhaps even that generation just following us had been made modest Frankophiles, but Anne of Holland, memoirist, seemed since then to have been lost to other, younger people somewhere, gone missing, been forgotten or misplaced in the rubble of the tearing down of the Berlin Wall and 9-11 and the dubious tragedies of Princess Di (Princess Die, Princess Dead) and Michael Jackson and the NASCAR driver Dale Earnhardt of all people, and the replacement of real life, not to mention reading, not to mention spelling — with tiny screens — which is saying a lot, if obviously, if about so very little.

Still, it is hard to remember anything if you never even knew it, so that Anne Frank was suddenly once again big now, even bigger all of a sudden, good for her, welcome brand-new news to plenty of people, young people, including my students. She was not a ghost, zombie or vampire — all ubiquitous — except that she was, kind of, and helpfully so. She'd seen a war on terror, been victimized by evil-doers, come from a dysfunctional family and even, as everybody today, gotten a tattoo. Cool. Awesome. "Awesome!" Her story had its familiar elements and was ready it seemed to me, for a revival, for this renaissance, jumpstarted by me in the classroom. And the "kids" just loved it. They read it through in one sitting, took a reading comprehension quiz, then wondered together if maybe she'd written other books, and what Anne Frank was doing now, no kidding. Sigh. And, yes, welcome to my world.

*   *   *

So that in my new, original dramatic play Anne was also very big, really big, huge, in fact fucking enormous! She had to be, consistent with the urgent, exaggerated, oversized need — demand — for her, my own and theirs, this response in over-reaction and overstatement and overcompensation, at least as I saw it. She was a giantess, a mutant, over the top and towering above other, normal-sized people, trees, houses, even community colleges. And of course my days spent at Jake's side only caused her to grow even that much bigger. That little dead Jewish girl had loomed so very large already and so very long in history, in my own imagination, if not in my students', those to whom I had assigned the original *The Diary of a Young Girl* for reading and study and research and analysis, and then the play and then the film version, so that I just plain went for it out of my own reckless need and anger and I blew her right up even larger, into Macy's Day Parade-style Anne, the Attack of the Fifty-Foot Anne, the Anne Who Ate Amsterdam, Tokyo or Los Angeles – boy, could that big little girl shovel it in! - a heroic Anne Frank, with big appetites, whose sheer size would demand attention, notice, respect. In my play, she would not, could not, be ignored. You could grieve for her or resist or deny her but you could absolutely not miss her, in fact had to make sure she would not step on you, on purpose or by accident.

Her story — a sequel, if you will — would, I reckoned, certainly impress the youngsters new to her tale and affirm something for their parents, might please or delight or, even better, frighten the very little kids and the older folks too, and so keep Anne immortal and dangerous, and thus bring some beauty by way of justice to a world gone mad.

Yes, my Big Anne would gently crush students into consciousness, make them into well-rounded human citizens of the world who would never, I imagined, be careless again, not with history or their allegiances or my assignment or, God help them, punctuation or spelling. They would not only read the famous bestselling book, a classic, but reread it, and love and care for this story, the character, the history, the title, not to mention celebrate the author of the brand new play about her, written by me and starring one of their own, redeemed by his immersion in the story, and its rewriting. It would not be about me, none of it, and my rude behavior in class, my lack of patience and procrastination, my dereliction of pedagogical duties. No, I was not the problem. I was the problematizer. I made problems for people, a provocateur, as the President from Texas was the Decider, making decisions, all of them bad except that I made good problems, which arrived with answers, or so I imagined.

And now with Jake tacitly or obliviously or duplicitously or semi-consciously giving me permission to proceed, to create, to turn life into art, I was all about making the opening night on schedule, catching up, making changes, changing perspectives, changing background and foreground and rearranging as needed. Something or someone might fall from the ceiling, the sky, a tree. Somebody might call an ambulance. Identities might be assumed, or confused, or irrelevant. Memory might be compromised. Go figure. That's what was happening everywhere, all the time! All the stage was my world, or what was left of it, completely out of proportion, tentative, asking for someone who was not there, and receiving as cruel recompense someone who was too, too much there, a weird gift to myself maybe.

*　　*　　*

I did a walk-through, checking for verisimilitude, or something like it. The play's set was, finally, magnificent in its way, if kind of busy. As one backdrop, Sasha and I had constructed a diagram illustrating comparative sizes, with silhouettes: Human woman (average height 5' 6") Asian elephant (female, 9'), African elephant (female, 9'), Eiffel Tower (917') Twin Towers (missing, of course, drawn in broken outline but once 1,368'), Rock of Gibraltar (1,398') with Big Anne standing between the figure of the African pachyderm and the crime scene ellipses of the missing buildings. For another scene there was a pair of doors, one tiny and one huge.

And afterwards, I reminded myself at each decision, me, Hope, Hopey, Ms. Watterson, Professor Watterson, "Teacher," my favorite lately, Mrs. Hope, the mother of Sasha and the wife of Jake, if my play were indeed a success, even bigger things would happen, for all of us: yes, proofreading and history would be reconciled once and for all, redeemed, linked forever in the minds and hearts of my audience to the advantage of all and both. Words and details would matter, and use of the correct ones would perhaps even save lives. My credo!

Yes, I was clearly out of mind.

Yet there was even more, some of it not so realistic, some pretty darn close. Realism and wishful thinking were not worth trying to separate. I wished, planned, dreamed, anticipated that donations to our small town's local food bank would overflow their big drums, set up in the lobby of the theater. Democrats and Greens would be there, registering voters outside. Amnesty International club members from the high school would host a table. Veterans for Peace, Tay-Sachs screeners, Asian bone marrow donating match-seekers, homeless shelter volunteers, Sierra Club docents and Audubon bird watchers, all were invited and would, I expected, be assembled. The local ministers, rabbi and imam would all attend, as if in some terrific barroom joke about clergy walking into a theater. Naturally, reviews would be glowing, ovations would be standing, cut flowers and bouquets would be heaved from the orchestra seats and balcony because, well, most of them would have been purchased by me in advance and strategically distributed among friends in the crowd for laying down on stage or throwing in the direction of the cast and, just to make sure, why not, nicely affirming both my ambition and answering my desperation.

And perhaps, I dreamed or wished or thought-choreographed, as a further result of my soon-to-be successful debut play and its likely enthusiastic reception, right-wing attacks on Mexican immigrants and gays and lesbians would also be checked, why not that too, and local hillbilly nativists, shamed, Minuteman Militia troops disbanded. Tea Partiers would back off, gun nuts turn in their weapons, the weekly anti-drone war vigil at the roundabout in the center of town would at least double in size, the Armed Forces Recruiting Center would close up shop and I would soon, very soon, be able to go home, pet the indifferent cat, and welcome my completely recovered hubby and his perfectly fine, healthy, brilliant perfect-recall brain back to our family, not worry about his stalker and easily finish, finally, quickly, that last big batch of unread, ungraded Composition essay drafts from my Tuesday-Thursday morning classes before the final version was collected and final grades were due and Christmas vacation, or so I imagined. I was, needless to say, thinking big, very big, and then even bigger still.

*   *   *

There had before Jake's accident been a couple of very minor roles still left unassigned, but the principal members of the cast, those already playing Anne, Margot, Peter, the other Peter, Mother, Otto Frank, the Van Daans, Mr. Dussel, Mr. Kugler, Miep, Bep, Hello (yes, Hello) and during and in between the tumult of the week I'd been able to fill the rest, with some occasional double-casting. Ali starred as The Allies, naturally, all four of them at once, in a military officer's uniform motley of those countries, a patchwork quilt of Stars and Stripes and Tricolor and Union Jack and Hammer and Sickle. He could fill in as needed elsewhere, but perhaps just as a small extra background cow. I did not want to overwork him. I could fill in myself, here and there, or just lose parts as needed or, not needed.

There were still plenty of other details, technical challenges to deal with, not to mention catching up on rehearsals lost to all the time I'd spent at first the ER and then the ICU and then the private room with the view from its big picture window and even bigger flat-screen television and an aquarium, too, with four plump goldfish swimming obliviously in and among plastic toy hospital room furnishings, a light-hearted replica of Jake's actual room itself, with a shy, pretty fish hiding under an adjustable hospital bed or nibbling algae off of a masked anesthesiologist or, could it be, watching a nurse fluff the plastic upright patient's tiny pillow? In this pleasing underwater diorama meant to parallel our own full-scale medical care experience, some attentive doctor fish always came when you called for help, checked your vitals, adjusted your pain medication, helped you to the commode though it was always of course still a fish.

Yes, for good or bad and absolutely nonetheless, everywhere I looked now I found that I saw dioramas, sets, theater, more and more accidentally or self-consciously contrived scenes of life or near-life requiring, even demanding, narration and elaboration and development. Stare at the same mistake long enough and you arrive at some kind of perfection. Once you noticed a stalker, for instance, the whole world was just chock-full of them. Fail to recognize your poorly disguised husband of twenty-five years, attired as, say, Rex Harrison in a houndstooth hat and tweed coat, and the next time he saw you he didn't even know you. It could happen. It had happened! And so then, why not, it could and would happen again, on stage, in a restorative reversal, a revision as easy to make real as unreal, which I would make.

* * *

Saturday morning. Big show that night. So much to account for. There were plenty of moving parts to the production, mechanical and electrical, a computer program to control it all, projections and lights and sound, from up in the tech room, and backstage all kinds of smart machines to help the human crew to work ropes, pulleys, lights, music and sound effects. Costumes and sets were all about perspective. We did the lead actress up in extremely oversized shoes and body padding and coordinated hydraulics and wires, or in some scenes, just dramatically under-sized the props which the normal-sized actress used, fitting her into a miniature set like poor Alice in her shrunken Third Reich wunderland. Perspective would indeed be my singular if overly employed tool; it was perhaps, finally, my only one beyond the power of suggestion and something like consensus reality. It was a mean trick, if easy enough, a gimmick, or it was an obvious and generous interpretation of other people's mistakes, tragedies and failure to run spell-check and grammar check, to protect us from ourselves and others. How to make the world both so much bigger and its easy metaphors and corollaries helpfully smaller and more manageable yet still resonate?

It was not really much of a creative process. I admit that

I relied on my vague and unreliable recollection of a short-lived 1970's television show about adventurers lost in a land of giants and my girlhood fascination with the famous, tiny Clock Family of *The Borrowers* books, Father and Mother and precocious miniature girl-child Arietty. I had tried to deny it, but then given in, to all of it, to everything. Such was the power of having nothing to lose, of desperation, of avoiding making small, useless judgments about beginning writers' problematic ordering of topic sentences and thesis statements and instead risking making potentially very big mistakes about what was possible to dream up, to pull off in front of an audience of people who actually chose to attend your class, err, play. Such was the weird power I was finding in myself, of all people, and of improvisation, of making do, of mimicking and repurposing, as they called it lately.

Giant Anne's old-fashioned pitchfork was only a tiny plastic cocktail fork. Her overalls were made purposely too-small, too uncomfortably tight-seeming, ankles exposed in the helpful cartoon realignment of the off-kilter and off-register. Objects were not to scale. She milked and fed my daughter's old plastic toy farm animals and bathtub creatures. You get the idea. History in cartoon miniature is so much easier to tell. I'd tried to explain to my students the easy trick of emphasis, the "frame," and of foreground and background, of big ideas reflected in big sentences, the powerful impact of brevity, of repetition and of repetition and also of more repetition as a way to prioritize and weight the relative import of people, places, things and ideas, the "rhetorical situation" it was called in our writing textbook, but it was a moment you could still miss if you blinked or did not recognize it calling attention to itself, however loudly, especially if you did not know to listen or look because nobody had told you, maybe you hadn't read the chapter, or you'd missed that day in class, or had not yet figured out that life itself was a series of same, as radical or not as reality, to crib from Lenin, not his real name either, of all people.

So that my Anne herself was exactly as tall as was required, as radical as she needed to be according to me, as real and unreal and as tall as the picture-perfect farm's silo and the rustic old red barn and the iconic old Holland-style windmill, too. Quaint, rustic, threatened if the Atlantic breached the famous man-made defenses of the below sea-level nation. She was in some later scenes represented only in a big, unwieldy papier mache human-woman hand reaching from stage left into the set in order to stroke the head of a child or pet an animal or, occasionally, to squeeze to death an SS guard in her fist, like Queen Kong. She was occasionally only a shadow, or a silhouette. She was Gulliver and Jack's Giant and Polyphemus and the BFG and the scorned and radioactive doomed fifty-foot sci-fi girlfriend monster except that she was also still, always, the fourteen year old Jewish adolescent girl now grown up to be a very large if also kind of sexy middle-aged woman who had so defined the worldviews of so many — if still not quite enough — further transformed dramatically to become a whole and complete and beautiful exaggeration of empathy and resistance and courage but by whom you also could be squashed, accidentally or on purpose, if you were not careful.

*   *   *

These, then, were the stakes, clumsily if sincerely, hurriedly contrived: immortality and its terrible saintly burden, or obscurity and a kind of giant, yes, giant and exaggerated freedom from it all — the diary, the legend, the responsibility, the tedious annual rereading by schoolchildren worldwide — along with above-average height and weight and being forgotten to death. Big people die younger, on average, than do average-sized people. Giants' bodies' skeletons cannot bear them, their hearts give out, and they often fall down and hurt themselves.

It was all of it so clumsy and obvious, and, yes, that suited me fine, just fine, you bet, thank you, especially with Jake struggling, or not, to re-Jakify. Easy tropes, clichés, exaggerations, visual puns were my welcome refuge and hope at a moment when what passed for reality was just unacceptable. So it seemed to me that clumsy and obvious and unsubtle and even slapstick were totally acceptable just now, as theater and pedagogy and parenting and living, especially with the attacks on the Towers and invasions of two foreign countries (and counting) unconnected to them, terrorists, drones, airport check-ins, Orange Alerts, a generation for whom horror had still not, so far, caused them to respect words enough to proofread or to keep in their homes, in their minds, a safe place — closet, underground cellar, attic — for runaway slaves, for Jews and other persecuted minorities, for themselves, for their completely imagined audience, and for the future or, worst of all, the past, often spelled as passed.

*   *   *

Totality and consequences and gigantism and, yes, here it came, all of it, with the sound of cowbells, because it had to happen, with the appearance of a whole third and final act herd of diary (sic) cows, inevitable if docile grazing-creature pages of long-hand written confession, all of it begging to be responded to, laughed at, I dared you, begged you. I had been provoked, and so I lashed out, and here's what I had come up with: Each animal, constructed out of cardboard or a cow costume with a person inside, was covered not in black and white spots but handwritten notes, girly-script, with loops and flowers and short, recognizable excerpts from the book, organized to fit the canvas, for instance: "Dearest Kitty: I hope I will be able to confide everything to you, as I have never been able to confide in anyone, and I hope you will be a great source of comfort and support." And so on, out of obscurity and into possible vulnerability to the total irrevocable loss of context, of apprehension, no longer a journal entry, but a manifesto, a pasture-full of word-ful ungulates chomping and chewing and regurgitating and chewing again, and finally digesting and then being milked, their wholesome milk going immediately after its fast, light, safe pasteurization into old-fashioned quart glass bottles or, processed into powder and shipped in big sacks with "Non-Fat Dry Milk: Donated by the People of the Netherlands" printed on each and the famous black-and-white photograph of the young Anne Frank, all to feed a needy world, not to mention my imagination, my gently subversive re-ordering of history and memory and focus.

*　　*　　*

She'd once been so very powerful and so was at first a bit intimidating, even to me, a character in my own play struggling to find herself and always finding, alas, way too much of herself. Like me! She was heavy on everybody's mind now, as I'd intended. And just plain heavy. When she sat around the house, or the attic or the dairy operation, boy, she really sat around. She wore a fat suit. My giantess Anne Frank was a very big role for any actress indeed.

Naturally, Anne's spread was an organic dairy operation, and kosher, too. Methane-powered and absolutely no rGBH or hormones. The free-ranging happy and free anti-fascist cows produced good, healthy milk and the animals were treated kindly, humanely and grass-fed. They each had names, of those figures in the original book for whom I had not found parts in the play, and wore them on name tags, "Hello, My name is _____," some with cowbells. They spoke and sang and tap-danced. The set suggested recognizable tourist brochure elements of Holland, of course, but with modern wind generators in addition to the iconic old mills, solar panels and Tibetan prayer flags a la Mendocino, California, in addition to the distant silhouettes of ancient earthen dikes and heroic Queen Beatrix Herself and a very, very big wooden shoe, presumably one of Anne's, if, always, also a dark swastika flying in the distance like a bad cloud, behind and above it all. The weather was balmy, skies clear, but always with a chance of Nazi. No kidding. My idea, basically, was that in this case, for this particular play, at this moment, too much of a good thing was just right. I could and would control scale, change size and emphasize, heavy-handedly, the power of intervention, of revisionism, of proofreading, of memory. Plot was far less important than identifying if not completely realizing the details of my big, impossible dream of rehabilitation and renewed attentiveness, of reading fully and running spell-check and grammar check again, avoiding repetition and remembering to identify credible experts, integrate quotations correctly while citing them using MLA rules and appreciating the consequences and larger context of one's writing. The extremely large adult Anne supervised the whole operation, and when she sang to the happy diary cows and calves in the big opening scene, they certainly did sing back, suggesting a harmony-making little herd, a jolly fat bovine Von Trapp Family singers-style ensemble, with one especially clever animal telling the wonderful old joke about why cream costs more than milk, because it was much harder for her to sit on those tiny bottles.

And it turned out that Anne had in my alternative universe (and hers) in fact married young Peter Schiff, the teenage boy of her erotic dreams, who appeared here as a handsome if only averaged-sized middle-aged man wearing a sweater with patches in the elbows and smoking a meerschaum pipe. He adored her, as he should have, and among their friends here at the commune were members of the brave Dutch Resistance, including the other Peter, who the play suggested might also be Anne's lover. Lucky woman, her husband and political comrade was okay with that. She had her needs, after all, being a whole lot of woman for only just one average-sized man.

And in a nod to both time travel and even more wishful thinking — both also popular tropes just then — these good Dutch people had freed up their below-sea level nation from Nazism so that — good news, everybody! — most of the worst of the Holocaust hadn't, it turned out, even happened at all, not in this particular alternative universe. Anne Frank had made sure of that, in a terrific scene in which she summoned help from Ali ("ally"), from the audience, from the future, asking, demanding as in the perhaps most famous scene in theater ever, that everyone stand, stand up, and clap if you, they, we all believed, to clap together as loud as we could so that we might rescue Anne and ourselves from the tyranny of time and error and cowardice, applaud, please, as loud as you have applauded in your lives, people.

I know, I know, I know: *Charlotte's Web* meets *Animal Farm* meets Peter Pandering, but why not? Fine. In scientific studies this phenomenon of mass assent or shared delusion or trust or faith is called "The Tinkerbell Effect." After all, why not have a delusion?

I would further provoke it, and graciously embrace any and all comparisons, flattering or not, sincere or sarcastic, it just did not matter, to the talking and singing and dancing cows and chickens and goats of every fable or children's story ever written, with the human and non-human characters all weighing in on politics and love and solidarity, the obvious problem of the play being Anne's enormous size, of course, and how she and the rest of us were meant to deal with it. And how were we, the audience, to deal with?

How? By considering the interrogatives, as that one, each delivered by Ali, in something like his custom-made role of "The Narrator." They were fully half of the play's dialog, and made for plenty of too-short and too-long questions, self-answered, unanswered, rhetorical, and polemical, but plenty of opportunity for him to shine. He was just terrific, a stout Egyptian-American in a dark suit, sort of Rod Serling as Master of Ceremonies, with a big oversized bow tie to suggest the awkward pedagogue, trustworthy father-figure, avuncular nerdy authority and beloved chronicler of a small, inconsequential town's history.

Act One had introduced Ali and the scene, the characters in their weird wonderful world, with some back story and, finally, the arrival of Big A herself. In Act Two we began to appreciate the problem, or problems, of her new life and those of her futuristic fantasy mini-kibbutz, including introduction of elements of a new journal, written by the grown-up giantess, in which she confesses to fear and anxiety over her haunting by the ghosts of her own girlhood and her struggles with a too-large imagination.

Anne spoke a truly magnificent soliloquy in Act Three about how she was tired of being looked up to. Literally, of course. How difficult it had been to be so much larger than life, and so defined by death and absence, including her own. Of being a case study, stand-in, object of affection, the subject of interminable middle school and high school and college writing class essays, a lot of them plagiarized from *CliffsNotes* and the web. Larger than life was, indeed, a difficult life for anybody to live, Anne's larger than after-life success as a prosperous dairy-woman in her hypothetical fairy tale-dystopia notwithstanding. Or not sitting down. If you were going to be this big you would be taking up other people's spaces, after all, filling in their missing places, their own absences, and creating a clumsy comparison whenever you were in the room, the 800-pound Jewish girl-woman martyr in the corner of it, an embarrassing juxtaposition, between what you could be and what you were not, and that troubled her, not to mention the head injury sustained by Peter Number Two when he fell out of the hayloft onto Peter Number One, who as a result often could not remember who he was or, worse, who she was, go figure, and imitating my own life.

The play's heart-wrenching dramatic dilemma was choreographed around the appearance of a giant question mark-shaped cloud, or smoke, either way, rising from below, in between and in front of both the gray storm of European domination by fascists and the sunshine of a free and sunny Holland, with Anne seeming to have to choose between the dairy or the diary, between the failure of real life to pay attention as closely as it should be paying attention to us, or as we'd like it to, and the possibilities of imagination and love and the vitamin and calcium-rich milk of healthy and well cared-for domesticated animals.

And, yes, the late addition of a key character in what was becoming experimental theater, as in experiment and perhaps mad scientist — why not, I was writing to catch up, to save my husband? A cat. Not our own housecat but, of course, a dear, dear kitty stuck up in a tree. A small, cute Asian cartoon girl-cat whose companionship and solidarity has meant so much to so many young girls and women across the world, inexplicably but undeniably — me hedging my bets, taking no chances, nonetheless and, again, why not? — across time and space asking but mostly listening as they wrote to her and talked to her and esteemed her as no other.

Why, the whole play asked, had I felt that I needed to write all of this as if it were fiction, as if anything at all were fiction, as if there even was fiction and fictionalizing after history, reality, the Holocaust and community college?

Because, perhaps, was the answer, there were as many consequences to dressing up like a teacher as being one, or as a playwright, as dressing up like a heartless old kitty cat, or as "Kitty," the diary, the journal itself, which was, yes, my own role finally. It was a totally non-speaking part, a person wearing a big papier mache head: white head, yellow nose, black whiskers, pink ribbon behind my pointy ear. I was the diary. I would be the autobiography, the story of one young girl and not the other. I would out-Hello her, out-Kitty her. And thus I imagined I would take something from her, away from that crazy, sad Chinese girl, and put it into my dream, my reordering, my syntax, my play, a play on life and on words. I would argue a fairly didactic if still completely satisfying argument for an appreciation of, yes, rereading one's work out loud, asking questions, proudly identifying a thesis statement, making a "promise to the reader," not just talking about the weather, as they say, but finally doing something about it. The swastika-clouds and the ashes of the six million plus, yes, and I would make exactly the right word choice here, insert a comma in-between Hello and Kitty once and for all, to ease the suffering and the confusion of so many who cared, to set right those millions more who certainly knew that "Hello" was a greeting, damn it, and also a Dutch name, yes, sure, but that "Hello Kitty" was a very, very strange name for anybody, human or animal or cat, a provocation, a syntactical uncertainty, a burden, a threat and a question which required answering, a call for a fireman with a ladder to rescue, please, a stranded furry house pet up on the high branch of a tall tree.

*   *   *

And so the Fire Department would arrive on stage to remove me with their ladder, and our oversized heroine would decide for herself, naturally, because she was autonomous but only after hearing from you and from me and the person sitting next to you and from everybody else in the Las Palmas (sic) Civic Auditorium whether or not to abandon the Anne legend, grown so very out-of-control, for real-life average stature and normal risk and human mortality. Whether, ladies and gentlemen, to continue in an infinite half-life of over-dimensionality among veterans of the Dutch Underground, herds of singing and dancing ungulates, a cartoon girl-cat and the triumph of good over evil, all of it a kind of disappearing act from history and people's ambitions for it, and for her, soon to be a major motion picture, who knew…?

Or to go back to being that toothy adolescent portrait forever on the cover of the book, one of the most recognized and beloved teenage faces in the world, if also to the sad foreshadowing of the life of a dark and mysterious beauty who never was meant to live, a first-time writer, a debut memoirist, a martyr, an accidental icon whose most secret thoughts were given to the world by her angry, sad, guilt-ridden father?

*   *   *

Saturday afternoon. Quick run-through, tech check. I stood in the wings, and watched, and yelled, when not up waiting in the tree. Yes, the play was beautiful and dangerous, not the least due to its invitation to be ridiculed or embraced, to take such questions seriously or not, which Ali ("ally"), in his main role of The Narrator in this perverse *Our Town* rip-off made clear, offering the existential question of who appreciates, who values life while they are actually living it ("The saints and poets, maybe – they do some") which is to say changing it, perhaps fixing other people's easy errors and risking the consequences of that particular civic arrogance, all toward keeping Anne alive or maybe keeping her dead, or both at the same time, one Anne big on the cartoon farm-commune and the other Anne emaciated, angelic, a transparent if ubiquitous ghost.

He stood there and insisted that wonder as this can be, must be distinguished from wander, friends, conscious is not the same as conscience (no, not exactly, though sometimes maybe) and must be, always, not because some nasty old teacher tells you to or you will get a bad grade if you don't or even be awarded fake extra credit but because, finally, nobody wants to have to live in a world where perpetual remedialism is going to risk getting those European Jews hiding in your attic killed, injure a good man, or constantly have to explain the difference between big and small and good and evil, especially to people you think might know, and do know better. There was more, all of it under a single extra-bright spot, and sounding a lot like me, go figure,

90   — *The Dairy of Anne Frank or Show Biz is My Life!* —

the author and the real-life inspiration, as I liked to call myself, for the play, "Based on a true story." There was more. Upton Sinclair and Sinclair Lewis are not, were not, ever the same person, he continued. "There" is not "their" is not "they're." Arose is not a rose. Every day is not everyday. (I am not Gertrude Stein, and neither is anybody else lately.) "It is" is not "its." There is in fact conscious and there is unconscious, and there are conscientious and conscience, too, and consciousness, and all of them may be used, must be used, should be used by all means, please, but used correctly and on the right occasion. A part is not apart. There is no un-conscience.

Or maybe there was, is, as in amorality, which I did not really believe in, or Hitler or the famous if now famously reconsidered so-called banality of evil. There was unconsciousness, if you wanted it, and it's (it is) really not that hard to find, concluded Ali in his big speech, except that he had that night not concluded, he had only just begun, going somewhat off-script, ad libbing, developing the material right there on stage, and making me proud.

*   *   *

Meanwhile, my real-life husband was now fully conscious, and he was conscientious, too. Or had been, once. Who even knew now? Not me. He was not really himself. But who was? Perhaps there was no going back. He had cared for his family, gone to work, paid his insurance, which featured a scarily high deductible, been faithful and a good father. Nonetheless, he seemed still not completely aware of his surroundings, even as he was being careful about bathing — we are a good, clean family — and keeping up with the news and asking about his students and, yes, doing some light administrative work from the desk in his new, less cheerful and expensive hospital room, this one with a roommate, his assistant showing up every afternoon needing his signature and providing help with managing the department, approving textbook orders, assigning classes, reporting to his president and the school board, reviewing the minutes of the English majors club meeting, preparing for an upcoming audit of the Writing Lab. He was realizing life, but seemed not to recognize it as his own. It was a pretty good one, sure, and he was more than only competent at it, anybody could see that. The new room lacked an aquarium, its main feature being a drape which separated the patients. The place started to look like his office at work, which scared me. If the school found out he could not really ever be himself, but could be taken care of here, working from home as it were, home being this hospital room, then would he ever be discharged?

*   *   *

For good or bad, you can see that the play was meanwhile turning out to be even more autobiographical than even I'd planned, not that I'd been able to plan much at all, not that I had resisted going in that direction, no, not at all, playing with the cat now transformed to playing the cat, which was maybe both the best and worst thing you could say about it. It was unabashedly mine, all mine. I was, after all, the director, producer, stage manager, costume designer, dramaturge, semi-autobiographical main character as well as understudy for a couple of parts, in addition to being the woman dressed in the pretty Japanese cartoon feline costume at a later key moment in the play, especially because I am afraid of heights

The show had gotten, as you can imagine, quite a buzz. We were already sold out, with limited standing room only by the morning of the performance, with volunteer valet parking attendants (Boy Scouts) and senior citizen volunteers as ushers. All profits would benefit the local homeless shelter. It was a big deal so, each and every action requiring a reaction, the city decided officially that because of "the nature of the material" it now anticipated protesters, or so announced the Mayor, for reasons at first unclear to me.

"Protesting what, I wonder, exactly?" the Chief of Police asked me at the hospital late Saturday afternoon. Chief Myers shook his head. I sincerely appreciated the question. It was insincere, but fun. I also appreciated his visit, the attention, my celebrity and the "anticipated" violence or civic unrest, which I took as an endorsement of sorts. I posed in a photograph with him, and posted it on Facebook. If the Chief of Police seemed to like the play, well, perhaps the crazies would not show up outside, and we'd have the imprimatur of John Law, theatergoer, and fill the house too.

Still, I did not so much appreciate the late introduction of an another, additional plot element, and the introduction of more characters, Chief of Police Myers, say, and protesters, too, who were not even actually there, not anywhere, and would have to be imagined, made up, in the stage version of what has happening or not happening, either way.

"Does it even matter?" I asked. It was a question I was asking a lot lately.

"I guess not. Not to me," he said, helpfully. "It's a line item, a budget thing."

He stood with his arms crossed, surveying our tiny, quaint town square from Jake's scenic third-floor hospital room, or perhaps looking for somebody deserving of his anticipation, suspicion, interrogation while the potential criminals, whoever they were, wherever, I figured, gathering unseen, un-seeable, in a fictional but unrealistic cabin in the nearby woods or a secret bunker or church basement or lay in wait — take your pick — in another room, just down the hall, up on a stage somewhere of their own weird imagining.

This is a small town but there was by now just paranoia enough to go around. More could always be found, it seemed, assigned, manufactured, or brought in. This was America after all.

And of course The Chief, as I liked to call him, an otherwise good guy, was eager enough to pull out those big high-tech and hitherto totally unused law enforcement line-item accoutrements for which the city had paid almost nothing or been given or coerced into accepting by the state or county and which had until now been in storage: bullhorns, plastic shields, tear gas, percussion grenades, walkie-talkies, all of it expensive Department of Homeland Security, Department of Defense surplus pushed on Las Palmas, just short of being driven to the city by the President and the Joint Chiefs.

"Betty would have loved this," he said, completely changing the subject. "She loved occasion," he said. "She loved theater. She loved just everybody."

"She loved you, Chief Bob," I said.

He smiled. "She did not discriminate, I'm afraid. She would have loved the protesters, too." I was lucky to have him there. He was empathetic. And he was armed.

A lone traffic control officer arrived to accompany The Chief on their way to find the crowd control stuff, dust it off, put in some fresh bullets and batteries. Neither usually even carried a sidearm. The P.D.'s traffic guy would presumably write you a ticket for interfering with his boss or even inciting a riot, whichever was going to happen because everybody knew that nothing and neither were gonna happen, probably.

"An equestrian squad will be there," said the Chief, "for crowd control," as he prepared to leave. I liked the way he hitched up his utility belt when he said it, cowboy hero style. It disappointed me that as a teacher I could not rely on the comfort or affirmation of such a gesture. Of course, as playwright I had more choices than I could handle.

"I didn't know we had one," I said, gratefully, if not meaning it, not one bit. "Pardner."

"Well, it's mostly," Chief said, smiling, "old Randy Forster and his son-in-law David."

"Two horses, then," I said, finding an image in my head, despite not having looked for it, not resisted it quickly enough. "I can work with that."

"What do you mean?" he asked.

"Sorry," I said. "Thinking out loud."

*　　*　　*

We'd been all over the Internet and shared and friended on Facebook and reported on by the wire services. There was a short piece and commentary on National Public Radio and a handful of newspaper editorials, too, some lauding my efforts and others attacking me, with all kinds of angles on the historical Anne Frank and the literary Anne Frank and what was sacrosanct, and historical revisionism and co-opting or stealing history and how the past wasn't even passed, that old chestnut.

Yet it suited me, all of it. This was my moment, mine, nobody else owned it, and I suspected that when my husband finally woke up from his unconscientiousness about my identify as his wife, or his absurd medical condition or dream or his own parallel universe, and when he loved me again, or when the confused local evangelical congregants and famous out-of-town "God Hates Fags" protesters had arrived, not arrived, been ignored, counter-protested by good Samaritans or arrested by our complete and total compliment of six officers (two in the saddle) plus the two oldster wannabes from CPR, when the curtain fell on Anne Frank and later, in a few months, when Ali transferred, finally, after graduation, to a four-year college, somebody would call me by which I mean call me up, as in call me out, on all my wishful thinking and wishful-experiential writing for the modern American stage and not ever call back with contracts and offers and residencies and I would be a happy nobody once again, returned to grading Composition essays and offering editing marks, or not.

*　　*　　*

Saturday night. The show was a go, the parking lot full. There was no intermission. After Anne's own big speech there were fades to black, and one completely entertaining alternative ending after another, each more provocative and impossible than the previous, with two stage hands wheeling out the big colorful cardboard applause-o-meter, an homage to game shows and 1950's-style audience participation. Each speech, each ending, each resolution of or further complication of the problem got a big hand, but then the curtain went up and there was another ending, with yet another appeal to the audience and yet an even bigger applause for that one, and the next. Would the endings never end? And was it possible somehow that each time Anne got a little smaller? They would. And, yes, it was.

That first big ovation was followed by a gratifyingly heartfelt response for which I had hoped, to that defining moment which I'd imagined or contrived or which possibly just wrote itself, as they say, when "The Narrator" (Ali Omar Nassef, in the starring role) walked in with his hammer and nails and set up a ladder and fixed the homemade sign at the entrance of the farm, the set, the world, at last switching out those crooked oversized letters "I" and "A" and offered a truly heartbreaking mea culpa, about language and responsibility and the importance of using spell-check, all exactly as rehearsed, in near-Shakespearean delivery, albeit with a Middle Eastern accent, for maximum pathos and satisfaction and, just like that, returned Anne Frank to her tragic if exemplary place in history, dead again, sure, but also living and alive in everyone's shared consciousnesses, if martyred once more anew as she was expected to be, poor girl. Anne would in this version be forever small — meaning normal sized — living dead in a room that could be an attic or a barracks, letting the murdered not rest, nor the murderers, not abiding in the ranch house setting of the rolling hills and pastures and wide open rural environs of their imaginations or of mine, lost and happy.

*　*　*

And here arrived that shameless rip-off of yet another familiar classic play, a defining moment from that uber-theatrical moment in Peter Pan where the audience is told to clap, please, now, if they believe in fairies, clap, powerfully, in a kind of epistemological group CPR-event to revive dead "Tink," which in even the very worst amateur school productions the audience is always eager to perform, or at least pretend to do, to act, to rescue or aid or repair, as if reviving a lost life or, in my case, stopping Hitler and imposing racial tolerance and peace in our time (and restoring my husband to me!) could be, would be, might be somehow that easy, elegant, even fulfilling, as at least rereading your own work before you turned it in.

In the next ending in the line-up, better or worse, more

or less satisfying, more false or more true — who knew, finally? — Anne hit a palm tree by accident while driving a tractor, knocking her husband Peter down and out. In another, two local police officers arrived, on two last-minute Shetland ponies, to confront Nazi brownshirts protesting outside the farm. In another a cardboard Hello Kitty was, yes, stepped on and crushed flat by Anne's giantess foot in a very, very large rubber boot but of course bounced right back, like an inflatable clown toy, in perhaps that moment most closely reflecting my own happy-drug-inspired dreams and, yes, frequently, nightmares.

And in one more penultimate un-final scene, emaciated and bloated farm animals were covered not in handwriting but in red and black and white swastika flags, simultaneously starving and needing to be milked. An ancient, stooped and lonely Peter stood alone, thin and gray, with Anne's photograph beamed behind him into the night sky like the famous Batman call, smoke rising from the camps behind it all in the shapes of spindly once-human forms. In another, Ali stacked cans upon cans of evaporated milk in a pleasing supermarket endcap display aisle construction, with a dramatic lights-out at the end, like trying to shake off a nightmare or startle oneself into consciousness, and so on and on until that moment when a direct democratic majority vote by the audience put an end, a happy end, to it all, finally, and the lights went back on and the results of their decision about which kind of liberation (from too many choices) our characters, my characters, would enjoy, would be were tallied up.

*   *   *

Either way, or both, or all, the show itself, the performance, was a great big surreal success, in no small part the result of all the audience's enthusiastic standing up and clapping and sitting down and then doing it again, not only for one storyline or another but for, yes, itself, for its own power of choice-making, for its collaboration and trust and engagement and empowerment and, I like to think, for peer editing, real peer editing and honest proofreading and multiple revisions and drafting and consequences. They all just ate it right up, esteemed and newly energized and eager to imagine even more possibilities, real-life variables available again, and relieved of the burden of choosing only one very best very limited future, so excited at the possibility of many, even too many, more. Immortality, or at least a multiple-choice destiny.

I could likely have written even further unconclusions for a play already mostly composed of ending upon endings, its beginning, the inspiration, that now nearly-forgotten trespass upon history and language long reapportioned, its perspective shifted to focus on the potential for freedom as constructed by a responsibility to language, and inspired I see now by the late short story writer Grace Paley's insistence that "Everyone, real or invented, deserves the open destiny of life," at least for a while, including Anne herself and the gang at the socialist dairy kibbutz of my dream world.

* * *

Which is how it finally ended, or pretended to, or perhaps had to, considering practical and time constraints. Life is not theater, and that's really too bad. Everybody in the hall was a winner. The curtain dropped and so I was finally brought out on stage to see the audience's choice — everything, impossibly, all of the above! — to accept my own applause, just like that, exactly as I had planned, and another final standing ovation with the cast. I embraced my star "star student" there under the lights. Flowers appeared at my feet, just like that, if exactly as I had arranged, as I had imagined, as I had of course arranged and rearranged and imagined everything to that point. Sasha ran out to hug me, right on cue. My mother-in-law waved from the front row, sitting — now, standing, clapping — with nearly all of the writing students from my two completely abandoned Composition classes and much of the college's contingent of contingent faculty, right there with the tenure-track teachers and coaches and custodial staff and administrators, all of them except, of course, Jake.

And after photographs and many bows, and the slow, reluctant exodus of the full house out into the lobby, street, parking lot, past the donation bins (gratifyingly full) and outreach tables surrounded by engaged citizens, the lone remaining protester (a man with a small sign about Obama the space alien, with a cartoon black-skinned version of *ET*) who smiled at the crowd, a thick mini-phalanx of law enforcement, a few piles of aromatic fresh horse shit, I also went out, briefly, for drinks with the cast to the watering hole across the street. I left them after one quick round to return to the theater to briefly secure the props, begin to strike the set, make sure the swastika was turned off, put out the lights, lock up, so I could get back to Jake, only just down the block at General General, waiting, I believed, for a debriefing, and to share my success.

*　　*　　*

Back at the hospital, bouquets in hand, I discovered he was missing, his bed linens stripped back, the stack of "Hello, My Name is ＿＿＿" blue-trimmed white name tags, all blank, scattered like playing cards on the floor of his room as if there had been a commotion, perhaps an attack or even an abduction, or some kind of struggle, the get well cards knocked off the dresser, clothing strewn about, an almost too-perfect scene, looking like it had, as everything lately, been staged, purposely and purposefully constructed.

I paused to consider the symmetrical arrangement of those name tags in their playing card formation, which seemed overly, absurdly communicative, as if somebody had dealt them, a winning hand, to suggest a message if not actually deliver it. Arranged like that, blank name tags connected in their blankness, they seemed another ghostly dispatch, repeated, of impossible forgetting and the twisted empiricism of randomness, hurt, powerlessness, the opposite of where I had just been.

A nurse found me before I could panic further, or act like somebody panicking, first at Jake's disappearance and then at the powerful if clumsy communication from chance or accident or fate, if that was communication at all. She had actually been looking for me, she said, a real first at Patton General. Finally, I thought, somebody at the hospital with a clear mission, something definitive to say, and at a helpful moment, too. I did not recognize her. Maybe she was new. Weirdly, she had a list with her, a physical piece of paper. She read from it in order, reciting as if she might get it wrong somehow, or perhaps be held responsible for some mistake or oversight later, or was only performing a read-through. One. He'd announced he was checking himself out, she explained, saying he had to be somewhere. Two. They'd called me, left a message but of course I'd been enjoying my success, she said, and probably was out at the cast after-party drinking a quick beer, she speculated, my cell phone silenced. (Not a beer, a Tom Collins, thank you.) Third. Chief Meyers, who they'd also called, had shown up just after Jake had gone missing, only minutes after he'd been last seen, walking out the front lobby, encouraged by a Security guy and an administrator to stay, please, Sir, but declined, been here and left, and, finally, that El Chiefo had called just now to say that I was supposed to meet him at the Sleepy Bear which, she reminded me — and whoever else was watching or overhearing this totally contrived-seeming scene — was actually the former TraveLodge, now simply called the Sleepy Bear, which I of course knew because I had grown up here, but perhaps she had not? That, she said, was it. It.

This nurse, whose badge read "Nance" seemed to want to be further acknowledged. I looked around for an audience or my imagined surveillance cameras or a narrator or somebody offstage whom I'd perhaps put there myself and forgotten, a friend to feed me a line for just this moment, scene or occasion.

Nothing. We were alone.

So I thanked her, saying "Thanks, Nance" but she said, as she must have a hundred thousand times before if she was real, and a real nurse, that her name was Nancy, no kidding, and it's possible that I began just then, finally, after all of it (It) to finally suspect the impact, for good or bad, collateral and other consequences, of my own experiment on each and all around me, on and offstage, major or minor player, hero or villain, loved and unloved. I speculated that my own influence, experiential intervention, hyper-awareness — "theatricality" it was sometimes called, pejoratively — my perverse, exaggerated sensitivity to and care for and defense of language (who cares, after all, if somebody cannot spell, not even their own name, and why?) perhaps accounted for or had even caused (!) the nurse's exaggerated and charmingly stilted yet almost if not quite welcome performance, and maybe that of everybody to this point. And perhaps that my intervention or modest resistance had itself even created this nurse herself, "Nurse," or "Nance," which of course should have been spelled "Nancee" if she were so committed to whatever it was she was committed to, another player, a new character as it were, in my meta-drama.

It was as if we were all situated in the workings of some big atomic pinball thought-and-action machine which I had invented, constructed out of my amusement, frustration, self-pity, disappointment, boredom, procrastination, then hyperactive out-of-proportion over-creativity. I had as a result become the biggest bumper in the mechanical thingie-world, the strongest flipper, perhaps the entire gizmo itself, and also the garish princess or astronaut or harlequin or wizard who watched over and controlled the whole game, in this case Anne Frank, if you can imagine it — and I know, friend, that you can if you have gotten this far! — yes, an Official Diary of Anne Frank pinball machine, why not, keep the little Jewish girl out of Bergen-Belsen if you can, avoid the S.S., with a nifty trap door and drawings of the hiding place, and the rest of it. Pull, tilt, but game never, ever really over.

*   *   *

And was it possible, I wondered, that even Miss Chinese Kitty's actions had responded to this scenario of mine, and not provoked it, and that I had gotten cause and effect, authorship and audience all mixed up? Was it possible that her temporary international migration to Las Palmas, California, USA, of all places, adjacent the adequate aqueduct, getting on a plane to fly here, to presumably study English and cartoon cats and husband-napping at a tiny community college in a small town in Central California, looking for a husband, setting her sights on my husband, de-arborizing our totemic palmy civic bookend mascots by exactly one, and now lying cuffed to a hospital bed herself, had only been a response somehow to my own construction and reconstruction of reality, magic unrealism and not just the autonomous actions of a nut?

After all of what had occurred, why not? Sure. Everyone deserved that open destiny of a life, perhaps even Tiffany, to whom I had denied that possibility, whose life I had interrupted as much as she had interrupted mine.

Yet one person's open destiny was certainly also another's opportunity to refuse, reject and resist. Mine. Me. That was my opportunity, as destiny un-opener, too, as director of my fate and others'. And I was going to make sure that there was, finally, going to be none of that kind of freedom for her, my feline foe, my animal antagonist.

And just to make sure, I left the weird and possibly partly fictional lady nursey and exited the hospital by way of Qing's room, checking in with my Security buddy and peeking in at her, glad to find her sleeping (like a kitten) behind a very closed, very locked door, in her bed, handcuffed to it, foot-cuffed, actually, and going nowhere.

*   *   *

The motel was all of three blocks away. I ran, the Tom Collins forgotten or evaporated or perspired out of me, perhaps scared away by my own body, a welcome chemical or alchemical physical accommodation of the needs of the moment, of body over mind over matter, like the famously slight-of-build panicked mother able to pick up a small automobile when it was required of her, to rescue her child trapped underneath it, that old story likely both hyperbolic and apocryphal, urban legend, and just exactly what the occasion called for. It was a cool night, and the air on my skin felt comforting, so much so that I stopped momentarily to consider an old VW Beetle parked and looking not all that heavy for a car. Hadn't I just thought of that iconic vehicle, and the baby under it, about to be rescued by its Hulk-mother?

I was there almost immediately. Sure enough, Chief Myers's police cruiser was parked out front of our town's only independently owned motel, the very old-school one-time Trav-eLodge with its once-familiar sign's final five letters long ago extinguished after a threatening letter from the chain which once owned or licensed the place long ago. The "Trave" persisted as a crumbling two-story stucco monument to once-popular 1960's discount family lodging and entropy snug-up against the railroad tracks, because that's where you'd want to go to get a good night's rest, after all. Jake must have walked here, stumbling around in his semi-conscious, semi-Jake state.

The Chief seemed to be waiting for me there in the night, standing, smoking outside his car with the radio on, not the police radio or scanner but the FM radio, playing the oldies station, a comfort at this motel people recognized for its tired old teddy, the bear sleepwalking or walking slowly to sleep, on his way to being tucked in but caught forever in his nighttime sleep costume even after the place had lost its lodge-ness and now was just a flea-bag motel with a leftover totemic spirit animal. I assumed that Jake had somehow identified the place as safe, and perhaps identified with its ursine mascot but mostly I did not, could not, assume anything.

"Room 202," the Chief said, pointing me up the stairs to the wide-open second floor landing, next to the rusty ice machine and ancient soda dispenser, where a light burned behind the ratty drapes of a room with two, if arguably the two most important of its golden numerals, fallen off, leaving only the zero and on either side of it the outline of what was gone, and tiny nail holes. There seemed once again to be a theme here, forebodingly, of course, no kidding, involving still the further rearrangement of language and communication, in a clumsy palimpsest testifying to the mutability of pretty much all expectations about words, letters, numbers and symbols, but hey, I was up for it, why not, even getting used to it and still riding high on the success of my evening's own restorative effort, emboldened and feeling strong despite it all. Tiffany safely locked away, one part of the world repaired. Now, on to the next, I told myself, armed for sleepy bear.

Inside, the television was on. I knocked. It took a moment but Jake answered the door, wearing his striped hospital-issue pajama bottoms with a t-shirt hand-painted by Sasha for Father's Day, something from her four-year old girlie-girl yellow and gold and purple puff-paint and glitter and late-unicorn period, and which made him look even more psychotic and lost. I recognized the heirloom garment from the suitcase I'd packed quickly more than a week ago now, and left in his hospital room closet, an object meant to trigger something based on its uniqueness and familiarity. Terror and loneliness inhabited my husband's eyes, as if he did not know how to even answer a door, much less perform whatever follow-up to that mechanically simple if profoundly vulnerable gesture was necessary or anticipated. He was not better. Still, he backed up into the room and let me in.

"Sit down," I commanded, gently. I closed the door

behind me, walked over to the desk in the room, picked up a complementary pen from the stationery set, which was not a set at all but a cheap Bic and a matching writing pad which read "Disabled American Veterans," featuring an American flag and cheerful, stoic U.S. soldiers in wheelchairs and on crutches and with missing limbs, the kind included in mass-mailed donation appeals meant to encourage guilt and giving and fatalism and patriotism, here obviously recycled to better, or at least different use.

*   *   *

And here, dear Reader, is where things got complicated, if also incredibly obvious, predictable and yet somehow completely and elegantly discouraging, too (some deal, this!), where elements which I had myself contrived — as if there could be any more contrivance to this point in my story and even one more unlikely likely event — as if in a time-travel movie — rebelled, reorganized themselves, took their own route to their own darn destiny, suddenly autonomous, leaving me, their author-creator standing by the side of the road, or, actually in room in a dumpy discount motel by the side of same.

I pulled from my pocket that blank name tag I'd taken so dramatically from the hospital room, understanding now why I'd picked it up off of the floor, and knowing what I had to do, should do, would do, what some character in a play might do, if not necessarily a good play. I hesitated only briefly, weighing my responsibility to Jake, to art, to storytelling, to love, and I turned my back to my wounded husband and wrote a name on it, and I pasted the sticker to my blouse. This was meant to be a dramatic and inspired gesture, a modest surrender to the meaningful compromise that is fate, not to mention a strategic smart move. I could practically read the reviews, in quotes, as in "a dramatic and inspired gesture," and so on, say critics, rave audiences, agree playgoers.

Or it was perhaps too-easy and risky and selfish and short-sighted, a pathetic or mean gesture, one person trying to control another, others, a trick and a deception and a contrivance, a means to an end, and an ending. Like that.

The lonesome wail of an approaching freight train did its part as if on cue, for persuasive atmospherics and a sense of urgency, a corresponding cry for help, like the audio track of a film, anticipatory and urgent. Then I turned around toward Jake, who sat on the edge of the queen-sized bed, with the coin-operated magic fingers, atop a horrible orange and turquoise floral print spread which may have been there since the year that the dangerously sleepy motel mascot first began his long, endless trek to his own impossibly lumpy bed, to nowhere, to obscurity, to here and to there and to now and, yes, to the now that is in nowhere, finally, the encouraging reminder of the moment in its immediate place and present tense.

I turned and stood in front of my husband. Jake looked first at my face, then read the name tag, went a little cross-eyed at first, looked again at the tag then back at my face and reconsidered me, and then, yes, he smiled.

And so, patient and persistent and dear Reader, fresh from one dramatic success, I embraced another and was for my proactive guerilla theatrical gambit mightily rewarded, at least at first, by which I mean also punished soon after. Now, here! So briefly optimistic and confident was I that I wished momentarily that there had indeed been an audience at this seedy flophouse of a motel, though I am fairly shy about that sort of thing. A warning, especially for parents and young readers: Up until now the play (and my life) had been very much family fare, drama for all ages but very soon, indeed immediately, things would get hot. I hung the "Do Not Disturb" sign, quickly latched the door shut, dropped in the chain, secured the lock, turned off the television and the overhead light, and drew the rickety plastic blinds. I sat down with Jake at the wobbly edge of that sagging bed with its horrible polyester print spread from the Vietnam Era and I quickly removed my skirt and undies and I turned back to him and asked Jake if he'd like to ask me, please, how the show had gone. He would, he said, and he did, and so I told him. He seemed pleased at the success of the performance, but I could tell also plenty eager to get on with things, obviously on the same page as me now and prioritizing quite correctly, and reassuringly, all of this corroborated by the shapely expression of erotic interest prominent in his PJs.

I took his hand and held it, and, thankfully, he let me this time. I moved it to my chest. The two of us were quickly completely naked and reconciliatory, which is not really a word, but a just-so neologism for now, useful, so who knows about its future, its possible embrace, perhaps a new phrase for a New Age of bespoke democratic language? For his part Jake seemed at first not to know just how exactly to next proceed, what to do exactly with this sexy new old friend with the familiar mature womanly body but I did my best, which was pretty easy, and soon he seemed to begin to remember, and engage, and perform despite his funny, mixed-up brain, administering those elegant mechanics of erotic mutual aid that is love-making not between two unfamiliar and horny young newbies — that joyful, fevered rush to fornication — but instead the moves shared between cooperating elements of a long-time couple, lovers who have known and cared for each other since their bodies were young, for richer and for poorer, in sickness and in health, and during which he sometimes called out with the coaxing and encouragement and need and self-congratulation and demand and urgency which is, in my experience, the progress of the animal act itself. I did not say much except to coax him, gently. And, yes, of course, pretty quickly still because it had been a while for him, for both of us. It had been awhile since I had heard my name — mine, not hers! — which I waited for, hoped for, needed to hear, counted on as a clumsy way to affirmation and recognition, first perhaps as an interrogative, "Hope?" — why not? — and then more assuredly, as an exclamation and reunion or homecoming holler, "Hope!" and that during and after I would, besides being relieved and gratified by his ecstatic narration of our sex, wonder only what had been wrong with me for a full week, what had I been thinking, and only that I wished I had tried this back in the hospital room, shooed out the so-called medical professionals and Jake's mother and locked the door and unplugged the machines and brought him, yes, back to his senses, to all of them, where lived his mind and memory and his man-body together so that I could hear him growl, as now, hollering "Yes, yes, yes!" or some other selfish, selfless, affirming, congratulating exclamation, along with the proud and perfect Anglo-Saxon verb, noun, both of which, together or apart might be the answer to so many questions, to so many of our problems, all in one heck of a big, yes, climactic moment, right?

Except that, indeed, he looked me straight in the eyes, then in the breasts, at the two of us connected to ourselves, at ourselves, to each other, me coaching him out of his fugue state to performing out loud that anthem of our entire fugue nation, world, planet, universe, and because of my own inheritance of multiple meanings, instruction and advice, fucking his brains out, fucking his brains back in, perhaps, my hubby called out for her instead, she is hope, she who he had been hoping for, hoped for, for "Tiffany" and then, finally, heaved and grunted and laughed with the otherwise deep satisfaction of physical recalibration. And then he laughed again, and so my husband seemed in all others ways except just that one to again be Jake. And that, as they say — or as some people say but I almost never do — was that.

I got up, bravely, hurt but at least clear on the difficult circumstances and challenges facing the contemporary novice lady playwright in her times and, wrapped in a blanket, opened the door, walked out to the banister and signaled to Chief Myers as I had planned, as we had agreed, giving him a big fake smile and the required and presumably assuring thumbs-up sign. He would believe me, and my performance. He had to. And, as if in just exactly this kind of moment, scene, from just this kind of play, he gave me a big toothy, sleepy lascivious grin and offered his own thumbs-up back to me, an "avuncular old guy" if I had to describe him in notes for an actor who would portray him in a future play, with his big moment, the vivid ghost of his beautiful dead wife at home to remember by way of actorly motivation, and just to make sure, I crawled back into bed with Jake and made him do it all once again, just to be absolutely sure and unhappy. I was, I admit, this time without the name tag — a stupid name that was and always had been both a proper noun and a verb — still hoping hopefully hopelessly that he would holler "Hope!" this time 'round, as both the absurdly didactic message of our little scene and of course in re-recognition of his own loving wife, no questions, no pretending because that was all and everything only that I wanted to hear, of all things, my given name, Christian name, my hopeful name, because that was so far in my amateur writing experience the too-easy and perfect and simple and sure way, and because it would be funny to me — not just ironic, but relievedly, sincerely fun and funny, too! — and I was absolutely not going to let him fall asleep on me, not without trying again.

There were worse ways to show him that he was himself and that he knew (or should know) that I was me and that we were us, in other words to realize life completely, right there, unlike in the play by Thornton Wilder.

He and himself would reconcile, I hoped, and his brain would recompose its broken song to itself via the sturdy middle-aged woman-flesh cupped in his hands, the smell of our sweating pheromonic solidarity, the physical act of it which would realign his synapses, in other words that he would, as had the audience, damn it, see the error, understand the writer's intent, appreciate the context, stand up and choose, applaud in his way, wake up, depart his Neverland, appear on a windowsill, burn brightly, and so on.

No, except this time I had not staged much beyond this big scene, which was a mistake of misplaced confidence, not fully thought out, wishful thinking, although his performance was magnificent, sweet guy, dear man, if completely without dialog the second time, and followed by deep sleep, the healthy kind I could tell.

*   *   *

We moved back home together the next morning, regardless. "Hi, Dad," said Sasha. "Hi, Sasha," he said, just like that. "This is Tiffany," he said, introducing me. I had warned her, of course. There was hope, it turned out, and hope realized but I was now Tiffany. We'd agreed to play along, if that's what it took, and consistent with the doctors' advice. They chatted, a reunited father and daughter. She'd painted and hung a "Welcome Home, Dad" banner, which he seemed to like. He was, it seemed, still Dad. Then she went off to a girlfriend's house, just like that. There was not much else to do for the occasion. Kids are certainly resilient, emotionally limber, or maybe just don't know better. What's to compare to? "It's all good," I often heard my own daughter say, to her friends and, so far, it was good enough I guess, if you didn't mind being called Tiffany for the rest of your life, your marriage, and so being good with being Tiffany.

Bad, in other words, but perhaps livable, endurable, and of course the result of my own miscasting, of myself, of others, all of it a psychological experiment gone wrong, the hubris of a minor artist besotted with her own seeming power, a revenge fantasy, not to mention overreliance on one organ over another, and now my happy, horny husband wanted to play that particular scene over and over again, desire affirmed, hope realized if not "Hope!," and all it took was this one small accommodation by me, which I guessed I could pretend was only temporary, would perhaps get old, a cruel fate, the sex vigorous, a kind of physical therapy, convalescence, our second honeymoon or, in his and Tiffany's case, a first.

*　　*　　*

The newspaper review that Friday was strong, if concentrating more on the audience than the playwright, the phenomenon of their provocation and surprisingly robust engagement, the collectivist choose-your-own ending or endings. That suited me. It was a small-town paper after all, eager to bring everybody on board by way to further newspaper sales, sell more subscriptions, secure more ads, including for the theater. Okay to flatter your readers, if honestly. The local community radio station (on the daily "Arts Talk" show) reported little except that there'd been no violence at the event, which made it sound like a failure, but seemed to like the play anyway. Our old cat offered little in the way of a critical position that I could detect. "Hello, kitty," I said, not even thinking, then realizing my mistake, sparking my unhappiness. Jake seemed not to notice.

We went to the theater together one last time, me driving, and Jake helped me take down the last of the rest of the set. We put most of it in the garage, for storage, next to the bicycles and tools and camping gear and cardboard bankers' boxes marked "Dad" and "Mom," respective quotidian miscellanies of my parents' material ex-lives, and some marked "Sasha-baby" or "Sasha-soccer." I couldn't imagine another staging of the play but just in case, I thought, and then tried not to.

*　　*　　*

Nearly forty *The Diary of a Young Girl* student mid-term essay drafts remained, faithfully, faithlessly, resting (or not, likely angry, fulminating, being resentful) just exactly where I'd left them on the dining room table three weeks earlier, abandoned, ignored, enshrined and otherwise transformed into something or nothing or everything, the MacGuffins of my own story. I also gathered the wigs, hats, trench coats and other props collected over the past weeks of Jake's undercover exile and packed them up for donation to the theater department at school. We talked about when Jake might return to work. We talked about Christmas break, and maybe taking a trip. We drove his mother to the airport and stood in the TSA line together, taking off our shoes and jewelry, and then redressed on the other side of the checkpoint to sit and wait for an hour with her, to listen to her motherly self-congratulation as regards the healing power of her visit, still occasionally calling me by my real name and probably confusing Jake.

We took ourselves off of the happy unhappy drugs and slept through many consecutive nights in each other's arms (he in Tiffany's, of course, lucky him!) and we were both grateful to wake up rested, refreshed and not remembering much except just exactly what we needed to, it seemed. I kept the name tags handy, thinking I might try again or, perhaps only to remind myself of my failure and of the limits of my power and the clumsy sadism of choice and destiny.

I occasionally looked out the window to the back yard, just to make sure "she" or, yes, "I" was anywhere but there, which she was, somewhere, far away. I had three more weeks of teaching, if I wanted them, till Christmas. And, no, I didn't. I considered not sharing news of Jake's recovery and homecoming at all, in other words lying, to the neighbors, or swearing our friends and his mother and the Chief to secrecy, or even asking him to pretend not to know or recognize anybody ever again. I checked in with my substitute teacher, leaving cheerfully affirming and grateful messages which I hoped she would not ever return. She did not. I did more of nothing about most of it.

So that family and civic and professional and neighborhood and academic life, all of them at once, crept slowly back to abnormal except for the element of my own new if modest celebrity as an artiste, agreeing to occasional interviews and a feature profile here or there, a prophet received well enough in her own land but also building a reputation in towns and cities and villages full of eager believers.

Meanwhile, I accepted the offer of the Chamber of Commerce to be Grand Marshall at, of all things, the annual Martin Luther King, Jr. Day Parade on a Saturday in January. And got good at being sexy Tiffany around the house, with Jake, who was doing well, returning occasionally to the General Patton General Hospital where his complete (nearly) recovery was a thing of celebration among the proud, pleased doctors and nurses who had done so very little to help him. They checked for swelling and asked him to follow with his eyes pencils and tiny flashlights, and to answer questions about the date and occupant of the White House, in between nodding and pointing at his CAT scan and other tests and arguing for his complete recovery. They quietly assured me that the one remaining symptom would likely resolve itself, for which I had no real response, not with the rest of him sound.

*   *   *

Thankfully, the real Tiffany was at least gone, long gone, far gone, checked out, returned to her parent or guardian, a wealthy industrialist (is there any other kind?) who'd found an easy enough way to buy her back her freedom through the time-tested and sometimes completely appropriate, fair and just strategy of extremely and precisely targeted local philanthropy. It turns out, that, yes, the city would happily accept a new palm tree as recompense, a gift, an exact twin of the first, that one on the left which had been struck and killed by the ambulance, and so, it seemed not have to consider changing its name or, worse, live with the confusion of misnomer, the potential butt of jokes and, like Jake, existential duplicity. Some clever wag (I think it was me) suggested asking for even more trees, as long as we were asking for trees. Las Palmas was plural, after all, and we did not have to stop at only the two iconic palms. Las Palmas could mean ten or twelve expensive and perfectly matching mature palm trees, fifty, even a hundred. I thought they'd look good, geometrically arranged, a forest of introduced non-native arboreal overkill, a celebration lined up in greeting and symmetrical suburban jungle celebration, a possible tourist destination and the chance to always be who and what we were no matter how many trees were lost.

But people cherished what had become familiar, were looking for something that looked like genuine restorative justice, more restoration than justice, not for vengeance, and for easy symmetry, sameness, equilibrium, the way things were or had been or ought to be or have been, past or past perfect or past imperfect.

Ambulance and hospital bills were also taken care of. The theater and the college both received generous endowments. Ally Nassef got a scholarship, and was himself profiled in the newspaper, announcing his decision to switch majors, to Theater Arts of all things, and to change the spelling of his name, legally, and forever. Discussions were held among attorneys and administrators, two groups eager to accommodate nearly any change, morally flexible, good people in a situation requiring that kind of professional response. A quick civil settlement was reached to avoid criminal prosecution of Tiffany. Agreements were made. Papers were signed, her custom German luxury vehicle auctioned off to benefit the CPR. People with credentials and degrees and well-paying jobs spoke and wrote a lot of long sentences just like these, with purposely passive construction and dramatic if welcome overuse of the verb "to be." Things were getting done. Things were done. Yes, as a result, all criminal charges were dropped. That's a funny phrase when you look at it, but then what isn't? Nobody picked them up. Not us, anyway. The charges were dropped, lay there momentarily, then just disappeared. We actually made money off of the whole deal, Jake and Sasha and I, if you want to know about it, accumulating a little something extra for Sasha's college fund — a big something, a lot of something, in fact — along with potential time off from teaching for me, ironic since it would be time off of already being off, far off, way off, and perhaps time for that imagined and relaxing family vacation over the upcoming holiday break or when we could get around to it, and money for that, too.

*   *   *

And so, energized by the opportunity for even more procrastination and denial, working my way into my new nom de amour, back to talking to the fat old tomcat, I began writing another play, a second one, go figure, initially thinking that it came to me naturally out of the experience of writing the first, or out of nowhere, but mostly not thinking at all, just writing, or thinking about writing when I was doing nothing or something else. This exercise quickly became a series of short moral-ity stories and overly-instructive vignettes with obvious Ovidian ambitions, about transformed lives and politics, and in the first one confusion, once again, over spelling and the responsibility, civic and spiritual and political, of choosing just the right words, of the consequences (or not) of choosing the wrong ones, with talking animals here again too, sort of *Metamorphoses* meets Ani-mal Farm but this time featuring exclusively ducks, of all things, instead of diary cows. And with vital and frisky middle-aged sex aplenty, go figure, because, well, I had done that now myself — and it had worked hadn't it, sort of? — and I was pretty sure people liked it, wanted more, and yet I still hadn't finished read-ing or even looked at those student essay drafts from the now nearly-ended semester, wasn't sure I could or would, not ever, and was considering — as I now did for nearly everything — reconsidering, the multiple and perhaps nearly infinite variable outcomes for that particular story of pedagogy, perhaps for all stories; indeed, I intended to speak of old forms changed into new entities, ideas with lives of their own, independent and un-controllable, of generation and regeneration.

All or most of the new script was there already, buried not very deep in memory it turned out, and pretty easy to pluck out of my psyche, as if bay leaves from a hearty cooked soup, or a wisp of somebody's hair, probably my own, from an otherwise perfect casserole, a bit of broken eggshell from an omelet. Cu-linary rescue metaphors abounded, dear Readers, as I was home a lot now, not in class, not working, and instead cooking big healthy mostly-vegetarian meals for my lovely reunited family when I was not thinking and not writing and not grading and not not-grading either.

The plot of the first episode or mini-drama was based almost entirely on a single line of writing which I had forgotten, an episode, if barely that, the smallest part of a bigger story memorialized by me in an old notebook years earlier, my own writing and learning journal from back when people produced those, when journaling was a word, however unfortunate. It was an instructive sentence I had once kept close then lost, but had carefully, sloppily copied into that now faded old black-and-white speckled old-school Composition book but which I realized had been waiting there all along. It was offered by a fellow community college student in a long-ago adult creative writing class I'd taken one night a week just after I'd married Jake and we lived in the City, long before Sasha was born, when I'd wanted to be a writer myself briefly, when I imagined that I could but told myself I could not, and I was learning how to teach and busy teaching other people how to write a topic sentence and a thesis sentence and a supporting sentence and the three-step method of quotation integration just everywhere in the daytime, the two of us saving to buy a house; Comp 101, Intro to Literature, Fundamentals of Research, nonfiction and creative writing, too, all of it. I used to joke back then that with my faithful, if battered old Honda Civic with the "Impeach Reagan" bumper sticker, a full tank of gas (or even half a tank), my bag of books, a clutch of worn dry-erase low-odor black markers and a classroom whiteboard I could teach practically anything, anywhere, to anybody.

One finds in one's recollections such confidence! Also,

brave delusion and clumsy and wonderful foreshadowing of something like hubris, disaster or comeuppance, if also sometimes even triumph. It's as if all of life had already been written, by someone who should know better, known better, who should have at least written it better, have double-checked and run it by a tutor in the Writing Center before even living it, much less memorializing it.

She had been an older woman, a returning student, probably my age now I see, a mostly non-reader reader reluctant to take seriously at all the kind of work we'd been assigned for the class, Flannery O'Connor to John Cheever to Grace Paley herself, stubbornly ignoring the teacher's ambitions for us, for more, for everybody. I am not sure if she felt intimidated or lacked the patience, could not or would not read or otherwise find a place in her life, in her own worldview, for this kind of highfalutin storytelling. She bragged that she was working instead on a so-called romance novel which was going to be a bestseller, she promised, a blockbuster, this despite the perhaps too-subtle suggestion of the instructor, a kind young man teacher fresh from grad school who reminded me of Jake, and the urging of many students, that the class was not about esteeming much less writing bestsellers, and that their predictable mechanical mimicry of form, of easy plot, of prurience and stock characters and clichéd dialog was a mistake, too easy, a sucker punch to the gut of the universe. This too-kind instructor later offered gentle encouragement that if she were committed, indeed, to writing a romance that she might at least try, please, to mildly subvert the genre, develop a critique or a problem or a wrinkle beyond what was required of it, and attempt something more like literature or real life or, adjectivally, real-life.

Naturally, she ignored the teacher's and everybody else's advice, would have none of it, or seemed not to, and wrote instead an elaborately and almost perversely unconvincing story, if plenty lurid and talky and full of pastels yet emotionally so very uncomplicated, the kind of predictable non-story story which readers of that type of fare seem to desire, welcome, even demand. You know, the ladies' romance formula: heroic and insecure yet surprisingly beautiful woman protagonist, in this case a single mother who hides her dark or troubled past (including living in mysterious circumstances on the outskirts of town with her perhaps bastard child, for whom she has worked and sacrificed and struggled) mostly chaste, but with the political vacancy and otherwise clumsy moral opportunism of creating a world in which Cinderellas, wannabe rich ladies who shop, play dress-up, find ways to be taken care of by older men get by, connive, plot and conspire to acquire even more in life. So did she, and all too well, and it was as if she were going to somehow force all that she wanted to believe might happen to her and her doppelganger into the 250-page manuscript she'd mostly completed, in careful and plodding order, with chapters and conflict and scenes and setbacks and a dramatic arc and resolution and loss and then, yes, happiness forever, no kidding, for our cardboard-cutout heroine with exactly the right man — wealthy, handsome, loving, an "older gentleman," a silver fox (actual phrase) whose beloved wife (no kids, helpfully) had died tragically (what else?) but whose grieving, it seemed, could indeed be healed by her, of all people after all, no kidding.

This stubborn lady writing student, Mona was her name, a tired if overdressed plump single mother who herself lived, yes, outside of town in mysterious domestic circumstances and sold real estate as I now re-recall and cared for, it turned out, an adult special needs young adult child, shared an excerpt one night in workshop, her week to be at-bat in class, as per the schedule, a chapter toward the end with her big clincher love scene shared with the whole class, each of us — eighteen or twenty newish writers in possession of a copy each of her manuscript, distributed by the handsome Jake-like young male teacher — with each of us reading a page or two, out loud, and she sitting there not listening like she was supposed to, not taking notes but instead watching, gloating, nodding, as if to show that she had made fools of us all, succeeded, did not need "Literature" particularly, or a critique, art, readers, teachers, other writers which was perhaps true, finally, at least for her.

Except that at that big sexy clincher moment, when you thought maybe the perfumed and otherwise tastefully choreographed coitus with the lonely, handsome, fit and still-virile widower would once again be invisibly censored or poeticized but however it would happen, or not happen, would at any rate powerfully subordinate the heroine to male privilege and class warfare, while nonetheless securing her new, improved position in affluent society, with security and wealth and social acceptance and esteem as his sexy, well-appointed love-slave wife, she had turned her conniving, tragic, sexy, strong-willed, beautifully but softly vulnerable heroine into, of all things, a duck, this the result of the unfortunate misspelling of the word "quake," as in climax, as in orgasm, real or faked, who knew, who cared, which she'd offered in the near-immortal line, which it was my fate to read out loud and to choose, cruelly to read as written on the page, and which I had immediately committed to memory, embarrassed but imagining its import at the time — "As he took her firmly, but lovingly into his arms she felt herself quack with pleasure" — a vaguely political gesture if sadistic on my part, though at the time I imagined I'd delivered it for everybody, for Writing, for Art, for what?

How could I have forgotten this? Or had I, ever? Had I been ashamed of myself? And had that moment of false triumph, now embarrassment and revelation, been simmering, to use another handy cooking image, or festering or lingering or waddling around like a duck itself in my brain all this time, for decades, without me knowing it, only to have it years later show up as a version of itself, the inspired joke or weird gimmick or trope or lowest common denominator rhetorical appeal that marked my debut and would, I hope, mark, yes, my next big theatrical success?

Her single if singular error put the entire class, normally respectful and forgiving enough, generous and empathetic, into loud unsalvageable laughter, fits of giggles, then guffaws, the pressure of weeks and weeks of having politely endured her stubbornly composed and condescending nonsense, uncontrollable finally, a catharsis burst of bottled-up energetic disdain, anger, contempt, betrayal, perhaps even empathy, in its way. And for me, obviously, the elements, all of them arriving, disassembled and unrecognized by me, in a kind of template at last for organizing the design or redesign of my own later imitation of life, imitation life, real life, similarly imagined life story.

Perhaps I'd apologized, or had I? I wanted to believe my action was forgivable, even justified, both simultaneously. Poor Mona took it as well as could be expected, this bit of frivolous group shaming, of our mixing up of the sin and the sinner, scapegoating, and she accepted the embarrassed apologies of the workshop at any rate all well enough, and with the intervention of the teacher. Or seemed to, pretended to. She of course abandoned the class that night, presumably fixed the typo — just one, after all, in an otherwise excellent, even perfect awful very bad manuscript — and a few short months later this Mona sent a copy, signed, to the class care of the instructor, with her real name in parenthesis, of the just-published Harlequin Romance novel with her fake name on the cover of it, which you can still find today in its terrifically successful "Love Inspired" imprint series, still actually in print after probably hundreds of thousands of copies, the first of many best-selling titles she produced (look it up!) toward both taking very good care indeed of her grown-up disabled child and feeding a fantasy of irreconcilable vicariousness, long ago moving out of her home to her imagined, and apparently fully realized new digs, good for her.

*　　*　　*

That occurred back in the late 1980s, of course, which may account for much of the achievement and reward of the perfectly welcome and elegant duplicity and cooptation of art reflected in Mona's effort, of commerce over verity, ideology over humanity, a duplicitous time if also a mini-epoch in the slow positive movement of recognition, expanded rights and more generous care for the disabled. One step forward, two steps back, perhaps. Her kid got proper care and lived in a big house with servants and we never had to see her again.

So much of a decade, a memory or an anecdote turns out to be so big and so encompassing that, finally, anything which you say about it might be true, or might as well be. And, no, that is perhaps not such a terrific or valuable lesson or take-away after all. But all of it worked well for the Director's Notes, which I had already begun composing in cheerful anticipation of the production of my next big (or perhaps small) play.

I had struggled once, long ago, to make sense of Mona's peculiar if instructively limited success, if that's what it was, her building of her own kind of shining city of McMansions on a hill, by way of the trickle-down theory of literature, this privatization of the emotions for repackaging as solipsism and self-help, the running of the arms race to what was once called alienation, fought by a contra army wearing new, improved bootstraps, with the smiling visage of the chiseled good-lookin' demented old cowboy actor-as-president a full-color backdrop to it all, if you can imagine or remember any of that, remembering or imagining being so much the same thing.

And so it was that now, all these years later, I found in all these remembered details some maternal affinity, of all things, satisfaction in the particular image of the disabled daughter (my invention, as I never knew if it was a boy or girl) living some-where on her restful and luxurious cloud of material security, in comfort and care, with her justifiably proud "author" mother, if you would like to know something I have never (had never) shared with anybody before, and certainly not before that mo-ment in which I had to make decisions about what to do with my own odd circumstances, a mother myself now and my own husband's brand-new wife, too, a person whose struggle with the examined life she had perhaps lost.

*   *   *

With this flashback and a new, renewed appreciation of it, I found that I had another opportunity to wonder yet again if anybody (else, or at all) ever really realized life as they lived it, I mean besides me (Hope or, now, "Tiffany") and Mona the romance novelist and Anne Frank of course, who probably also realized death as she died it in that death camp, each of us with our significant blind spots and prejudices, sure, but I was certain-ly glad for the opportunity to try, and try again, which seemed pretty close to the real thing, maybe even better. And besides, I had actually realized both myself, hadn't I, on-stage and off, for good and for bad, for Hope and for Tiffany and for Ali-Ally, despite my apparent confusion about where one ended (life) and the other (the realizing – every, every minute) began, if there ever really was such a place to begin with or, yes, to end with? Not to even think of asking the question of why.

*   *   *

Fast forward, again, if slowly: That first episode of my newest new play, which with the confidence of the newbie I assumed would also be a big success, depending of course on how you measured success (and I did not anymore, especially not after reflecting on Mona's) relied on some terrifically overly overconstructed confusion between the noun for the waterfowl and the act of lowering your head just in time, a verb, and of course the further slapstick hilarity of the costumes, with the old man's discovery of his sexy fiancé transformed, costumed now suddenly in yellow feathers and big duck feet and bill, a hairy-chested Everyhunk committing cartoon bestiality on a bird, the sudden and totally expected-unexpected occurrence of a major earthquack (sic) to boot, 6.8 on the Richter Scale at least, and so on, two more people (and counting) doomed by their easy failures as regards language and love but, yes, ultimately to be redeemed (stick around, people) by same.

It was really just a follies act, a vaudevillian revue, a cabaret circus-happening, unapologetic but in its way a kind of apology, as well as a thank-you to somebody I would never meet again and did not really like at all but whose example of single-mindedness and selfish self-distortion, of recreating what passed for reality into one's own image, was the personification of that power, vanity, honest selfishness of both the saints and of the poets, every, every minute.

Realizing, I realized, finally, was a kind of valuable super-solipsism, a self-confidence, self-promotion and yet, of course, I had as a result of this terrific hyper-realizing become somebody else, hadn't I, at least in name, if not a very good name, notwithstanding the association with the luxury jewelry company and the Truman Capote novella, where Holly calls the famous store "the best place in the world, where nothing bad can take place."

And in this new, big area of further possible regret and recompense where nothing bad could take place, and me learning to answer to a new name, I found now that I could not justify awarding actual real grades or providing evaluative comments on my students' final essays either, delivered to me in week twelve — because I was still the "teacher of record" — by my substitute, who had penciled in her own scores anyway. I thanked her and wrote her a big check.

Most of the final essays were actually just terrific, especially and considering and nonetheless, as I had never actually ever read the mid-term drafts of them at all, not offered comments and missed four weeks of the quarter and did not provide any direction, so busy was I directing and redirecting history and management for others, or sitting at Jake's bedside. And most of the students had come to the performance, to support me and Ali, which I figured was more important anyway in the scheme of things, key to their real educations, civic literacy and political development, to moral instruction, so besotted was I with my newfound power if also still somehow correct.

And, no, Administration would likely not allow me to let them decide on their own grades, to cast a vote on their own essays, not engage the "make your own adventure" YA fiction model of awarding grades, alternate reality, not create a group consensus built on a standing ovation or even a secret ballot. Too bad.

So that in a morally confused pedagogical decision which conveniently also let me off the hook and also rewarded these students, I did that other teacherly thing which you are never, ever supposed to do, not ever, as a teacher, along with saying "No!" outright or giving people the answer (as if figuring it out themselves were ever somehow helpful or "instructive" or generous) and I gave them all A's, "for affort," I liked to tell people, some of whom found this gesture of mine lazy and solipsistic (yes, indeed, yes!) and others generous and wise, some who found my joke tasteless or mocking, reckless or disrespectful of the students and of teachers and of the profession itself, some going along with it as if all life and each of its many characters had the potential for this variety of terrifically ironic and funny premise-constructed situational humor suddenly just everywhere, the conceit of what is called lately, yes, the "dramady," a fun portmanteau word which promises something for everybody if not much at all for anyone in particular and which, as I mentioned earlier — much earlier, sorry — annoyed me then and annoys me still, but not as much, considering.

Some people I met after the incredible success of *The Dairy of Anne Frank* doubted I had ever even been a teacher. Or a student either. Or a parent. Or if I ever even should have been. That's three "ors." You can imagine my special pride at that, of my particularly ironic sense of achievement at these multiple choice assessments with all of the same answers, all correct. "Live and learn," I would occasionally say, when I found myself telling the story, which happened more than you'd think. I would smile and nod my head wisely and self-deprecatingly.

"Or, in my case, just live," I'd add. Ha, ha, ha. And then, go ahead, write a play about it, friend, and quick, before you forget, and give yourself the best or second-best part and the best possible chance at every kind of failure, and then find a completely unlikely amateur star right there in your own back-yard or classroom. And why not bribe the audience with the chance at direct democratic participation — yes, that too! — but mostly find something totally ambiguous and disturbing and yet painfully funny and you just plain go for it. Give your characters some open destiny of life, at least for just a night. Some of them, if not all. And not too much of any of it, please. Oh, and it is handy to create an antagonist, preferably with exaggerated comic attributes.

That was my take, my advice, my experience. It's what I said on the radio interviews and when I spoke to a few re-porters on the telephone, met some genuine theater types who also nodded, or shook their heads, in agreement or perhaps in a shared sense of regret or shame or embarrassment, having them-selves also come too close to irony, which is like the warning on prescription drug bottles, "May cause restlessness or drowsiness, and not to be used while operating a motor vehicle or heavy machinery and only under the supervision of a professional."

Sometimes, I learned, it was hard to tell people anything at all, and sometimes it was just hard to tell, period. I enjoyed my new time alone at home, spending days with the pet, both Sasha and Jake back at school, the piles of ungraded drafts and those fully graded and excellent student papers finally abandoned at last to the recycling bin in violation of the department's rule that we keep them a whole year. Holiday decorations were now arranged on the front lawn, me drawing sketches and dreaming up set designs and other gimmicks meant to prejudice the performance of my next twisted little fable toward esteeming the audience while also challenging them, once again.

*   *   *

All this as offers came in from all kinds of places — a feminist playwrights' collective, a guerilla street ensemble, and an avant-garde theater troupe. Each asked if I wanted to collaborate on staged versions of, respectively, adaptations of, you guessed it, *Dairy of a Mad Housewife*, Pushkin's *Dairy of a Madman* or Grossmith's *Dairy of a Nobody*. Disappointing, but still. I wrote back, politely declining or, rather, declining politely — both are acceptable but the former is preferred — that I was lately lactose intolerant and pursuing new creative possibilities. I drew a happy face, and an unhappy face next to my response, together a nod to my new standing in the world of drama.

Nonetheless, I appreciated the offers, the recognition. I had, after all, the entire Feminist Surrealist Collectivist Diary-Dairy oeuvre totally wrapped up, and could say no without hurting anybody's feelings. Me, more than anybody in the country, probably the world, not that anybody else had wanted it, not until now. And now I was over it. Though uninterested in that particular theme, collaboration with these fellow theater people intrigued me. I wondered if working with others who knew who I was might make up for the special humiliation of Jake introducing me to strangers and friends and colleagues as her, as Tiffany, or the further embarrassment of him seeming to ignore what everybody else called me. In fact, I'd already had and discarded my own early sequel idea anyway, the story of yet another huge and powerful woman, an evil Midwestern monarch in a post-democratic dystopian U.S.A., (dystopias popular lately in novels and films) this one managing her own oppressive soft-ice parlor and all-American burger joint, wearing a huge crown and writing a very big, evil, nasty memoir about how she controlled the lives and fates of other people. *The Diary Queen*, it could have been called, except that I could not summon the false pride, contempt or weakly satirical smart-ass worldview required to even begin to embrace that unlikely premise. Imagine.

I'd been there, done that, after all. So I stuck with further scenes involving animals and homonyms, multiple meanings and multiplicity of character offered in short, meaningful parables offering important life lessons for humans, and more chances to recognize oneself. *The Tail of the Bare Bear*. Something about a hare and his hair. A clever furry camp survivor named Eli Weasel. There was still the endless possibility and impossibility of punctuation, the promise of finding meaning where it was not meant even to be considered, much less proofread, corrected, read out loud.

* * *

In conclusion, to crib from so many student essays: Still, sometimes, or perhaps more often than you'd think, maybe even frequently, it is difficult to comprehend, especially at the time, who, finally, is in a comma and who is not. Punctuation is a funny way to live, with all sorts of bodily functions suggested, in a period, say, and in a colon but people almost never fall into these, and never into a semi-colon.

There are rules about spelling and usage. A coma, as it turns out, may indeed be used in real life and/or on the stage, to separate elements in a list, to connect independent clauses, to set off introductory elements and, finally, to distinguish parenthetical elements, as your mother and your father. There are more, in between, sometimes requiring ellipses. My own favorite rule: You should, when in doubt, use a coma to avoid confusion. I just love that.

And soon it occurred to me, with my developing playwright's chops, my burgeoning theatrical career and my life in art, my sudden and accidental audience, my husband returned to me, my life as an artist subsidized by tragedy and triumph, my pretend identity becoming easier to live with, that what you don't know can hurt you as well (by which we mean as badly) as what you do know. And often as profoundly, cruelly. And sometimes that what you don't know or only forgot can also help you plenty, too. And help other people too, who are perhaps as a result aided even more than you are. Ali, for instance, and Chief Meyers, and an entire town — our town — and its lousy little free weekly newspaper, too, which acknowledged its error in its Corrections column and printed loads of Letters to the Editor mostly celebrating my play and demanding the replacement of the palm tree.

But let's stop here, shall we, just before the end of my story, of somebody's story, as I wind things up, sign off, and consider together what pass for events and scenes in my own life and the fictional and fictionalizing ones I'd created for myself, by myself, with others, for others, the wish-fulfillment super-historical, supra-historical, super life-history of your favorite real-time remedial rewriting super-heroine community college writing teacher, who resembled me a whole lot, especially if you squinted a bit or attended your local community theater on a Saturday night and waited for the house lights to dim, even only slightly, if dimming just enough to suggest that somebody else was in control of so much but that you, yes You, sitting in the orchestra, might also play a role in this bit of magic-making and digression and its denouement.

In such a purposely contrived scene you might hear one of us — me, you, Anne Frank — say that I had all this time perhaps been lying to you, to myself, had written unreliable narrators, constructed an unbelievable cast of characters and was, as they say, my own worst enemy all along. And probably should have known better. And now did, lucky me! And now, perhaps I really was her, as much Anne as Tiffany, or the memory of her, of each, a character with her name, or hers, assuming either even existed in the first place which, I sometimes tell people, she did not, Otto Frank having discovered, excised, edited and otherwise (other, wise) brought his lovely, sweet, smart lost daughter back to life through, of all things, a book.

But guess what? People will not actually contradict you about much when you are a semi-famous playwright and your husband has a special name for you and your real name is in the papers. Besides, I have made Jake, still slightly brain-damaged, very happy, and she could have been named something worse, or more suggestive, Minnie or Strawberry Shortcake or Barbie or Barbarella, all of them young women trapped in their autobiographical what's-in-a–name-would-not-they-all-be-sweet-just-the-same story?

My enemy was, to put it clearly, something of myself. You already knew that. And thankfully, it turns out, if you are, finally, your own worst enemy, how bad can that really be? Because you might as well be your own best or worst, friend or alley. You can't have too many of either and/or both, even if they are all the same people.

Maybe anybody can do anything well. Or as well. But not everyone can do everything well. Some can do some things extremely well. Few people, I notice, do much at all. I need to get back to work. I have papers to grade.

GOING CLEARER:

AN INTELLECTUAL AUTOBIOGRAPHY

—Andrew Tonkovich—

I'D ALWAYS PROMISED MYSELF and anybody listening (nobody at all, so that I was talking only to me, quietly, so as not to appear delusional) that unlike the sad, passive masochists or hapless hope-ridden ones who lie there on an elevated mechanical bed in a hospital room dying in pain — or dying all doped-up or otherwise extending, enduring their lives out of futility, misplaced tenacity, greed or in some weird curiosity about or anticipation of insight which never arrived — that I would, despite all personal previous history, action, details of my weak autobiographical record to the contrary (and notwithstanding my general cowardice) respond to the diagnosis of my own terminal illness with action if not quite resistance. This might, I had speculated, stupidly, occur through a usefully focused gesture of surprising generosity and vigorous humanity or, alternatively, one of vicious revenge and dark cruelty, or perhaps manifest in only an entirely symbolic statement or expression of destruction or creation (it did not matter) or even an actual practical, real, genuine physical act of same. This, then, dear Reader, is that gesture, though not realized as I or anybody could have anticipated. No, I'm not dying at all, in fact just the opposite. I feel just fine, great, tip-top, and am healthier than I've ever been, thanks for asking.

I'd had no real experience of either or any of the above, not really. But I imagined that, upon learning my hypothetical terminal fate, I would at least somehow do something about it.

I was a young man after all, just barely thirty, and not prone to producing speculation or long sentences or the variety of overly exuberant elaboration that you read here, and will encounter so much more of below. Sorry about that. Honestly, I did not always talk, much less write like this. I was, I see now, mostly illiterate. I lived alone, a kind of poster man-child for the condition of either satisfied or lonely, financially comfortable, single, a non-voter, assenter to whatever those in power offered, an all-purpose if soft-spoken complainer, not that I bothered or cared to complain, an un-civic-minded un-citizen, non-volunteer and non-blood donor, and so on, able to check off every box as regards the easy estrangement from everything except my "work."

I mumbled to myself but had been generally laconic, a word which I now learn in the process of composing this memoir — the first installment in my autobiography-manifesto-confession, written from top-secret exile — is based upon the conversational behavior of the extremely reticent Spartan peoples of the Greek peninsula of rugged and mountainous Laconia, from whom you generally do not hear much, ha ha ha.

Now I know. Now you know. Now we all know. Of course, those quiet Greeks always knew but did not, ironically or not, tell anybody about it.

And once you know something, it turns out that you (or at least I) desire, need to know even more, perhaps even everything, as insisted upon by the excellent Russian short story writer Isaac Babel, his work lately added to my fast-growing personal library, the books now starting to stack up, shelves bought, shelves installed, bookcases full.

"I was just a kid at the time..." begins that classic story, which is about, among other things, recognizing the nearly impossible collateral consequences and variables involved with see-ing, perceiving, decision-making and remembering, always, not to underestimate people or opportunities, for good or bad, to "imagine," yes but in the more immediate and specific sense of that task, responsibility, with specificity and color and details and action.

Yes, it turns out there are challenges and big responsi-bilities to knowing just everything, or trying to, the biggest one being mostly the problem of having to know about some very difficult things indeed. This is also, of course, the best part.

Alas, there is finally just no going back, no return to ig-norance or shallow happiness, not to making empty promises to oneself, or speaking and thinking in short, stupid sentences or to living the unexamined life as had I to that point of my own, as a one-dimensional cartoon-person residing in the City of Lake Forest, Orange County, California, which is not Sparta, not at all, and which lacks both lake and forest except for man-made reservoirs occupied by stricken, overweight, permanently un-mi-gratory Canada geese living on their artificial beaches of safely sterilized sandbox sand and upon the rolling super-green turf of the golf course next door and in the stout, high branches of rows of introduced giant eucalyptus groves planted on the edges of each planned geographic-topographically symmetrical cubby-hole of the city's warren of civic and commercial life: gas station, apartments, single-family units, shopping area, school complex, multi-denominational worship center, self-storage yard, as if the residents were, finally, only another ill-tended agricultural crop arranged in plots among hedgerows, protected by the giant socio-politically engineered windbreak of those lanky, aromatic, beautiful Australian trees.

*   *   *

I actually liked the fat Canada geese, which seemed to have claimed this unlikely habitat as their own, surviving on handouts of Wonder Bread and good year-round weather, no predators. The golfers I largely ignored, noting occasionally a stray white or pink or bright orange golf ball exiled to the parking lot, floating in the complex's fountain or swimming pool. No, I was of course not dying after all, at least not in any way other than in that everyday protocol in which everybody is always dying, if pretending not to be, and so slowly that it seems not to matter until it does, and then, well, it is finally or immediately too late to resist, isn't it, sometimes, even to stop living and just lie down and expire, the body so accustomed to itself?

Or so I might have further speculated, uselessly. I was myself perhaps only just a kid at the time, as Babel's stand-in narrator, if ostensibly a grown-up. I was in reasonably good health beyond that big, clumsy, awkward mortality problem which confronts us all, and I was reasonably if perhaps averagely unhappy too, also reasonably slightly overweight and physically weak, reasonably sad and lonely, reasonably overcommitted to working at what turns out to have been an almost stereotypically clichéd job, an accountant, an auditor, a bean counter. All of this I must have certainly suspected for a very long time but did not acknowledge, could not, would not, even in a whisper to myself. I had been so very reasonably distracted — if that is not exactly the right word — that the urgent always-terminal condition of my own life (and yours) had become not any more or less imperative or angry-making or relevant to me except, finally, for one desperately mortality-affirming passion: my joyful engagement with clever, funny assassin movies, mostly those starring the terrific actor John Cusack of Chicago, Illinois and most-famous young graduate of the Piven Theater Workshop and then, yes, suddenly and immediately, one more element, a life and death-changer for sure. And that is my story, which follows, about how I escaped the Prison of Belief and now reside elsewhere, everywhere, from where I write this unshy memoir.

*   *   *

In fact, it was only eight short weeks ago (well, actually quite long, busy, completely life-changing weeks) that I read, quite accidentally, a terrific award-winning nonfiction book exploring the so-called religion of Scientology. It is told through the story of the life and career of one of its former adherents, a good-enough, even brave man, yes, but still too scared or weak to condemn it outright though courageous enough — more than so many — to tell at least some of the truth, by which I mean explain, review, affirm somehow its elaborate and obvious lies, all so very easily affirmed if you were so inclined, yet so open and obvious in their lousy, brazen construction, so as to attract very little attention and, no, perhaps not even falsity but something else entirely.

My resulting new life-affirming engagement, anger, my active undistraction — sudden and welcome and completely unexpected and, yes, exactly the right word! — which arrived almost immediately upon learning more fully about the criminal sci-fi cult which sells its nutty ideas to gullible, ambitious, greedy and confused people — people I didn't know or even like, for Pete's sake! — taking their money, minds, lives — challenged that previous program of active distraction, inaction, passivity, fear, modest if numbing success or what passes for it, the relative security and comfort I'd been a happy-enough participant in, victim of, collaborator with, though of course I have kept all of that to myself until now, dear Reader, for reasons you will divine forthwith, in addition to the most disappointingly obvious one: that nobody I knew around here shared their own "intellectual autobiographies," read or talked about books (except the Bible) or explained themselves, much less took on Life and in my case beat Death, which I am pretty sure I have now but will of course leave you to decide.

*   *   *

Here's how: I found and spontaneously borrowed an abandoned or at least unattended hardback copy of the veteran journalist, screenwriter and playwright Lawrence Wright's excellent *Going Clear: Scientology, Hollywood and the Prison of Belief,* published by Alfred A. Knopf in 2013, from an unseen neighbor or perhaps visitor here in my vast and discouragingly average apartment complex, albeit without them knowing it, or so I imagined. He or she, a stranger to me either way, had left the book in the downstairs laundry room in my quadrant of The Arbors, in Building C, accidentally or on purpose, who knows, but it seems now a gesture or mistake or unlikely reaching out, as people now say, some behavior not so unlike evangelizing, as that copy of the Good Book left by invisible Gideons in a motel room and discovered by the broken man, its message — of this one particular book, this copy, right here and now, in a motel room — saving him, or the religious tract distributed by the proselytizers, or the firm hands placed on the head of the innocent with the required requisite hollering or screaming or weeping and, yes, also, the connecting of the two wires to a flimsy machine which reads electrical conduction in a kind of skin test of perspiration, that Rube Goldberg gizmo which we are meant to believe is useful to the trained Scientology "auditor," a kind of priest or religious clerk but which anybody can see best measures only sweat, vulnerability, credulity, sap-hood, suckerocity, markdom, foolishness and susceptibility to the big con.

The book itself, with its entirely easy-enough revelations about The Commodore himself, the flim-flammy "Electropsychometer" and the secret Sea Org inner sanctum, and the past and future goings-on over at the Galactic Confederacy and of its one-time interplanetary dictator Xenu, was in its way my own skin test, my own measuring of conductivity, good conduct, bad conduct, heart palpitation, mind and body health for even as I picked it up, yes, my own heart raced, I perspired suddenly in excitement, my hands trembled, I felt a chill, a shiver, in which a fierce and immediate clarity of perception and an exaggerated if pleasing sense of new and unfamiliar purpose embraced me. Imagine, just from holding the book, this one book! I now almost wish somebody had been there to see it, to remark on whatever physiological manifestations were occurring, heartbeat accelerated, brain-waves rearranged, psychic animation kicked in, rapid eye movement recording it, all the physical manifestations of my exposure to this one book, this fundamental text, this singular and single time-portal to my new life-path. The book seemed to glow, and in my hands it felt warm, alive, and radiated a palpable if invisible energy, leaving me breathless.

Yes, as if in some perverse (well, what else?) and excitingly weird intellectual-existential mental-homeopathic experiment, only just briefly touching the book — only that! — indeed did to me just enough of something impossible to measure physically as, empowered, I then opened and read a very short passage from it and it — the book, this copy! — slowly reached into my consciousness to change everything in the area of my perceptions, my circumstances, finding a still inexplicable and completely impossible way to trigger a transformation of the interlocutory spatial elements, expanding neuro-air-muscles all around, the cosmic vibro-particles and anatomic dust-motes which surrounded me, as if I were now invisible or perhaps super-duper-extra visible, either way, something beyond what was too easy, too material, too available for others to see but with the accompaniment of the book, or The Book, as I would soon begin to call it, was made real? Some deal!

*   *   *

—*Andrew Tonkovich*—

It comes in a dark black dust cover with lovely design qualities, shimmering metallic letters of silver and gold done up in pleasing typography, tiny triangles organized to suggest something like compass points, but with the enduring monarchic symbolism of glimmering Pharaohic or divine metaphysical direction. At the bottom of the cover, author Lawrence Wright is identified as a Pulitzer Prize Award-winner. On the back, underneath impressive blurbs, the Library of Congress or the publisher or whomever is in charge of these classifications indicates in tiny four-point caps that The Book is in the category RELIGION/ HISTORY but the forward slash between the two words is so very thin and lightly printed that it seems to read at first apprehension only RELIGION HISTORY, which puzzled and engaged me.

Such was my immediate and improbable fascination with every small if clearly important aspect of the volume, its classification and intriguing syntax, promise and details, even its too-lightly rendered punctuation mark, that I sensed a change in myself immediately, a physical transformation, the disappearance and reappearance of that too-thin line, seemingly innocuous or even imperceptible, which had formerly bound me, divided and separated me somehow too, and imagined that along with me there in the laundry room was a host, an audience of other readers and thinkers, perhaps the author of The Book himself, his editors, the publisher, the proofreaders and fact-checkers and artists and the agents even, a whole congregation of individuals who had at some point in its production touched this same object, in all kinds of forms, but which seemed now to gleam under the too-hard, too-bright fluorescent lights of the apartment and condo-conversion complex laundry room. I felt dizzy, and thought that I might fall down. Or fall up.

But then, just as suddenly, I felt immediately physically robust and strong, the result (I see now) of just simply discovering and then holding and leafing through this particular book in that particular laundry room on that particular early evening after work on a Thursday in late spring, where there had never been left or shared or abandoned anything at all before except lemons, offered anonymously in a small basket with a certainly helpful if perhaps redundant hand-written note, "Free," a joyful reference to both the gesture and to the fruit, presumably picked or fallen from a local backyard lemon tree, but suggesting, I see now, so much more: portent, fetish or token.

They were good-looking enough lemons, large and plump and well-shaped fruit, with perfectly formed little nipples at each end. Their presentation suggested a serene still-life, with the perfect wicker basket for presentation and the hand-written single word note on a three-by-five card, and the book itself, all of it displayed on the hinged fold-out clothes-folding table, and I was never even sure, finally, whose lemons, whose lemon tree. There were no fruit trees at The Arbors, too bad, though every other kind, artificially introduced and encouraged, from brightly orange-flowering exotic coral trees to tiny blue Norwegian pines, perpetually dying, to the massive native live-oaks and spread-eagle sycamores with their pleasing cherry-bomb seed pods which I remembered fondly from childhood each time I saw them, despite myself.

This interior scene, still-life or diorama called attention to itself, or so I understood suddenly, with the addition of The Book, as if a provocation out of the stories of Aladdin or Alice in her Wonderland, though I was there to acknowledge it, perhaps not only notice it, perhaps also to destroy it by removing this one element, a singular detail in a beautiful contrivance, as easily as a person could miss or misunderstand, add or remove a forward slash, or even add one.

*   *   *

So that I appreciated even before actually reading that single paragraph or, later, a page of The Book that the limits upon and limitations of my engagement with my perceptions, with my life generally were being challenged here, or at least would be if I took The Book for myself, challenged even if in a very small way, and so I simply set aside the problem-mystery of to whom the book actually belonged and I just took it. I stole it, or I borrowed it. It was not mine, but I made it mine. This act was surprisingly easy, if atypical, for an otherwise obedient and laconic (!) rule-follower as myself who'd until this moment never even taken a piece of "free" fruit, suspicious about the premise and of the provocative adjective. But for now, for that early evening, that moment, the book ($27.95) suddenly, easily belonged to me and, better, I might have thought to myself even then, to all of us, a residential apartment lifestyle community, a city and county, a nation even of lemon and book-takers and diorama destroyers, re-arrangers of moments and scenes and punctuation. Free!

Like the lemons in the basket. Free! Or as the basket appeared then, without any lemons, perfectly and totally lemon-free! That is how I was thinking all of a sudden, about The Book and more, too, so much more. And even more than that.

Indeed, I see now that I had acquired just enough insight about so much, into both nothing at all and everything that might be, so as to understand that I needed to, was being required to read the entire book, immediately, by way of completing a circuit, fulfilling some kind of promise or responsibility (perhaps to the leaver of The Book), receiving the baton from a runner, real or imagined or invisible, as if in an urgent foot race, a relay race for meaning and perhaps even some purpose to my own previously non-urgent existence.

In this way I understood all, as if time stood still for the moment or two it took me to physically reach for The Book, open it without guile or shame and read that fateful, as it turned out, paragraph about how newly initiated pre-Clears (on their way to Operating "thetans") could, it was alleged, practice, exercise, show off their newfound Sciento-logical powers post-auditing by exercising telepathy and thought-and-action control of other human beings through visiting a public place, say, the local mall, sit there in public on a bench with other disciples and use their newly earned L. Ron Hubbard-y superpowers to physically interact with our world, to cause strangers walking by to blink on command or as they were walking out of, say, Radio Shack or Hot Dog on a Stick to sneeze, to scratch their noses, smile for no reason at all except to express the whim of the pre- or potential Clear or, amazingly, eat their just-purchased hot dog treat as commanded mystically by the new and totally hegemonic people-puppeteers.

Observing these human dolls dancing to the will of the practitioner, more correctly called, yes, a "manipulator," the disciple, newly-ordained, could get a startling glimpse of his or her own potentially bigger power as a fully realized and elevated being, for now possessing just enough understanding of the profound and urgent power of the science of the mind as something meant for themselves. Reading about it in The Book I understood not just the episode of obvious farce but the telling of this episode in The Book as meant for me, as in meant for me to know about, written for me, and that the author, Lawrence Wright was in fact speaking to me, imagine that, directly through this text, which I understood to be a manual, a life-instruction scripture, a guidebook.

Imagine that, I thought. I looked up from the page to smile, to laugh, to wonder and be delighted that someone else had apparently also actually read this crazy-wonderful revelatory book, this actual physical copy in my hand — for could it be, that the absurdity and, more thrillingly, the revelation it offered, so easy to apprehend, and to enjoy, in its way, perhaps too easy was transforming my own life even now? — and that this other reader, this person might also be standing, near me perhaps, another convert, hiding and waiting, about to leap out of a closet or from behind a door, to affirm or confirm or to join me or yell "Surprise!" or "Ah-ha!" or "Gotcha!" and pat me on the back, shake my hand?

*   *   *

It was by then dark out, quiet. Indeed, I might have welcomed, enjoyed the appearance of just such a person just then, a fellow reader, a new reader, an immediate fast friend, long-lost pal, distant or forgotten relative, formerly-estranged sibling, potential lover, dead but revived mother or father, long-steady political comrade, war buddy, someone, anybody to corroborate and to affirm. It could have, might have, been the individual who'd planted the book there herself, himself, it turned out, just for me — me! — as a provocation, a kind of gag, a squirting boutonnière or joke corsage, or tiny metal windup handshake gag buzzer, the equivalent of a quarter coin cemented or Super-Glue'd to the sidewalk or a tiny hand-scrawled sign taped to my back reading, yes, "Kick me."

Alas, there was no one. I was completely alone. But, wait, no, I was there. Me. I clearly saw myself in the scene, sitting on the flimsy white molded-plastic chair under the fluorescent light of the laundry room, holding The Book, a reflection. I was indeed the person reading The Book, reflecting, the individual consciousness able to appreciate the revelation, the joke, the insight, the lemon, the lights, all of it, and whether or not others, or only another, had similarly seen the light, I was content and empowered with this vision of myself, my selves.

*   *   *

I marked that page using the jacket flap. It seemed important, and the least I could do, to indicate my commitment thus far to the project, to show I'd been there, perhaps even somehow to communicate to author Lawrence Wright my involvement in all of it. Perhaps, I speculate now, even only just touching this book, or only reading the dust jacket, maybe only glancing at the author's handsome photograph (photo credit: Kenny Braun), receiving some instruction, as in the relationship of the devotee to the ancient illuminated manuscript, would have been all and only what was needed, at least for me. That it might have been enough to inspire what would happen next. I was ready, so ready. I had not read a real book at all in many years, all of my pseudo-reading being financial reports and accounting ledgers, statements, spread sheets, Excel files, memos, emails, occasional letters, IRS and other communications whose prose did its job, yes, but, all of it something certainly not illuminated, that was for sure, not calling out my own self, not thrusting or inviting or compelling me into this awareness of my own potential power, soon to be realized, and big-time.

*   *   *

I see now that my time in the laundry room was for this non-reader and non-believer a version, however cracked or warped or exaggerated or indeed ironic, of that moment of epiphany spoken of by religious proselytes in their "I-see-the-light" story, the kind you hear recited to a man, woman or child-convert trying to explain their new devotion to Jesus, Yahweh, a guru, Tibetan Buddhist rinpoche, whatever. And I saw suddenly a much bigger truth, a kind of universal vision, a short-cut revelation, that it might indeed be the same for all of the devotees of all faith-hucksters — probably was, yes, I was sure of it — and not just for the followers only of this perfect all-American sci-fi faith meets Ponzi scheme that is Scientology but for all of them, each and all, from the emptiness suddenly filled, the easy indoctrination into the blinding light, the narcissistic babbling-in-tongues crowd, recovered alkies and cleaned-up junkies, petty criminals, snake handlers, knee-scraping rosary-claspers, unsatisfied or "purpose"-lacking suburban white nativist Orange County Republicans, confused liberal do-gooders, immigrant Mexican store-front iglesia hand-clappers, pillow-cushioned meditators and self-realizers of every stripe, not to mention women-hating Promise Keepers, Ugandan homophobe Methodists, self-regarding uptight Lutherans, unironic Islamists, mindless-over-matter Christian Scientists, the catatonic-seeming members of the standing-around Watchtower Society, spooky vegetarian Seventh-Day Adventists, on and on and on and on, with all of whose fascinating and disturbing worldviews I was of course passingly familiar but had been somehow too busy to care about, and certainly not object to, much less commit — within only a few short hours it turned out — to destroying, just like that, each and every one of them, one at a time. A vision, indeed, of all-ness, of one-ness. A mission, inspired. And to think that I had not to this point yet even read the entire book, only a few sentences, such profound provocation had it caused, such an altering of all.

*   *   *

That Scientologists would, according to The Book, indeed go to a very public place and believe or insist or project that they could cause other people yards away from them, across the way, to do something, anything, and that this power justified or affirmed their having allowed themselves to be "audited," to be assessed and cosmically invoiced, then paid their bill to the Church, credited L. Ron Hubbard with healing them, getting them off heroin or booze, prospering and believing and anticipating immortality one way or another, pretending that movie and TV actors — short, handsome scary superstar Tom Cruise and fat, sexy Kirstie Allie, John Travolta, permanent child-bride Priscilla Presley, singer-songwriter Beck, fake television news journalist Greta Van Susteren, albino Texas bluesman Edgar Winter — were their friends or colleagues here or on a faraway planet, struck me not at all unreasonably, I thought, as an urgent problem which needed addressing.

No, I did not know how, and still do not exactly know why me in particular except that it turns out that I had been quietly angry about this for a very long time, if perhaps no angrier than anybody else, and, yes mostly (if quietly) at myself. And perhaps I guessed that night that this — the mass deception — was perhaps why, and that I was just as angry about, with, on behalf of, anybody and everybody who should have been angry. As a result I felt not angry at all and saw instead that I had to know more — perhaps everything — and that I had to act, not only for myself but for others, many, if unseen.

*   *   *

But can a person catch up on their own missed, ignored or overlooked outrage, their credulity and also, simultaneously, the sadness and injustice of those large and small betrayals by others of their fellows, even, lo, perhaps travel, as it were, backwards in time and recover those powerful, difficult emotions in order to retroactively find redemption, even salvation?

Why not?

It helps to have read that, according to the cosmology of kooky as described in The Book, a person is said to be a "Clear" when he or she has transcended his or her own reactive or subconscious mind and as a result suffers none of the ill effects that it causes, none at all. (I am making none of this up.) A "Clear" is said to be "at cause over" (in control of) their "mental energy" (their thoughts), and able to think clearly and so both avoid and somehow exploit the problem which early made them so incomplete, unsuccessful, unfulfilled, losers and unhappy.

As in, perhaps, instantly appreciating the total fuckuptitude of a putatively democratic culture and free, open society which identifies, esteems, sings and talks and claps and whispers and hustles its constituents, its fellow citizens, about what is not there and never was and, worse, fails to help, rescue, avenge the most foolish of the fooled, the most victimized of the victims, the poorest of the poor, the innocents out looking for their little lost pet doggy or accepting the lies they are told and then finding themselves, even worse, taking a personality test, checking their E-meters and signing up for a "billion-year contract"?

Again, why not?

Just look at the photographs in The Book of L. Ron Hubbard, would you, please? He was an ugly, ugly, ugly man, with a smirking smile, weird lips, the full-on crazy eyes, too-broad forehead, big clown nose, a physically strange and obviously disturbed individual — charismatic, some people said, unbelievably — but somebody you would today, right now, physically make an effort to avoid if you saw him coming in your direction, walking on the sidewalk toward you in his dumb admiral outfit.

Yes. Yes! It turns out that a person can catch up. Yes, indeed. And appreciate. And learn. But there are consequences for sure. The good news is that these are mostly overwhelmingly positive consequences, with unexpected collateral consequences, rewards, improvements, life-extending results, happiness and good health, realizations of powers within and without all made accessible and, best of all, inexplicable good luck and powerful sex appeal, too, and satisfaction, all of it or at least some, depending on the person, in this case me.

The bad good news is, yes, the extremely long sentences and digressions. Sorry for that. An enthusiastic intellectual autobiographer as I am — a newbie, an amateur, a convert — finds that he has a lot to say, to explain. In my defense, I had nothing to say for so very long before this. I have, it seems, some catching up to do.

I had once limited my communication to telling other people what they owned, what they owed, what they were saving and saving up, working as a real, licensed auditor in the everyday sense of the word, the actual sense, the not-crazy sense, as in a Certified Public Accountant and not a confessor or interrogator here from the Galactic Confederacy as once run by an all-powerful and knowing space-lord leader.

What else? It turns out, at least according to my own admittedly casual research — in fact a number I find now that I must have almost completely made up — that the occupation of at least seventy-five percent of stereotypically lonely, frustrated, depressed, alienated, one-dimensional fictional male characters as presented in popular films, literature, jokes, memes, tropes and comedy sketches are employed as, yes, accountants, auditors, CPAs. That's just too easy, and wrong. And yet the number might actually be higher. Still, pocket protectors. Short haircuts. Horn-rimmed glasses. Dockers brand pleated slacks and sensible shoes. And too bad, because auditors, accountants, tellers are good people, solid people, stalwart men and women. More of us should listen to them and, when possible, interrupt to inquire about their real lives outside the office, take them to lunch, recommend books (No surprise, I recommend *Going Clear: Scientology, Hollywood, and the Prison of Belief* by Lawrence Wright, ISBN-10: 0307700666, ISBN-13: 978-0307700667), in no small part to affirm that they live real lives, which they might then as a result notice themselves, and embrace, as did, indeed, as have, I.

My own sense, speaking from personal experience, is that this provocative interrogation would lead to difficult, surprising and helpful answers, unexpected and salutary actions, and of course immediately destroy a lot of careers and wreak havoc across the financial services industry, most private busi-nesses, non-profits, associations, the U.S. government, the In-ternal Revenue Service, wherever proud American women and men add and subtract and multiply and divide and amortize and then report on it to their higher-ups. And, no, that this would not necessarily be a bad thing, no, not at all.

*   *   *

Perhaps only just being there in the laundry room, where I opened up and began reading from the beginning of the rest of the five hundred and sixty page take-apart of the crazy disciples and sad human space-rodents would have been enough, just be-ing that close to it, in close proximity to a book lying open now on that faded linoleum countertop, but of course after taking in the chance excerpt and the historic black-and-white photograph of the leader plugging his wires and clips into, of all things, a to-mato plant (why a tomato, why not an apple or a yam?), I opened it up again and began reading right there during the wash cycle through to the loud buzzing of the finish of the first load, and then through a second load and two dry cycles.

It was comfortably warm if moist, humid, in the laundry room. An hour went by, then another, nearly. I stopped reading long enough only to take in the rest of the photographs dis-tributed throughout, mostly of Hubbard and other, even more very ugly people, and then to flip back to my favorite, of L. Ron himself displaying his prowess with his flimsy device, affirming its viability, turning loaves into fishes, into tomato plants, love apples I think they were once called, into human stand-in entities for psycho-spiritual energy potential.

Laundry washed and dried, very dried, I walked outside and back upstairs to my modest one-bedroom-with-balcony condo conversion, did not fold my sheets, shirts, underwear or towels and instead ate dinner (leftovers from Pick-up Stix) while continuing to read *Going Clear* through nearly to the dawn — through the completely manufactured war stories and early pulp writing career, the publication of Dianetics and then the move into Scientology, through the failures and cons and rip-offs and scams and abuses and criminal larceny of L.R.H. himself, his henchmen and wives and victim-collaborators, and the story of Mr. Haggis, the screenwriter and TV writer, with the revelation, the breakthrough as it were, the quantification right there of indeed just exactly how much anger and empathy a person could apprehend after nearly 30 years of life. A whole lot, it turns out.

I had, honestly, never read a book like this. Of course, again, I had not actually read a book in years, not since college. I had been an illiterate of sorts, only just hours, minutes, earlier. I'd belonged to the accounting club at Cal State Long Beach, graduated in four years, landed a job immediately, and what else since then, what else in nearly a decade? Now I could not even remember any of it, and saw only a void. I had never travelled outside the country, never been hungry, never desired much, and only watched along what I could of the world on CNN, if only half-interested, half-heartedly. I'd had perhaps only half a heart to this point, or half a brain. Fifty percent of one or the other, maybe, but of course another number I had made up, confidently.

I did however indeed enjoy one hobby, one pursuit: clever, funny assassin films, especially those of the actor-director-writer John Cusack. I recommend starting with *Grosse Pointe Blank,* in part because of the wit, beauty and curly hair of the actress who plays his love interest, a British talent named Minnie Driver, with a great name too. And the music, by The Clash, and the acting of funny comic Dan Ackroyd, a Canadian by birth, as a competing hit man, an actor who is what they call a comic genius but all of it explicable only, finally, via appreciating the work of Cusack, who also helped write it.

*   *   *

The continuing side effect, symptom or happy consequence of reading this particular book which, by the way, features blurbs about Wright's earlier work by the esteemed journalist Dexter Filkins, *The Wall Street Journal, TIME* and super-duper-smart *New York Times* reviewer Michiko Kakutani herself, was noticeable: immediate improvement in my physical health, energy level, feelings of well-being and attitude. Stamina. Intellectual curiosity. Anger. Anger! Energizing, creative, healthy anger. Generosity! Joy!

Finishing it that early morning after reading all night, I put down The Book, possessing and being possessed by a new vigor and clarity, energy, self-understanding and the physical manifestations of seemingly universal empathy, the empowerment of the experience of reading story after story from the life of Haggis, who wrote and directed many excellent films and TV shows himself — but the best of which is *Crash* — and of the regular disciples and of the members of the elite Scientology inner circle called, yes, the Sea Org (don't ask!), of the billions of dollars spent, stolen, the coercion and violence, and all of it made me, to say it again, very, very angry and happy indeed, and filled with empathy and an emotional and corporeal strength I'd never before felt or even imagined, much less understood. I impulsively touched the wall of my room, a gesture of affirmation and triangulating and grounding actually used, as it happens, in Scientology, toward somehow adjusting the parameters of my new life, stretching my awareness, finding myself and understanding.

Then I let loose and hit the wall, punching it hard, and putting a hole in the plaster. That was definitely a first for this auditor. My knuckles bled, and it felt good. I liked the feeling, the modest pain, the swelling, the bright red on the wall — my blood tasted sweet — though doing that once was enough. I felt alive.

*   *   *

Frankly, I recommend this experience but as you will see, I can't do that publicly — recommend anything or hit walls or otherwise call attention to myself — which is why I have not and will not mention my own real name anywhere, have changed a few others in the testimony-confession-manifesto which follows, but of course have unshyly included the real names of the hoodlums and criminals and betrayers of humanity whose exploitative missions almost immediately attracted my unfettered attention, my interest, my passion, as it were after reading about the biggest, ugliest one.

Yes, I had until reading the book, staying up all night, attacking a wall, been a blank, and a blank slate. Empirically there is in fact nothing at all except for my discovery of The Book to account for my conversion, if you will. I did not seem to have a brain tumor or serious psychological problems. I'd experienced no apparent trauma, though my knuckles throbbed for a few hours. I had to this moment been noncommittal and unconcerned about matters of faith or religion or spirituality, uninterested, only peripherally engaged and never personally victimized, not really, or so I'd thought until then. I had never been to church or synagogue or mosque regularly, not to religious youth camp, not been baptized or otherwise ritually humiliated, and certainly never raped by a Roman Catholic priest or forced to get on my knees and mumble something to somebody who was not there, not ever. More to the point, I had never known, worked with, or even been approached by Scientologists, engaged or invited to take the famous personality test or consider joining their cult or given one of the hundreds of pulp mystery-detective or sci-fi novels written by The Commodore under one of his many odd names.

I saw that I was as a result especially, counter-intuitively, yes even somehow more vulnerable or, if you prefer, receptive, available. What I now understood as my own slow, cumulative betrayal had been, perhaps like yours, only modest, garden-variety, an acquiescent and gentle coercion, like the childhood game of indoor dodge ball played on a rainy day at junior high school, where the average child could effectively avoid the sadists in the gymnasium by running just slightly faster than the slower, fatter, stupider, weaker, frailer children (who would be struck violently on the fleshy places of their bodies where it hurt most, or even on the face) and shut out the injustice of it all, not to mention ever once tell a teacher, coach, principal or adult, as if that would do any good.

*   *   *

I was, after all, educated in above-average public schools, earned my AA degree, kept my nose clean, whatever that means, was generally hygienic beyond only my nose, was well-enough compensated at work, owned my condo conversion unit outright, and through it all was exposed only vaguely to the holy rollers, snake handlers and evangelizers, so that I say again that my now-urgent and overwhelming sense of betrayal was not just my vicarious own but one which I experience as ours, friend — his, hers, yours, everyone's — a collective affront so ghastly and large — the forging of documents, the larceny and faked military career, the front groups, the army of lawyers, the shake-down and intimidation and victory over the Internal Revenue Service (!) and other agencies of the United States government, the bribery and donations which held special metaphorical as real, political meaning for me, of all people, yes, an auditor — that its cumulative harm could not be contained, focused on only one person.

And yet it was. On me, of all people, as they say. Perhaps for all people. I had been both a sad cartoon of an auditor and yet also a real one, with a real license, a job, benefits they call them, a calculator, computer and spreadsheets, a trusted and licensed professional with a reasonably, unreasonably good gig in a mid-sized, stable firm, only your average phobias, little love or apparent need or desire for it, someone I see now with pity, or could except that, happily, I have no room or need for pity anymore, or sadness, or even anger. I had plenty of that. It is never too late. It probably is, sometimes. But it was not too late for me. Or for you, or the rest of us.

No, neither was I prone to philosophizing or self-assessment, I see now, nor introspection. There had been no form to fill out, nobody asking me, no personality test. There were only things, objects, appointments, the reliable markers of a quotidian world. And even more things. There were alarm clocks and bills and Excel, with a two-week paid vacation and preprogrammed reminders on my laptop.

I was an only child of older parents, now both dead, over whose deaths I had grieved reasonably, efficiently, customarily, then donated their effects to the Salvation Army — a big tax deduction! — but not thought much about since, or about my new identity as a genuine, real-life grown-up orphan.

So that I was it seems in so many ways more than ready for what happened to me — yes, what I made happen! — as the result of reading that one very special, singular book of award-winning reportage, suddenly, and embracing my own perceptions and then powerfully taking grand existential liberties with other people's perceptions, responses: transcending, over-assuming, over-empathizing, taking liberties meant to be taken, not given or bought or awarded.

The book's indictment of one specific if spectacular faith delusion, perhaps, yes, the worst of them (notwithstanding Mormonism or the Moonies or Hari Krishnas) showed me in that good Friday morning early light of a late spring day in south Orange County, in my modest one-bedroom, one-bath unit with living room and kitchen, walk-in closet, storage locker downstairs and partially enclosed carport I'd lived in since just after college, a bachelor with no girlfriends (no girlfriend, singular) and no pet, no parents, that I had finally achieved that most dangerous of dualities: curiosity itself and the simultaneous, urgent awareness of curiosity, if with a vengeance.

I was reanimated, risen from the dead, still perhaps dead but alive at the same time. I was Paul and Saul both, riding my donkey to Damascus, struck down, but getting back up on it and, yes, reaching down and helping myself up to sit on the back end of the saddle, too, both of us, the old me and the new. Poor donkey.

I sang to myself. I listened. I sang of myself. And I sang back. It was a duet, and loud. Yes, because there were now two of me. One of me opened the sliding glass door. I (or he) took off my clothes and assessed my physical body in a ritual inventory. I performed a tiny dance, perhaps a jig or a hula. So did I. I clapped my hands, and heard myself clapping, an echo. I rooted my feet on the ground and twisted my torso like a helicopter. I did jumping jacks. My eyeballs rocked happily in their sockets, like a carnival ride. The landscape was disturbed. I sweated. I felt the air on my body. My penis flapped in jolly consent. I was alive, and conscious of it, too. I was John the Baptist. I was John the Cusack. I was Mercury astronaut John Glenn, orbiting myself, and Earth too. I was Johnny Appleseed. I was both Johnny Appleseed and the apple seeds he sowed and I was the worm in the apples, too, also the apple trees from which the seeds grew and the tree-blight and the orchard, and I was also the internal combustion engine in my old Camry which I saw parked in my carport below and, yes, the local auto mechanic who could diagnose the problem and explain to me why the "Check engine" light was always on, forever, and perhaps finally fix it.

Forgive me, I was, and am still new at this. I am alive. I am free. I once was blind but now I see, to coin a phrase. My digressions, scribblings, happy rants, poetic ramblings, secret journal entries belong perhaps more typically to a teenager, which perhaps I never really was, or once was but never acted like. I had been a very dead-alive young person and adult who went along and took advice and questioned no one and failed to scoff at the charlatans or tease the pious or question authority (like the old hippie lapel button) or challenge the lies, not of any of the liars, Scientologists being the least, worst, most obvious, but never, ever to object to any of it, lie after lie after dodge balled in the face lie, each and every easy assault on humanity and reason, too-bright klieg light conspiracy of blinding and then stealing from others their very lives when they could not see. But now I understood all of it, from the yachts at sea, captained by the spaceman idiot-savant to the Pope in his Vatican robes to the wall-worshipping woman-haters to the secret-sacred underwear-wearers, the bearded misogynist jihadis and the hooded reincarnationalists, saffron-robed "om"-ers and meditators, all of them, too, at the same time, lucky, lucky, lucky me.

*　　*　　*

Done reading The Book, I felt a little scared to abandon my new biblio-totem, transportative periapt or magic golden oil lamp, but would try, so confident did I feel, and so empowered by the shadow-person of myself I had acquired, and so I picked it up, glancing with satisfaction at the small if impressive hole in the wall of my condo, stepped out into the clear air of my new life, walked downstairs and returned the glowing, shining, beautiful book to the folding and stacking table in the laundry room, unlocked by staff at exactly 8 AM every day, as on this morning. The room was empty, but still comfortingly warm and heat-moist from the previous night's work of dryers doing their reliable mechanical rotation. Perhaps the owner would be back for it, and never even know, not have even an inkling. My unlikely if welcome secret life had begun with this modest feint, or was about to, after drinking a second cup of coffee back upstairs and, completely surprising to me, the recognition that I had walked down that morning still completely naked, if somehow also unseen and the desire, no, need or expectation suddenly to perform pushups and sit-ups after doing some easy stretching out on my little balcony, to breathe in deeply, observe brand new buds on the plumeria out there, which I'd assumed was long dead, a plant gifted to me at Christmas by the wife of my boss but which I had been too lazy or busy to care for, water, feed or dispose of and also to see, there in the enormous ficus on the other side of the community pool, a great speckled bird, a fat pheasant or grouse but with long sharp teeth, resting on a stout limb at exactly my eye level, consuming what looked like the bloody remains of what I surmised to be my downstairs neighbor's yapping white toy poodle, the one whose dainty if potent shit-bobbles were left everywhere on the grounds, if always on the same spots. I realized that something was wrong, or at least different, no kidding.

Or that something, perhaps everything, was now finally right, all right.

*   *   *

I cancelled my morning work appointments that Friday. I could do that, had just enough power at work, and had frankly never even used it, not the power or the time off. The circumstance seemed to demand it. I showered, and shaved. I cooked an egg-white omelet, for reasons I was not clear about but which made me feel even better, more confident, in control of some modest if powerful cause and effect, perhaps already planning...

I had never in my life cooked an egg-white omelet, never even thought to do it. It was a start, some expression of difference and purposefulness. Then I called back the office and cancelled my afternoon appointments too. I did not have evening appointments. I briefly thought about making some, just so I could cancel those too. I was giddy, reckless, excited, eager to consider all the details, the orphaned egg yolks in a bowl on my kitchen tile, the missing dog, the book, all of it there, it seemed, elements, as in elemental — all as a result of hearing the voice of Lawrence Wright which I imagined in my head — to the assets and property of the Church of Scientology to each and every faker who pretended at transformation, identity change, who entered into some bargain or contract for their billion years of immortality-slavery and saw that all of it meant only action and possibility to me, perhaps the first person, I lamented, in perhaps the most well-reasoned of my insights, to in some real, quantifiable way have in fact been actually transformed by Scientology — book thievery, punching the wall, embracing nudism and exercise, identification of an exotic bird — by way of abandoning my old self, recreating myself anew almost immediately and then using my facility for demolishing, and simultaneously creating, living and killing, birthing and aborting, I could go on.

And so I began that late morning to throw out most of everything of my old life, and invite so much, of a new one in, of someone else's even, of whose I was not sure. There was not a lot to toss, not really, but I managed a few Hefty bags. Out went anything which displeased me just then, which burdened me and potentially prevented my advance to the next step on my journey — chipped dishes, single socks, worn clothing, a drawer-full of crippled small appliances, rusted batteries, anything broken or blemished or incomplete or suggestive of the imperfection which had plagued my mind — out it went, into the Dumpster downstairs next to the carport, this time delivered fully clothed.

I watered that previously faded, withered plumeria stalk now revived out on the balcony and then thought to fish out the morning's eggshells from the trash. I crushed and mixed them, along with that early morning's coffee grounds, into the plant's soil with my fingers, cutting myself, but expecting like a child for my action to suddenly further brighten the leaves, produce flowers, as if in a stop-motion high speed film. Which, yes, it did, transforming the once-bare stalk but now revived plumeria into a leafing, healthy plant, with the fully appearance of three gorgeous large yellow-white blooms, a trio of small, happy faces. And my finger? When I washed my hands of the dirt, taking extra pleasure in brushing out the soil from underneath my fingernails, I could not locate the cut nor could I locate any evidence of it.

From then on, I see, I did not stop for life, to bowdlerize Emily the D. It did not stop for me, start, or even notice. It was only noon, after all. I felt great, but understood that I was now in easy reach of the possibility of feeling, being even better. I next drove to the nearby Whole Foods, that supermarket-heaven big -box outfit past which I had driven so many times before, that formerly ubiquitous "Check engine" light in my car not coming on at all now, its leftover outline silhouette not even visible.

I'd never before shopped at this mega-store Eden. Too expensive. Too careless or self-indulgent, and probably too much fun, I'd thought. Yet it was certainly whole, and it was suddenly there for me. And walking in through the wide automatic double doors was fun, yes, indeed, and just the right amount of fun. The other citizens shopping there were attractive and affluent and healthy-looking, the food excellent, the staff bright-eyed and eager. I ordered miso soup at the tiny Asian café inside the grand emporium, prepared by a small, grinning, lovely old

Japanese woman wearing a paper hat, an apron and see-through plastic gloves. The soup smelled and looked perfect, artistically pleasing. It smelled good. It was alive, the fermented bean curd doing its vigorous amniotic swirling and the deep-dark green seaweed spread like a tiny kelp forest on the surface of a little sea of bobbing tofu cubes. I thanked her. I dropped a dollar in the tip jar. She acknowledged my gesture with a nod. I dropped a second bill. This was, I felt, still not nearly enough to express my gratitude for her work, for the pleasure I would take in consuming her lovely food. So I bowed to her, too, like a dope. She laughed, but bowed back.

Then I was off to Sport Chalet, another place I had thought of as a huge-scale hypermarket of easy stupid dreams, just down the boulevard, where I bought a pull-ups tension bar and running shoes and high-wicking running socks and fruit-flavored gummy bear energy supplements, and I found when I returned home that I felt physically even better just two-thirds of my way through Day One despite a sleepless night and having only installed the exercise bar in the bedroom hallway and consumed my first 500 milligrams of nine essential vitamins and minerals in a base of wild ginseng and organic green tea in chewable "Berry Delicious" form. Fortified, energized, strong, I thought seriously about what the researcher and writer of *Going Clear*, Lawrence Wright, might have himself wanted or imagined his readers would do after reading his Book, or should do. Laugh, cry, argue, write a letter, take up running and vigorous exercise and light patio horticulture, eat healthy, tell others, leave The Book in a public place and imagine, like the crazy cultists, that they were physically changing people's actions, thoughts? Or perhaps even more, much more?

It was still only early afternoon. The Santa Anas were up. It would be a warm, dry day, the wind full of dust and particulate matter, whatever that was, some other kind of electrical energy you could feel, often famously encouraging anxiety. I got a nose bleed, then sat out on the balcony and held my head up, pinching my nostrils. From the parking lot of that Sport Chalet, in the massive shopping plaza, it had been possible to apprehend the pattern of humanity's traffic, to appreciate it as a series of repeated impulses and finite journeys, of failures and of the gorgeously displayed limits of imagination, broad and narrow, especially next to the open-space Southern California foothills covered in thin arterial animals tracks through the dirt, all of which I had apparently never, ever even seen before or considered.

There was so much more to see, to observe back at home. My downstairs neighbor, the old if fit seeming Middle Eastern man I'd noticed but did not really know, wandered the paths of the apartment complex looking for his pitiful little dead — and worse, shredded, masticated, consumed — dog, whispering "Toby, Toby, here, Toby," and then walked through the courtyard and out to the parking lot and toward the distant edges of the vast, green golf course next to The Arbors, searching up and down the length of the high fence for his beloved pet. The big, strange, frightening dog-eating bird was long gone. The neighbor-man stood there alone, perhaps grieving, resigned, then shrugged and lit up a cigarette, as he often did, underneath the tree where it had earlier perched. Children played in the community pool. The golfers stood around in the perceivable distance, in their netted enclosure, watching one or another of their group stooping and fussing and strategizing over his invisible ball, each of them imagining for him, against him, an easy-enough future, however complicated and pointless if, apparently, enviable.

*   *   *

As unprepared as I might have seemed, don't forget that I had seen — in fact watched carefully, studied even — dozens of assassin films, dramas and thrillers and comedies (my favorite) with the handsome if flawed professional killer falling for a femme fatale or ditzy, charming, reckless beauty, often betrayed but, in my favorites, redeemed or softened or affirmed as, ironically or not, so much better than what they had once been, cold-hearted killers. In the days and evenings that followed, I stayed at home, and watched them again in between exercising, *Grosse Point Blank* and the darkly, dangerous and unfunny *The Numbers Station*, handsome and smooth George Clooney in *The American* and *Wild Orchids* starring Bill Nighy, another favorite, another slim, handsome killer, and co-starring the extremely sexy Emily Blunt. In each I'd felt that I was picking up valuable lessons on how to kill, quietly, efficiently, anonymously of course, and how to be funny about it all too, in an ironic, suave and postmodern way. And because I felt I was learning, becoming, developing, I discovered that I was.

Most of achieving my new reality had to do with extreme physical fitness, military training (Special Forces), use of special tools and weapons, none of which I owned, but also the kind of whimsical hyper-self-consciousness which comes from doing something so very out of the imaginings of normal people as to allow for a worldview in which it both becomes necessary to and at the same time facilitates being one's own starring, leading man whether dramatic or romantic or comedic. That I felt I might now possess. And could perhaps fake the rest of it: poised, tall, singular in a crowd even with a disguise, attractive to women, grudgingly admired by both cops and federal agents, confident and assured if, yes, very, very troubled.

Such a person — me — would require equipment, planning, and the wearing of high-quality well-made dark clothing, and also being young (or old, but pleasingly craggy and still in great physical shape) and tough and cold and hard and handsome of course. Tailored suits, expensive gloves, shiny Italian dress shoes. Payment in diamonds occasionally, and a wall safe behind a fine art painting, and a hideaway in the country. Mark Twain warned about accepting jobs that required purchase of a new wardrobe, but I am pretty sure that he did not have ninja-professional killer-for-hire gentleman in mind. Assassination is apparently not the kind of work you can perform in ordinary street clothes, a Hawaiian shirt, say, a pair of worn Dockers, old deck shoes, unless of course you are disguised for the occasion, the mission, the "job," as somebody who actually dresses like that, under very deep cover, perhaps with a flimsy fishing hat and sunglasses and an adhesive moustache. But it was my costume, and, besides, nobody was actually hiring me, not auditioning or noticing.

Faced with this (my) wardrobe of stereotypically sub-urban ordinariness, purchased mostly at the nearby Sears and Ross Dress for Less, I simply decided to consider what I was doing — when I finally did put clothes back on for good — as disguising myself instead of only dressing myself, and as a result of another morning spent naked, felt especially insightful, secretive, sly. And then I got dressed and I felt it, my new job, and so it *was* my new job. Thinking it, of course, made it so. There was spontaneous transformation, instantaneous wealth, peace of mind, vigorous good health, I could feel it. If I could imagine it, I would be it. Think it and, yes, become it.

So that this way, and from now on, no matter what I wore, my outfit was now a potential disguise. After all, I was not who I appeared to be, or had been. I was not who I once was. And I was not who I was before that, either. It would make all the difference in the world or it would make no difference at all, and there lay my strength.

After a particularly good night's sleep, I woke late Saturday morning and began to compose what I at first called a roster, for lack of a better word, or out of some misplaced shyness at using a meaner word and yet saw it almost immediately as a kind of to-do list, if an unlikely and necessarily cruel one. It was indeed a roster, a list of names, immediately recognizable, one which you yourself could have as easily assembled if you will only admit it, not that anybody has asked you, too bad. It was the same names you'd have come up with were you only a casual reader of the news, a moderately engaged citizen with some even scant historical memory, even the remotest appreciation of cause and effect, an easily-enough recited hit parade of frauds, creeps, fakes. And you would no doubt have done the same if you had read that book, The Book, then stayed home from work yourself, called in sick but still felt just great, eaten locally harvested bee pollen and drunk daily probiotics and enjoyed Japanese food, received the micro-vision of the Speckled Killer Bird, done lots and lots of push-ups, pull-ups, sit-ups, jumping jacks (and for the first time enjoyed them all!) and been under the guiding influence of a strengthening, gentle, mystical anger derived from and at the same time built on collective, what exactly? — empathy, perhaps also for the first time in your life.

The names on my hit list were, after all, of only the most available, egregious, obvious exemplars of the bald-faced effort to take us from, to separate us from our faculties, from one another, and to steal what I understood now as my misplaced, hidden birthright of reason, of freedom, and of yours too. These were, after all, truly despicable individuals about whom people talked but, as with the weather, did nothing about. And did not, and here was the difference, even think about doing. Not until now. Not until me.

So went Day Two and Day Three. I fell into bed tired at night, satisfied. I took three deep, slow breaths after lying down for the evening, after staying up to read. Did you know that taking deep breaths tricks the brain into believing that the body is relaxed, causing it to step down, to back off its guard, to abandon the fight or flight impulse and to allow easy sleep? I also immediately developed a vivid dream life, having missed before this new variety of adventure. And a memory, too, also pretty vivid.

I had not remembered that I even had a memory, to sound both accurate and, yes, a little sophomoric about it. But then again, I now had no fear of seeming sophomoric or immature or naïve or retarded, not to anybody, and especially not to people out there who had believed in or allowed others to believe in a certifiably insane pathological hustler who liked to play dress-up in fake admiral or ensign or captain uniforms, not to mention all the rest of them, similarly oddly attired, with funny collars and robes and big hats, beards and other regalia of the hierarchies of pretend.

The new nightly dreams were something like taking an online course, or old-fashioned cable TV public access channel, low quality but sincere and gentle and intimate, like what used to be called correspondence classes. Indeed, events of my waking life began to correspond to my new awareness, and I learn by watching, as is advertised on television. Enroll now! Take classes through the mail. Master a foreign language in your sleep. I was reminded in one especially vivid and gratifying dream-recollection that I'd once had an instructor in college who, clearly exasperated and impatient at the lack of moral or political engagement by his students, walked in one morning and offered, patiently, that he had just been alerted by campus police that a giant wave of toxic sludge was making its way toward our classroom, one of a hundred in a building which would soon be destroyed, perhaps in minutes, and that nobody else knew about it and what, students, should we do? Run, get the hell away, leave, offered a couple of the mostly bored and apparently only mildly panicked students. A few stood up. He asked them to sit. Really, asked the professor. Really? What else? Nobody said anything, not me either. No, certainly not me.

It is too late and now completely unnecessary, pointless, to feel any shame about this episode. I am redeemed. I am an object lesson to myself — who better? — an A+ student of my own new self of apprehension. I learned from my own mistakes, and felt good about it, even as I was unconscious, in a REM-state. Damn, I love this story! I mean this particular anecdote, surely, and The Book too, but also this first installment of my autobiography, which you are reading.

You people in this room know something which others do not, said the teacher, patiently, carefully to the students, including me. That this entire building and its occupants will likely be harmed, be injured, perhaps die or otherwise suffer serious negative consequences (he talked like that, which further added to my gratitude and affirmation, not to mention the verity of the dream) and all you people are going to do is save yourselves?

There was no toxic sludge-wave, of course. You knew that. Just as there was, for me, once, not imminent death or a terminal medical condition. There was only painful knowledge and its relationship to responsibility, and human empathy. And you knew that, too. I hadn't known it, not then. I do now, you bet. Substitute Lafayette Ronald Hubbard for toxic sludge-tsunami wave and, besides the loss of a gratifyingly horrifying image and replacement with, instead, an extremely ugly red-headed white man from Tilden, Nebraska, you have pretty much my new dream and its moral, too. Moral: There is, for those who know how, indeed, work to be done, toward saving ourselves, and others.

*   *   *

I woke up on Wednesday, Day Six, refreshed, happy. I called in sick, lying with a joy previously not known to me, and completely, happily confident that they all knew I was lying, then took my yummy chewable adult vitamins, did a full hour of exercise including pull-ups, took a shower and prepared a healthy breakfast. I hated to leave the condo, so perfect and calm were my surroundings, as newly redefined and controlled by me. But I went out and purchased black clothes anyway — who knew when I might find a use for them, regardless? — thin black gloves, a black ski mask, a fancy micro-fiber jersey, all of it at the Salvation Army. I found a tiny battery-powered LED headlamp at a discount electronics big-box store back at the mall. This was more good fun if not much else. I went home, dressed, and stood in front of the mirror, shades drawn, posing, coffee table lamp in the "up" position to create just the right shadows, doing karate poses, and saw that I resembled an elegant if still slightly fat, out of shape secret agent man, James Bond meets a black-clad Tele Tubby, and hardly the picture of your typical cold-blooded professional killer. Yet it amused me, and it made me glad, and I saw that what I might achieve was within reach. I had already come a long way, fully enjoying my journey thus far.

Was I discouraged? I was not, not even a little. I got naked again, which was my new default position back at home, did more push-ups and pull-ups, drank a frothy-good glass of a delicious multi-grain beverage sweetened only with healthy agave syrup. I had not been to work for two days and already contemplated further absence by way of my new presence.

All of my actual real killing gear, which of course fit nicely into a military-style duffel bag, I purchased easily that week (in cash, just to be safe) at the local Sharper Image, which is just a fun place to shop even if you are not on a mission. Miniature gadgets. Listening devices. Micro-cameras and scopes and telescoped mirrors for peering around corners. Tiny knives. Wrap-around sunglasses.

Except for the weapon itself, which was simple to locate for sale online, from a local guy who lived right here in Mission Viejo, a city which likes to remind everybody that it has the lowest crime rate in Orange County. He mostly sold at gun shows, he told me over the phone, and at swap meets, and would be more than happy to accept my fake name, fake ID, and fake reason for needing what I first called a Lugar, confusing the moderate Indiana Republican ex-Senator (Richard) with the famous Nazi gun.

I was in fact actually thinking of a Ruger, and here is as good a time as any to point out that when you think something and imagine that you will as a result make it so from just thinking the thought really hard, being close turns out to be okay, not a problem, at least not with handguns. Sort of a "horseshoes and hand grenades" situation, maybe. Or that there are so many weapons that, say anything, and you will get one right.

He chuckled at my mistake, this good old boy-sounding man, and said that he had all kinds of guns for sale. Seemed like a nice enough guy, as they say. He also seemed bald on the telephone, and white. Probably large. Or so I imagined him. I asked him about ammo, whatever that meant, and a silencer, too, and he chuckled again. And then we met on Tuesday evening in the local Wal-Mart parking lot of all places where, inside, of course, I probably could have purchased a pistol, a revolver, a rifle or a retired federal elected official whose name sounded like one had I wanted anybody to know about it. I did not.

"Personal security," I told him, when he asked me in person, somewhat disinterestedly, about why I desired to own a small-caliber handgun. He was six feet tall, indeed bald and white, two-hundred pounds, bushy beard, suspenders, boots, in each detail of a rudimentary description exactly as I had imagined him (yes, exactly as I had imagined, anticipated, constructed him) from our brief telephone conversation. As I had expected and realized him. This was gratifying and, of course, an assurance and a portent, obvious now but then only an inkling.

He seemed not to want to talk at first. The Santa Anas, still blowing, were bothering everybody, if delighting me. But he brightened right up at the phrase "personal security," telling me that he also owned several weapons for personal security, for his wife's security, his children's, for his house and his dogs' security. I thought of my lush plumeria back at home, doing so well on the balcony now.

"Your house plants?" I asked.

"Theirs too," he smiled.

*　*　*

Beyond Netflix and the assassin-movie genre vigorously represented there, it turns out that You Tube explains just about everything else that you need to know, learn, own to become a hit man, a for-profit or indie assassin, a freelance, contract or all-around killer, all of it presented in short, reasonably high-quality videos. Except of course you need your own motivation beyond the craven expression of exotic violence so easily available, so easily imagined.

And a victim, or victims. Targets. Thanks to award-winning and critically acclaimed nonfiction writer, journalist and *New Yorker* contributor Lawrence Wright, I now had plenty of those.

Say, do you know what *TIME* magazine said about his earlier book, *The Looming Tower*? Its reviewer wrote: "Compulsively readable [and] deeply unnerving." Compulsive, unnerving, deep. Exactly my experience with *Going Clear,* to put it mildly, and these critics hadn't even read this one yet! Imagine. I made a note to somehow find Lawrence Wright, to thank him or perhaps just answer what I had come to understand was the question implied in The Book, his book, in its subtitle. "To break out of that prison of belief," I might tell him. Or ask him: "To kill the warden of the prison of belief? To free all the prisoners in the prison of belief? To tear down the high walls of the prison of belief? To free us?" And so on, like that, as the simple instructions written on the note in the basket of perfect, plump homegrown lemons left, like the book, for anybody, for everybody, for me.

*   *   *

What, then, is the precise if impossible alchemy required for creating the vocabulary and language or dialect of angerism, anger unmanagement, practical anger application, or whatever I will call it, my own fake catechism for my own scientific religion, my neologism, and for the making or remaking of my language, any language to reflect more accurately what we, I, am talking about? What is it which allows us to appreciate the gorgeous duality of life and death, of destruction and creativity simultaneously, or not at all? No, these are not the kinds of questions I would even have thought to ask before, much less answer (!) but here I was with a small arsenal of illegal weapons stored and with me at the ready in my condo conversion, a semi-automatic weapon and handsome carrying case, plenty of bullets, gloves, a black turtleneck sweater, a zip line, a hand grenade which my weapons dealer had thrown in — no charge — infrared sights, black no-scuff running shoes, and messages on the phone machine from work asking where I was, a healthier body in days and a new outlook on life.

I lived alone, as I had always (if now also with my own newly spiritually-accessorized Self) for some few more days with my gun and my books, doing my exercises and reading, not going to work, watching the singularly beautiful and aromatic tropical flower grow, larger and larger, and bloom. Plumeria is a genus of flowering plants in the dogbane family, *Apocynaceae*. It contains seven or eight species of mainly deciduous shrubs and small trees. People call it the lei flower: Hawaii, hula girls gently playing ukuleles, hair, a blossom behind the ear or hung around the neck.

And, yes, about to begin my campaign, my one-man liberation movement, for which there seemed little explanation except that I had used my mind after not using it for so long, was using my new mental and psychic and telepathic insights, and so had quickly achieved impressive physical and mental well-being, had embraced spiritual health, had quite possibly, no, probably indeed achieved immortality, and other special powers well beyond my experience, life, job description, all of it without advantage of an E-meter or a leader, only, yes, from reading a single black hardback nonfiction book, the white and yellow-faced plumeria became my symbol.

*   *   *

Not the Scientologists but Reverend Ron, denomination everything, denominations all, denominationally interdenominational, chief prophet of the all-purpose gospel of the holy prosperity hoax was my first, perhaps easiest, perhaps natural target, not a wild target at all, and a most obvious and available choice because he was my neighbor, closest to me, poor guy, his megasanctuary actually within walking distance of The Arbors, a short way up El Toro Road at the base of the Santa Ana Mountain foothills. He is the nation's favorite pastor in case you did not know it, one of our all-American religious heroes, motivational speakers, positive-thinking thinkers. People who assess and predict and consider these things offer that after the Reverend Billy Graham — collaborator in golf-playing and war-making with presidents — finally kicks off, Pastor Ron will likely take his place as unofficial but popularly acclaimed spiritual advisor to the nation, his name moved up a few notches to the near-top of the list of "most admired" Americans, along with Oprah herself. His bestselling book on a life of purpose, as Hubbard's Dianetics: The Modern Science of Mental health, has changed so many lives for the better! As, it turns out, did Lawrence Wright's, not to give too much away too early, with Mr. Wright himself likely not terribly eager to get credit for that.

Reverend Ron led a mighty congregation. He hosted a dozen church services a week, including a Spanish-language and family and rock music worship fellowship! He taught Sunday School. He offered couples' counseling, Bible studies and teen retreats. He ran a softball league for recovering drunks and junkies who got help from Jesus and from each other, but mostly from Big Ron himself. He wore elegant Hawaiian shirts, which accommodated his big barrel chest and comfortable paunch. He sponsored forty days of transformation, with nifty lawn signs. Imagine, this minister-man hosted a U.S. presidential debate at his famous mega-church auditorium, between the liberal Constitutional law professor who was, it turned out, just about as Black as anybody could take without saying it out loud and the old, white, shell-shocked, Air Force fly-boy tortured for years by the VC, and why exactly would anybody have wanted to torture him? Suddenly I knew, deduced, because I now had to know everything, after never having given it a thought before. And, easily enough, I found I knew the answer by simply employing my new powers of hyper-reason and extendo-logic, super-empathy and mystical self-confidence in the understanding that it was now so much easier to perceive things as exactly what, exactly, they were, seemed or portended.

But just to make sure, I looked it up on the Internet. Why, exactly? Oh, right, for dropping tons of bombs and Napalm on small poorly-armed men in straw hats or in tunnels and on civilians, women, children, reservoirs, dams, rice paddies, roads, huts, and helping kill hundreds or thousands of humans and water buffalo, jungle creatures, plants, trees, poisoning water, and the rest of it without even seeing them, not that seeing would perhaps have mattered.

But I digress.

And, yes, this too was also a first for me, digression, along with curiosity, and energetic thinking and writing and research, and energizing, sweaty physical activity and going to the local indoor shooting range, just up the 57 Freeway in Brea, wearing a disguise of course (fake moustache, dark glasses, stylish Hawaiian shirt) and doing quite well for a first-timer, putting holes in targets, if not always killing the silhouette, which always managed to advance on me after each session, in crippled antipathy.

You must certainly be marveling at my transformation, or are perhaps incredulous, even skeptical. Yet it's all even weirder if also somehow more benign: I had, after all, been an auditor before this, a human cliché, a Kafkaesque pawn-like character with no real sense of himself and little of others. I had been a type, a person surprised by free lemons, friendless, mostly sexless, a young man wearing middle-aged slacks and long-sleeved dress shirts, and sleeping through the nights with not even occasional anxiety or insomnia as a companion. And yet maybe I had now indeed been motivated — at least in part — by the numbers themselves, the data, me being, God help me, a "numbers guy," a quantifier and reporter of little successes, and of injustices and irreconcilable sums, an aggregator and an assembler, a dissembler too, in my way now.

Those particular numbers offered in the anti-Scientology book's introduction were impossible to reconcile, and equally impossible to let go. How, I might have struggled to comprehend, did the creepy cult-mafia leaders manage to acquire so much wealth, influence, and coercive power? The religion, Wright explains early, claims eight million members, but also says that it "welcomes" 4.4 million each year. Welcomes. How to figure that out? Its official association of believers (membership required) indicates actually only 30,000 and a recent, reliable survey says, according to Wright, that only 25,000 Americans identify themselves as Scientologists.

"That's less than half the number identifying themselves as Rastafarians," observes author Lawrence Wright, somewhat hilariously, in what might be one of my favorite early lines in The Book. The Rastas smoke dope and worship the memory of a skinny, dead, bearded fake man-god-emperor who stood about five foot nothing, dressed up like a toy soldier. They liked to imagine that they were important via a dubious if pointless connection to both — both! — Egyptian and Hebrew culture, tradition, fantasy and endless self-regard. And yet think of it, there are fewer Scientologists in our brave Republic than there are these delightful, largely harmless dreadlocked ritual stoner-pothead mystics with, I have to admit, some pretty amazing music, which as far as I can tell, the Scientologists don't even bother with, not as a group, and what good is there in even the worst religion with no songs? Instead, the Hubsters had Mark Isham, composer of film scores, and John Travolta, superstar actor, and the left-handed original Mark Super vii (non-quantum) E-Meter, available online in a handy carrying case ($49.00), and of course a butt-ugly dead solipsist hack genre-writer who favored dressing up in spiffy fake naval costumes.

If I'd had a little more of this kind of instant shock-training or education, I think there might have been no effect of it on me at all. Less, and maybe that would not have been quite enough. I was the Goldilocks of ex-accountant, newly-initiated exercise fanatic, health food-eating assassins-in-training of religious leaders. The 365-pages, plus acknowledgements, extensive notes, bibliography and index were just right — not too many, not too few — though I considered writing the well-known and successful professional author Lawrence Wright (Tulane University, class of 1969) and suggesting a glossary of terms for the paperback edition when it came out, a list in the back defining "enturbation" not to mention "going clear" and "blown" and all the rest of it, which you can easily skim past, ignore, if also delight in as you read through because it is all just so darn crazy but which might be fun to have at the conclusion by way of further arguing whatever it is, finally, that Wright is arguing.

What, actually, did I know about what he was arguing? What did I know at all? Not how to critique a book. It might have been the first book I had ever finished, certainly the only one I'd read in one sitting. I guess I am very lucky that it was such a good book and not, say, *Battlefield Earth*, the sci-fi schlock epic by Hubbard, which Wright helpfully points out is the favorite "novel" of one Mitt Romney, who is — because you and I and Mr. Wright absolutely could not ever make this up! — besides being a Republican candidate for president and hedge fund criminal con artist himself and also, famously, an adherent of the other all-American space-travel cosmology dreamed up by a crazy person, with plenty of godly sex and dress-up and financial commitments and pledges and tithing, all organized by horny, bigoted, weird, women-hating old white men with names out of some Midwestern 1800s can-you-top-this parlor game.

*   *   *

You can see that it's a challenge for me to tell this story in order, which is to say chronologically. Disorder, if a healthy, healing disorder, is its theme, but to review: By the end of the first full week after reading The Book, I had my fitness regimen, vitamins, my own copy, thoroughly annotated, of *Going Clear*, the hit list, my unconvincing but inspiring disguise and then my anti- or undisguise as Myself, and what else? More messages from work on the answering machine, and me calling back to say that I needed personal time, an excuse or reason which, cloaked as it was in the language of hurt and possible harm to myself and others, met with no resistance, perhaps because unlike me, myself, others had seen in me the potential for some kind of emotional retreat or the manufacture of a clumsily disguised need for "personal time," an odd phrase which seemed to me to point to a cruel distinction — my, your, isn't all time personal? — and which only encouraged my own withdrawal or maybe because, finally, they did not really care.

I washed my new clothes downstairs (professional killer costume or disguise, or both, at the same time) but I ran them too high or too long in the drier, shrinking everything including the black balaclava and the utility belt. No problem! I was ready, and so I commenced immediately in that other available direction sartorially, toward undisguise, which is to say my normal dress, at least around the house. The laundry room "Free" basket had been replenished with lemons, though no new book had been left, no clues about my mystery book club pal, so I left my own new copy of The Book, testing perversely some kind of reciprocity theory, the details of which I had not bothered to work out, but tried anyway. Empiricism was at this point kind of fluid. Perhaps I would flush out the owner of the original copy, or locate, provoke some heretofore unrecognized element of what I was understanding as my own story, myself as a character in it, perhaps even the hero.

I ignored (or had perhaps forgotten) that very basic assassin and assassin-move rule about not doing crimes in your own backyard, disguised or undisguised or not. Pastor Ron's massive industrial-sized concrete-and-glass God-complex adjacent the self-storage yard and the recently reclaimed, rehabilitated sand and gravel quarry (soon to be the site of yet another LA Fitness, as it happens), with the private if totally taxpayer-subsidized toll road above it all, lacked security on a weekday, which I knew from watching the place from the vantage of my own recently rented personal storage unit overlooking the parking lot (with valet parking), administrative offices, child care, baseball diamond, lawn, fountains and Sunday School buildings, meeting rooms, worship pavilion and gift shop. Renting a storage unit, buying high-powered binoculars, conducting surveillance — it all seemed right to me. I'd learned plenty from those films, you bet. If, for instance, you are needing to rescue a badly wounded if also extremely pretty young woman (say, lovely actress Malin Akerman in *The Numbers Station*) and want to protect her identity, her anonymity, get her to first remove her rings, bracelet and any other identifying jewelry before departing the scene in an attempt to flee the bad, bad men with machine guns and also imply your own deaths in the fiery cataclysm you have made of the place. The plastic explosives you have carefully if hurriedly planted will cause an inferno of extreme high temperatures and take care of all the evidence, and the two of you, a once-hardened but now redeemed-by-romantic love ex-assassin and a gorgeous, smart, willing, grateful and obviously deserving beauty, so that together you will have a much better chance at a new life somewhere, a new identity because of that one careful gesture of destroying your old one. Good to know.

*   *   *

I called the superchurch from home, disguised my voice, and told the secretary who answered that I, Bishop Lawrence

Wright, was running late for my appointment later that Wednesday morning with Reverend Ron. I used a British accent. It was terrible but fun for me. She did not object or interrupt, thus confirming that Reverend Ron would indeed be in shortly, embarrassed as she must have felt at not having previously written me in to his busy schedule of ecumenical power consolidation and religious/political networking. It's this variety of clever strategic thinking which you can develop from watching high-quality spy and detective and assassin movies, doing push-ups and pull-ups, and taking your vitamins and minerals.

I knew the purpose-driven evangelist's routine and so, disguised (or not so much) in a Hawaiian shirt myself (Reyn Spooner, originally ninety-eight dollars but only fifteen at the thrift store), slacks and sunglasses, followed him from his old Ford pick-up parked in the "Reserved for Reverend Ron" spot in the parking lot and entered the lobby just yards behind the relaxed, easy-going fundamentalist holy man himself, who waited as the elevator doors opened. Amusingly, in an overdetermined gesture of Fate's affirmation of my mission, he wore the identical shirt, same pattern, no doubt purchased new, at full price. He seemed not to acknowledge this bit of perverse kismet, the two of us standing there in our matching Polynesian tableaus composed in soft high-quality cotton. I smiled, he smiled back.

We stepped into the elevator together, me feeling my weapon tucked under my belt, hidden under the pleasing fabric land and seascape of island outriggers, sexy brown hula girls, volcanoes and palm trees organized in display across my chest — and his, too — and reviewing in my head the drill I'd practiced using the schematic, the easily available online architectural plans and photographs of the place, double-checking my watch to confirm the time it took for the elevator to close, first to hesitate briefly in its mechanical way, and then make its journey up to the reverend's third-floor administrative office, and imagined carefully exactly what was about to happen because I knew how important this was, to imagine, to create the scenes as I required them, planned them, to see them in my mind so as to make it happen: his death.

But before I could pull the Ruger, not a Lugar — from its comfy, snug, intimate staging area under my belt, I observed to myself that Reverend Ron, age sixty, suddenly did not look at all healthy, was a bit out of shape, and seemed to be sweating, wheezing, pale, suddenly gasping out of breath and, almost immediately I was witness — the only witness, happily — to the scene (as if in a movie) of the goateed host of presidential candidates and mouthpiece of the Almighty clutch his chest and fall heavily to the floor of the elevator right on his face, clearly and immediately stone-dead of a heart attack, what they call a "massive heart attack," unrevivable, not that I was the best or most likely candidate for the job of performing emergency medical triage or CPR or reviving, no, or defibrillating. In any case I understood what I saw, a miracle or the intervention of Fate or coincidence or dumb luck or timing, and an urgent opportunity to do absolutely nothing at all, and so I did it, quickly. I had, after all, a larger moral, ethical, political responsibility not just to save one life, but to save many, other lives, and so I assumed it.

Needless, to say, I skipped our nonexistent appointment. I simply pressed the "Close" button when we arrived together at the third floor, the door automatically opening — me standing, hidden behind the panel of buttons in something like shock or elation or surprise (all of which I was now getting used to, actually, almost counting on) and Pastor Ron lying stricken, dead, on the elevator car floor, well helpfully below the line of sight of secretaries, staff, disciples, janitors, administrative staff, assistant pastors or any security cameras which might have witnessed or even memorialized the episode. It's possible the tips of my dark running shoes were exposed, for all of thirty seconds, to whatever observer or witness, human or mechanical might have been present. I was otherwise anonymous and, I hoped, somehow irrelevant.

Thinking fast, thinking as would the actor John Cusack, I pressed "2" and, when the door opened onto the dark lobby-narthex of the great auditorium one floor below, I pressed the "3" to send him back up to his office while I planned to take the stairs down to make my escape. I stepped carefully over Reverend Ron's body, wishing somewhat panicked, certainly tardily, if also off-handedly, that the dead man, a dead man, any dead man were not lying there after all. It was a modest, gentle wish, a kind of all-purpose observation cum weak afterthought, an idea, not fully evaluated for all its problematic elements, just a sort of mental sigh, a passing fancy of psychic whimsy.

I glanced behind me back into the elevator car and, yes, even as I unconsciously sent that puzzling message travelling its way to my brain, it — he, the body — seemed not to in fact be lying there anymore. Gone. Disappeared. Absent. Or at least unseeable. The elevator door closed. I stood there alone in the lobby, confused, to say the least, now with even more to consider, another remarkable detail to reconcile, to incorporate into the larger story.

Shaken, if also still delighted at the progress generally of this extraordinary morning's extraordinary events, I took the stairs one flight down and back out to the parking lot, glancing to confirm once again what I already knew, that the place lacked outdoor cameras, as well, now, as the charismatic shepherd for its flock of obedient human ungulates, with me never having actually touched the guy and, technically potentially responsible only indirectly for his death only because I had, indeed failed to offer aid. This was a moral failing I was more than prepared to live with after having lived with so much, so little to this point, in fact planned not to confront at all. No one, I reminded myself, knew I was there, much less why I was there in the first place, and of course there was no actual appointment, only the inexplicable fact of a man with an unconvincing British accent who'd never shown. A man who shared the name of a famous American writer from Texas.

I would get away with it, I thought as I got into my car, whatever it was, and was much more prepared, budding sociopath or psychopath that I was, self-realized, centered, to be not in any way at all concerned, though of course I was more than a little bit curious about what, exactly, I had done, and of course how, having actually done nothing at all with such dramatic results, not to mention the curiosity of that fleeting further vision of nothingness, absence, of a corpse. Hmmm.

*　*　*

Still, I got only satisfaction and encouragement from the lucky circumstances of my failed attempt on Reverend Ron's life, success not mine at all, but notwithstanding, and a sense of many new places in the world open to me, physical places as mega-churches and parking lots and elevators, yes, all of the wide-open world now wide open. I listened for the sounds of police and ambulance sirens on my short drive back to my condo, and tuned in to the AM radio. At home, I searched the TV for Action News and Eyewitness News and Breaking News and every other real-time alarm-sounding electronic clarions, for the report of his murder, or was it disappearance? Nothing, not either way. I searched the Internet and then gave up, took a nap, watered the plumeria, ate dinner, and read, which is to say reread.

The next morning I found it, sort of, the television, radio and newspaper coverage of what soon developed into a puzzling story indeed, mysterious, alarming — less puzzling to me than the rest of the county, the nation, the world of course — of the "disappearance" of Reverend Ron. Kidnapped and held for ransom, run away as the result of some potential shaming so typical of these doomed men of the cloth (sex tape or misappropriation of funds), lost or missing, perhaps fallen down a deep hole somewhere, injured or dying or eloped like Sister Aimee with a parishioner's wife or daughter, even young son, who knew?

An investigation was launched, but without a body, reported the authorities, FBI and the rest, with no clues at all, the search was certainly going to be a challenge. His wife and family, congregants and staff were mystified, which struck me as just the right phrase considering the circumstances.

An assembly, a "gathering of concern," was organized after a week, attended by public luminaries, religious leaders, elected officials, law enforcement, a kind of vigil, a tentative funeral without a body, perhaps a kind of collective plea for return or resurrection. I found it easy to ignore all of that except, as one in my situation might, the relevant and puzzling reports that the Rev had been in good health, having recently undergone a physical, where everything had checked out. Still, I set up a lounge chair and binoculars on the morning of the big public wing-ding at the worship facility complex, and watched the massive parking lot from the open door of my storage unit above it, the scrub, the cars and the crowds, the traffic police arranged specially for the big event, me sipping comfortably on a terrific and tasty green algae high-protein smoothie concoction and thinking to myself what it would be like to be wealthy enough, not stinking rich, but with enough money to not ever have to return to work and instead fully embrace my new occupation, preoccupation, hobby, calling, whatever it was, which was a good and powerful thought if perhaps a completely different one than, say, about what, exactly had occurred in that elevator car.

*   *   *

Despite or because of the weirdly if salutary mixed-up ultra-extra-anti-empiricism in operation over the past week, things got only better! I continued my strict if enjoyable fitness regimen, bought more jogging shoes and expensive micro-fiber wicking socks, ordered the rest of author Lawrence Wright's books from my local independent bookstore using an assumed name ("David Miscavige," the former Sea Org leader, if you want to know) and felt just great. I'd been off work for eleven days so far, wondering casually how much longer I could stay away, but late that week, only a few hours really after my bit of speculation about a life of leisure and targeted killing, I learned that a relative I'd never even met, and knew of only vaguely, many times removed as they say, now totally removed, somebody about whom I had something like an almost apochryphilic familial sense, had passed away peacefully of old age and, it seems, extreme wealth, as her trust lawyer told me first over the telephone and then in a registered letter, confirming the details of, you guessed it, the significant inheritance which was now on its way to me.

As her only living relative, my late mother's distant great-aunt had left me, her sole heir, a fortune, as they say, and, no kidding, a chain of lucrative Laundromats, a dozen of them, half in Hemet, California, a retirement community below Mount San Jacinto in the geography of high desert and middle-class retirees where, just outside the incorporated municipality of Hemet proper, population 80,000, elevation 2,500 feet, was located, yes, the top-secret compound of the most hidden and protected inner sanctum of power, the Sea Org of Scientology, Inc, no kidding, which is legally a religion and does not pay taxes, has never been criminally prosecuted despite obvious lawbreaking including kidnapping and perhaps murder, and, yes, is well-known to threaten and intimidate its critics and apostates, and occasionally kill people's pet dogs by way of warning or threat.

But let's stop here and consider my recent and rather startling, if pleasing life changes so far, achieved in such a relatively short period. I was by now up to twenty-five pull-ups on the bar, had lost nearly ten pounds in just over a week as the result of my new self-developed combination vegan-caveman-lactose free diet, which included somewhat idiosyncratically both raw vegetables and raw meat, had stopped drinking alcohol except for a single very large glass of extremely nice red wine at dinner, was nearly a millionaire, owned a lucrative business — requiring almost no supervision or administration from me, had not gone to work for what now felt like months and, yes, felt terrific.

They say that being a millionaire does not mean what it once used to and, friends, they are just so wrong. It means exactly what it used to, to me. Naturally, I quit my job. My boss suggested I was making a mistake, if not very convincingly, and assured me that there would always be a position for me if and when I chose to come back, and warned me, however gently, that I would, someday. It sounded like coercion or threat, but I thanked him anyway. The next day a flower delivery man brought a lovely, robust plumeria, of all things, with a card from my ex-boss wishing me well, and I recognized in its arrival an occasion, another too-effortlessly constructed life-moment meant, feebly, to commiserate with or comfort me but, when located out on my balcony, next to the now fully rehabilitated and thriving first one, the two beautiful plants seemed in their perfect compatibility and easy affirmation of each other to communicate nothing but power and beauty and freedom, a celebration of robust brilliant color and good health.

I guess his wife liked plumeria, which are not cheap. I would send her, both of them, a thank-you note. Arranging this second magnificent flower out on the balcony, positioning it to keep the first one company, which was doing so well, I wondered if, with possession or custody now of two of these healthy, luxuriant tropical plants I was as a result a collector, albeit a newbie, a beginning aficionado, devotee, a plumerian if you will. I decided that I was, why not, perhaps indeed willing that too, and began investigating their care and how and where to buy these two plants their no-doubt easily available special food and fertilizers and, yes, to reconsider the balcony, previously a sorry interface between me and the outside world, instead as a plumeria portal, a greenhouse, a micro-eco-system.

You can see that I was thinking and seeing clearly, or perhaps even vividly, appreciating myself by way of this newly developing sense of interest and passion, and of course I was buying more books and visiting my local public library branch for the first time, which turned out to be just down El Toro Road across from the hilariously named retirement home — Freedom Village it was called, unironically — and of course watching and re-watching probably the absolute funniest of the assassin genre films ever, *Wild Target*, about a natty if dreamy hit man who falls in love with his victim, and reading Lawrence Wright's first book *City Children, Country Summer: A Story of Ghetto Children Among the Amish* and then, after finding this excellent and smart, reading his important if often overlooked memoir, about Wright's teenage experience of an American adolescence in Dallas, Texas called *In the New World: Growing up in America, 1964-1984.*

And, yes, I also began to consider the next name on the short "to-do list," confident that this time I would have the opportunity to pull off my proactive murder, constructed in my mind around the defense of rescuing a child in a burning house, a trespass as it were, the embrace of violence for the sake of a greater good. The first time I had been lucky, or so I thought, seen a coincidence, somehow two, a perfectly timed if impossible correspondence which, I kept telling myself, included the detail of my presence there only an irrelevant if certainly, yes, well, compelling detail of the story as the man was clearly going to have had a heart attack anyway that morning and his body stolen by whoever it was organized that part of events predetermined to occur. Or so I thought, speculated, imagined. Or, as they say, I liked to think. And now, of course, I really did like to think, in a concentrated and focused way, liberated in so many ways to do it, free to create my own fate and future, or so it appeared.

Going forward, getting clearer, I planned the next job but, reading the newspaper in between Lawrence Wright's other excellent books, noted the announcement, and then a long, fawning feature article on, yes, the author-spiritual thinker-former endocrinologist self-help guru, life-extension preacher and fraud, Dr. Mamout Maharishi, in the *Orange County Register*, our local, friendly if, true to the county's reputation, politically super-reactionary daily newspaper but with terrifically easy and ego-boosting crossword puzzles. In fact, as if in some weird and easy-to-dismiss confirmation of the rightness of my choice, indeed, of his own famous mantra that "consciousness creates reality," his first name appeared in the crossword on the very same day of the fluffy feature "news" story, with a sidebar about his upcoming appearance at UC Irvine, just up the freeway from me, for a small scholarly roundtable and, later that same day, a very big public address in the school's basketball arena. Long lines were expected, perhaps as many students, faculty, staff, community members attending as had lined up for the Dali Lama, the late Senator Ted Kennedy, President Jimmy Carter and Richard Branson, a rich man who wanted to sell everybody rocket ship-airline tickets to the moon.

The article noted that the doctor practiced, or at least promoted yoga, and that he also played golf (and had authored a book, *Golfing for Eternal Life*), so I began planning accordingly, embracing again the spirit of the project, in an effort to smoothly manifest my goals, reach my full potential, realize my imaginings, live forever, that power of positive thinking I felt I now possessed if not quite mastered. I enrolled in a beginning Pilates class which met on Monday, Wednesday and Saturday mornings at the local yoga emporium and fresh juice bar, the class populated by many sexy and trim suburban mother-types, an added bonus. Soon enough I was standing on my head. I took a healthy half hour in an ozone-free tanning booth after delicious wheatgrass juice and a cleansing high colonic or a Swedish deep massage at the LA Fitness, where I had just purchased a premium membership and often cycled a mile while going nowhere. I completed the crossword puzzle (edited by Will Shortz) in less than five minutes — granted it was a Wednesday, but still — and

I felt, as I had since reading *Going Clear*, just great. I had until recently never even done a crossword puzzle, not once and, yet, here I was gaining more than only competence, perhaps even expertise, in part due to reading and performing research but also clearly the result of my newfound adoption of power-principals of autonomous telepathological intuition. There were so many new and encouraging ways to measure my achievement, self-improvement and self-realization, physique and can-do attitude about life.

I returned to the shooting range, where I took aim, and this time consistently missed. This was disappointing. What was wrong? Perhaps my new body, renewed metabolism, muscle-memory had so improved as to need recalibration. I took a few deep breaths, and refocused my mind. Then I took aim again and thought really hard about hitting the target. I visualized hitting the target. I "became" the target, but got confused. Instead, I became the weapon. Better. Then I projected my own newly stronger and vital willpower onto the target, and on the pistol, onto the molecules in between, too. I listened to the better me, the real me, the new inner me and collaborated with the ur-shooter who lived inside of me. Then I chanted, too loudly perhaps (I wore noise-cancelling earphones) simply repeating his name, "Maharishi, Maharishi," pulled the trigger, connecting my truest intention with my trigger finger and with my mind, and on my next shots hit the bull's eye.

Yes, I thought (!) that it would happen, by which I mean that I thought it, made it happen and so I had of course created my own reality in which it would happen, had to happen, a whole alternative story fulfilled, in this case with me becoming an overnight (afternoon, actually) expert marksman-sharpshooter and that is, after all, as Dr. Maharishi himself says, what counts.

And, yes, I felt terrific. Why? Because, yes, I wanted to feel terrific, if terrific about my new secret mission, which I could not of course tell anybody about, and why would I even want to? I figured I would find Dr. M. out on the green, secure a round myself, and kill him, now that my sure-shooter precision skill was assured, with a poison dart shot from a blow- gun or perhaps slingshot a sharp icicle exactly into his eye and hit his brain, or launch a well-placed golf ball to the temple, imitating either some inexplicably weird if symbolically pleasing random and impossible accident or an act of God or otherwise untraceable motive expressed. Or maybe I would befriend him on an early morning predawn jog around the Newport Back Bay adjacent the luxury five-star hotel where he'd be staying, choreograph his drowning in the skanky, salty, beautiful water of the intertidal zone at the high-tide of the inland slough adjacent the Mercedes-Benz dealership and the rowing club. Or perhaps just shoot him in the face, drop the pistol and my gloves and disappear into the tall brush.

Embracing prudence and with still two weeks to go, I elected for further research. I purchased a ticket (in person, in cash, of course) for his talk at the basketball arena, and planned the route to finding my way to the panel he'd be featured on, titled, no kidding, "The Cosmic Vibration: The Ultimate Physics of Human Life Extension."

And in the coming days I only further improved my posture and digestion and excellent attitude through weight training, calisthenics, yoga, lost another ten pounds, firmed up my abs, finished reading yet another of Wright's books, and began reading English evolutionary biologist and all-around atheist Richard Dawkins's excellent *The God Delusion*. And, as I never get tired of saying, I felt just really great! I felt only great, all the time. In fact each day got only better and greater and more enjoyable and fun, and I found that I was getting more and more done, working on my "self," as people in the self-help world of Dr. Maharishi said, partly because I'd been able to quit my job (retired at age 29) of course, but also because I now swam an hour on those mornings I was not at yoga, jogged around the golf course, used my stationery bike while enjoying jazz or classical music on the radio, or ran at the Back Bay, future murder site (timing myself, natch) and was now up to 75 pull-ups, like Scientologist Tom Cruise of all people in the vigilante film *Jack Reacher*, an only average assassin-sub-genre type movie, and listening to audio tapes which taught me Spanish, a language I had somehow managed not to learn despite growing up for my entire once-meaningless life in Orange County, California, less than a hundred miles from the border. One of the first Spanish-language books I purchased was titled *Dianetica: La Evolucion De Una Cienci*.

I made smart decisions. I tapped into my positive energy-source. I grilled lean meats, ate fat wild prawns and sustainable oysters, steamed or braised fresh locally-grown organic vegetables, created lovely kale and edamame and walnut and cranberry salads, consumed only raw expeller-pressed nut oils, ate more kale and super greens, experimented cooking with underappreciated exotic grains, simmered rich, healthy sauces from the latest Alice Waters cookbook, toasted quinoa, limiting myself to but certainly enjoying that occasional single glass of extremely good organic red wine and, yes, sitting on an occasional late afternoon at sunset just outside my self-storage unit in my plastic beach chair, watching the slow dismantling of Reverend Ron's super-mega-church, his continuing absence having disrupted operations there, no successor, no leader, no shepherd.

I had not masturbated for weeks, and began noticing the change in my sexual chakras which until then I had not even known I possessed. My male energy, my chi, my life-force, was building up. I was filled with positivity. I began sprinkling such helpful terms in my vocabulary, which put me in a good mood and seemed to delight clerks, salespeople, people at The Arbors. My aura of confidence and strength became a nearly visible circle of gentle blue light around me and I soon enjoyed a new, open and healthy relationship with plenty of attractive young women, including sexy, sweating housewives in our complex and at the gym, who paid me a new, unfamiliar and vigorous attention, obviously flirting and often taking me home, where one after another I pleasured them beyond their wildest expectations, and it was also quite good for me.

Did I mention that I felt just absolutely terrific?

*　　*　　*

As you will now know, Dr. Maharishi made it to neither the planned academic talk at the school nor the public event. I myself pulled into the faculty and staff parking lot early that day near the greenhouse and the campus radio station's tiny studio, a shabby modular unit, where unbeknownst to me he was scheduled that late morning to first do a short interview. I had just arrived, planning, as any good professional killer would, to first conduct additional surveillance before the afternoon's, well, what to call it? Hit. Murder. Transitioning, I preferred. Self-improvement exercise. Guru-removal operation.

But, suddenly, I spotted the faith-as-science huckster himself, nice tan, designer glasses, handsome suit, exiting a shiny black late-model Town Car, the uniformed livery driver opening the door for him, which was parked, engine running, in the clearly marked blue-framed handicapped spot.

I had planned to pretend to be a fan; I was, after all, in my special own way. Yet it's possible that he and the driver understood my urgent flagellation as objection to the obviously, embarrassingly piggish parking behavior or maybe the greeting of another New Age noodler excited to see his spiritual hero. Or a groupie. Whatever, as the kids say. What. Ev. Er.

I honked, and then waved again, clearly getting Maharishi's attention this time. I was a buff young man in a stylish Hawaiian shirt and dark glasses (still no chance to wear my ninja outfit, despite now being so darn sexy) and saw him immediately clutch his chest, yes, even as the prosperity and purpose-filled late interdenominational, non-denominational capitalist evangelist had clutched his own, fall to the pavement and never speak again, not in this life or any other, Amen, Om shanti, Namaste, and good night, maharishi.

Wow. Again.

I pretended I had not seen this even as the driver leapt out of his seat and kneeled on the pavement to administer CPR or attend to his client. I got back in my car and backed out of my own spot, counting on the driver's attention being focused on the dead body of the otherwise immortal uber-consciousness now cooling its heels permanently on the asphalt pavement in the shadow of the giant water tower and the campus's own mighty eucalyptus trees, marveling at what had transpired and thinking, ever so briefly, if only a micro-second, the briefest of flashes across my brain, of what had happened to Reverend Ron. And, yes, as I glanced up into my rearview mirror I saw perhaps fifty yards behind me only the chauffeur, now standing alone, bewildered, two of the automobile's doors open, engine running, parked without a former passenger or a former passenger's body, if still illegally (minimum fine $250) idling his obscene, long tinted-window luxury vehicle in the handicapped parking spot. It was risky, but I immediately braked the car, closed my eyes, concentrated, moved around the live electrical connections in my brain, and thought, concentrated on the body of the stricken man. When I opened them and looked up and behind me in the rear-view, Dr. M. was back, reappeared, reconstituted if still dead, with the shocked driver backing away, clearly stricken, and for whom I felt sorry, but not too long or too deeply as I did not have time to hesitate, heal, move, or otherwise further manipulate the circumstances.

Of course, I had once trusted the mechanics of the empirical method as much as the next guy (Scientologists, religionists, "believers" excepted, so maybe not as much actually as the next guy, depending on which and who and how many of the next guys there were — and two fewer, now, if you are counting), but now I also embraced, anticipated, welcomed it, eager for more of it, all by establishing my distance from it and simultaneous influence upon it. Sometimes things just feel right, you know? And me, I felt great, as you also know. I felt, well, empirical. I felt I was the empirical method, somehow personified, direct and indirect observation or experience, the scientist and the experiment, too, the control, the controller.

I had, I now believed, now understood, killed two major religious figures, criminals of a sort, warriors against humanity, or I hadn't, or I had, hard to tell — either way, by accident or with my extra-super-mental intentionalization force field, a term I'd made up myself, go figure — or had I? I was an assassin, albeit if not quite as planned. But I had planned, in my way, hadn't I and, now, responded to circumstances successfully? And so I was the Uri Geller of murderizing, bending the spoon-like hearts of two corporeal entities just by getting physically close enough to these two easy frauds, sending them to the cornfield of violent if painless, quick coronary attack, like Billy Mumy in the possibly most famous *Twilight Zone* episode ever, except that I was so far a secret sorcerer and had been, until now, unable to control the perhaps reflexive impulse to further disappear the bodies of my victim, something like a cat burying its poop or a compulsive unable to resist rearranging objects, a possibly helpful habit or reflex or instinct under other circumstances, no doubt envied by real criminals, those not charged with the quasi-divine mercenary mission as was Yours Truly.

The next day another obit in the newspapers, another public grieving, if perhaps less than you'd expect. Ticket purchases would be reimbursed by the university. There would be a public memorial. But Dr. Mamout Maharishi had his enemies, critics, it turned out. A mistress, who came forward. With dirty photos. Sons who did not love him. Rational and secular scientists, long cowed or overly polite, who took the opportunity to kick him when he was down. The authorities did not believe the driver, whose testimony was of course both a challenge to the investigation and an endorsement, in its way, of the mysterious cosmo-illogical worldview of the late, missing, briefly evaporated (as described by the poor driver) then returned scientist-mystic with the always-positive thinking and endless-life message for sale, in his books, CDs, DVDs, apparel, seminars, cruises, even in his afterlife, as his bestsellers sold even more vigorously.

Yet skepticism, if not hostility, was also awakened, for at least the duration of the short news cycle, for at least a couple of days on the public radio, on the smarter and braver websites, in a few reports exploring his legacy, yes, that's what it was called, that afterlife which is dished out in portions, large or small, depending, like the high school cafeteria lady behind her Plexiglas cough and sneeze-guard. The testimony of that distraught driver seemed not to include mention of a waving male fan, his car, any of that perhaps necessarily diminished by comparison, this element of the episode trumped by details of the bigger mystery. I made a mental note, a very real discipline of mine lately, to next take up some kind of self-discipline regimen toward learning to more carefully control my powerful wish-fulfillment dyno-reflex as I could now not deny the obvious cause and effect so vividly dramatized a second time. I would also, I pledged to myself, find some way to vindicate the innocent if no doubt emotionally and perhaps mentally destroyed driver, who did not deserve to suffer the collateral consequences of my apparently sloppy and over-eager psychic marksmanship, a skill which clearly required fine-tuning, though I had, honestly, no idea how to do that.

When I arrived home, I took a small, modest step, locating his address and of course using a delightful alias, "Ayn Rand," and ordered the delivery to his home in nearby Stanton, a plumeria rubra, also called red frangipani, the most popular and easily available varietal, and a good starter plant in my own extremely limited but developing experience. This gesture I thought might not only bring comfort and distraction but also, somehow both communicate a message and perhaps even grow something of a similar environmental affect in his home, a posture of protection and courage.

It couldn't hurt.

*   *   *

Meanwhile, I was losing more fat and simultaneously building muscle like a son of a gun, feeling just terrific notwith-

standing the plight of the misbegotten Town Car driver, his absolutely true account threatening his liberty, and also receiving
regular communications, financial reports and earnings statements
from my socially-conscious financial investments advisor, my lawyer and the management company. The Laundromats were doing
great, reported the professional money man, and I now needed
to start thinking about some charitable giving, diversification, in-
vesting my money, buying real estate, who knows, even starting a
foundation. My new IRA investments portfolio was bullish, and
yet all I was really most engaged, animated by was my new-found
power for good by way of exotic flower cultivation and eliminat-
ing the next horrible person on my to-do list, which I now called
only my "Do List" or, after a while my "Due List" and then, finally,
amusing to me at least, my "Overdue List." It was the kind of joke
I could not, of course, share with anybody else.

I was, like the late and still missing reverend, totally
purpose-driven — with a vengeance, boy, you bet — and completely at one with the meta-cosmic physics and also, it seemed,
possibly reversing the aging process as I got stronger, ran faster,
my penis becoming larger and thicker, my eyesight improving, my hair getting thicker, richer and fuller, my smile brighter
(partly because I had begun to floss and got them professionally
whitened) and able to intervene and redress and avenge, doing
research and buying more and more books, done now with the
entire Lawrence Wright canon and moving on to the actress and
writer Julia Sweeney's important if also entertaining *Letting Go
of God; Under the Banner of Heaven* by John Krakauer, about the
crazy Mormon murderers of women; the philosopher Peter Bog-

hossian's *A Manual for Creating Atheists*, which is exactly what it sounds like; and pretty much everything by the late neo-atheist, antitheist Christopher Hitchens, as well as several poorly written, sometimes helpful if often confused (go figure) memoirs by former-Hubbardites, none of which seemed to appreciate fully the extent of their own victimhood, complicity and certainly did not arrive at the, shall we say, more radical if obvious universal conclusion about the exploiters of people like themselves, some of them other men and women on my list.

*   *   *

They had, so far, come to me, my targets. Or just been there, all along, right next door. The Sunday morning *Los Angeles Times Magazine* profile of the Archbishop Cardinal, pitiful prevaricator, defender and enabler of religiously-trained child molesters, caused me to plan a short trip up the long freeway to Los Angeles County. The reporter mentioned the particular Mexican restaurant in Venice, a mile from the beach and famous boardwalk where the capo of local Catholicism liked to eat lunch, surrounded by his supporters, sponsors. I drove up the 405 after a weekday morning's rush hour, when the eight-lane wide river of concrete flows smoothly, parked at a meter three blocks away, slipped into the back of the restaurant just minutes before the place opened, paid a Mexican guy two hundred dollars to give me his white shirt and apron and hair net and disappear for an hour, and started washing dishes, quietly daring any of the remaining staff to challenge me, the handsome white guy who'd replaced their colleague.

In ten minutes, his Holiness's party arrived, the famous developer, the obsequious ex-mayor, the reactionary councilman, an assistant or two, a group of men. I was unarmed, having come to a place of acknowledgement about the nature of my power, and trusting it. The whole thing took three minutes, if that. I grabbed a tray of tumblers and a water pitcher, walked out to the otherwise empty restaurant, and filled their glasses. God's emissary wore his robes and little red cap, as if to make this easy, easier, easiest. Good for him, I thought, working to control my mind, preparing the precise homicidal thought, focusing.

I poured ice water for the first old guy, then went on to the next and, sitting in the middle, reached over but before I could even touch pitcher to glass, the ex-Arch was, well, you know. Clutching. Gasping. Dying. Expired. I was suddenly extraneous and made immediately even more invisible in the face of his attack, helpfully obscured once again by the commotion surrounding the victim, and so quickly backed my way away from the table, turned and walked calmly to the kitchen, abandoned my apron and tray, and exited the back door and walked back up Lincoln Boulevard to where I'd parked my car, time still on the parking meter, having (I hoped) with this episode actually avoided the previously misdirected concern or discomfort or human sympathy which had so complicated my earlier actions.

*   *   *

Spring turned slowly to summer, the death of the criminal Cardinal reported only as exactly what it appeared to be, a heart attack, what an amazing expression, somebody attacked by their own heart, and with it the arrival of the big "Harvest Festival," a decades-old Orange County tradition derived from the confused era of the "Jesus People" and hippie and "born-again" reactionary evangelical crowd, and now the available default position of easy stereotype and too-available cultural-political touchstone, with colorful bumper stickers often accompanying the nearly ubiquitous "Not of this World" decals and "My boss is a Jewish carpenter" license plate frames, "Let Go and Let God," my own personal favorite, a mass gathering involving the assembly of enthusiastic believers in the invisible monarchical triumvirate of faith at, of all things a great baseball stadium event.

Announcement of its coming travelled across the county, with its appearance composed on billboards as well as in placards plastered on telephone poles. The "Brain Harvest" I began calling it, finding myself not only more attractive, well-read, sexy but now also hilarious and droll and clever and witty-funny too. It was a start, and then some. I was, as many people, not of course as funny or bright as I thought I was, but so much more amusing (and amused) than someone previously unable to startle or delight or amuse himself at all, much less others, not to mention possessing a secret so awesome and terrible as to energize my every action, public or private, imagined or dreamed. I was in new, unfamiliar and completely satisfying territory, reborn — born-again if you will! — transformed, sprung from my own big handsome head nearly-fully formed but still growing, still improving, and eager for so much more.

*   *   *

My next project would test those topo-psychic bounds of what I now called targeted proximity-elimination and my own still-developing powers of concentration and focus, mind-control and strength and discipline. Thousands would be reaching their hands heavenward in the big outdoor revival, on the field and in the bleachers, together singing easy-listening contemporary worship songs in their "Praise the Lord" t-shirts and other eschatological Jesus-wear, standing up and marching out of their seats and onto the infield for the traditional altar call, with a fiery sermon from one Pastor Jimbo, a sort of rock'n'roll minister who favored polo shirts over Hawaiian wear, a stylistic distinction if not a theological one, embroidered with the crest of his hokum ministry.

"I'll have to pray on this one," I said to myself, just for laughs, driving over to Angel Stadium in Anaheim to case the joint in my brand-new cherry-red Prius, with an oversized Harvest Crusade bumper sticker on it just for giggles, for cover, for verisimilitude or whatever the mirror image opposite of that was. I didn't want anybody to get hurt beyond my target, but understood that the next perturboration, another term I had coined exclusively for my own use, would need to be especially public so as not to risk connecting any pesky cause-and-effect dots between the sudden death and disappearance, and immediate reappearance, of one dead holy man and then another, and the unidentified man (me), now an announced "person of interest" from the university parking lot crime scene or, however unlikely, as described by the Mexican restaurant waiter who had since offering his testimony to the police apparently left the country, returning to Hermosillo, according to neighbors and friends and family.

And, if I did not control it, who knew how many others could be hurt, not that I was all that worried, but to be left standing there among dozens or even hundreds of heart attack or, better perhaps, heart failure victims, some randomly disappeared, me the lone, healthy (very healthy!) non-victim would be awkward indeed, messy, difficult to explain, if of course any of this could be explained, which it could not, thankfully. No, it could not.

Indeed, somebody out there might be noticing nonetheless somehow, putting together an impossible narrative's disparate pieces, broken or disconnected elements, perhaps another reader of the excellent and award-winning *Going Clear,* themselves using what I surmised now was its potentially adoptable or experientially derived power. Not possible, I guessed, that I had been its only convert, the only reader jettisoned into this consciousness, this hyper-aware and empowering exercise of mental acuity, vigorous physical health and invisible tele-homicidal trans-associative target killing. What a great blurb that would make for the next printing, or the paperback, if only, if only it could be acknowledged!

Or, yes, even only an average reader who got lucky, or a

preexisting atheist or skeptic avenger, a curious or bored or just plain random observer who noticed something right or not right or different or odd, as I had, and developed it. Or a neighbor — perhaps the neighbor who had left The Book there in the first place — or the manager at the self-storage facility or the florist, who might have wondered at the oddness of the exiled former Scientology leader ordering flowers, all of them unlikely but then, "unlikely" had got me, my victims, so many, thus far.

And what about the police investigators, detectives, FBI, computer types, algorithm builders, newspaper reporters and careful newspaper readers, or stay-at-home randomizers of bytes and bits and ones and zeroes who might purposely or even accidentally locate me, finding me in first the vicinity of Reverend Ron, then Dr. Maharishi, then the Archbishop Cardinal or suspect, somehow, that it was as lucky to have been random as not, as impossible or as possible, as pleasing, let us say, as an arithmetically composed non-accident as whatever influences, accidents, incidents had once lined up just right to create the experiences of, yes, why not, a young red-haired all-American sociopathic savant boy-man hack pulp writer named – again, why not? – Lafayette of all things, of all names who, despite or because of being the author of hundreds of terrible sci-fi and fantasy and private eye and nautical adventure tales, not only sold them, but believed in them himself and made so many others to believe. Well?

This was all and everything I had to do, to think and imagine. That, and purchase the matching one-bedroom unit next door, vacant suddenly because, yes, I had hoped it might be, to acquire an increasingly diverse and impressive collection of plumeria by now, all doing well, to meet up with young, fit women for once or twice-weekly assignations after workouts or yoga, and over the next few weeks find or create or circumstance (lately my favorite verb) or wish or otherwise imagine into existence the following, my only nagging concern the fate of the unlucky Town Car driver, under surveillance at home and under a doctor's care and still the prime suspect in an unconvincingly argued conspiracy story involving, alternately, the estranged son of Dr. M. angry (real) scientists who objected to his falsity and gooey fake physics, straight-ahead ransom-demanding criminal types who'd botched their kidnapping of the millionaire huckster and, most pleasing to me, a narrative involving his ascension, transcendence, spiritual elevation if eventual failure to transcend — not so very far, it seemed, from the truth or something like reality.

I arranged for delivery of a second plumeria to the driver, wanting to make sure that he understood, however obliquely, to apprehend some order and persistence and beauty just now, his world otherwise beyond comprehension except in the heightened consciousness-plane in which I now resided. "Say it with flowers," the old florist ads used to encourage.

*　　*　　*

Before the Brain Harvest episode — ultimately successful, with the death of yet another pop star football coach-style minister, this time captured on the JumboTron in the shadow of the Big A, and later played over and over again with him clutching his Bible, clutching his chest, yes, clutching at life and loss, with over a million hits on You Tube and aired on the national news — I'd achieved quite a breakthrough by way of the plumeria, my beloved co-conspirators, as I had lately come to think of them, stumbling by way of random thought on the exercise of mine that would help me to succeed in this and future projects. I learned that I could, indeed, influence the health of the plants directly, their population scenting both my units in a thick, pleasing perfume, subtly or profoundly, open and close buds, murder a plant, revive it, and so I often sat, needlessly, but somehow helpfully, cross-legged, completely naked of course, staring for hours and thinking at the plants, meditating, controlling, now exercising and strengthening my mind as I had my body. Soon I expanded my reach, also narrowing it, indeed succeeding as I had at the target range with killing and reviving small cactus and the nearby eucalyptus tree and, in an expression of poetically pleasing satisfaction, a healthy Early Girl tomato plant, this a modest nod to L. Ron Hubbard himself, the scientist and prophet who'd so influenced my life, second only to his biographer, Mr. Lawrence Wright, of course.

Indeed, that afternoon in the massive baseball stadium crowd, among the prayer teams, intercessionary posses, support groups, youth leagues, seniors, softball teams, Korean church groups, missionaries, Promise Keepers and excited, enraptured Christian rock fans, I thought less about thinking more, and understood some sense of now-measurable self-control, my own invisibility, the unlikelihood of detection despite finally, a few days later, a couple of alert or commentators beginning to spin a tale of a conspiracy against mainstream religious leaders by Muslims, or the malevolent covert agencies of the U.S. government — CIA, FBI, NSA — former disciples, grown-up molested Catholic boys and girls, Lyndon La Rouche anti-world government types, foreign-employed mercenaries, Kim Jong-Un, the confluence of aircraft "chemtrails" and fluoride and vaccination, death by poisoning, and so on, gratifyingly, each in their way but my absolute favorite, yes, assigning these deaths to the work of a secret Scientology hit squad using its network of weirdoes to undermine conventional religion and devil-psychology and deliver the nation into the auspices of the Thetans!

* * *

The famous TV minister and founder of the Holy Trinity TV network died before I could get to him. Or was it that televangelist Peter Couch's mere inclusion on the Overdue List was enough to take him out, my super-suggestion powers having found their own way toward fulfillment, in his case prostate cancer? I would have to experiment with that.

Too bad, there was, as far as I could tell, no real way of measuring, despite my increasing control, although in my super-consciousness I had constructed a kind of internal map, lay-out, ever-reaching if also ever-limiting my influence. My actual facility, however potent, seemed to have natural boundaries. I was not a witch or a magician or sorcerer, my range, as it were, was still, though I did not realize it then, completely defined by my understanding and application of the information and worldview of The Book, that defining experiential life-text, how-to and manual for going, and keeping on.

Meanwhile, I made a quick drive over to Trinity Worship World International, the kitschy wonderland iteration of a palatial afterlife, with a gift shop and reproductions of the Holy Land, its famous year-round riot of Christmas lights brightening a mile at least of the San Diego Freeway and environs of Costa Mesa. I was there to attend the memorial service for Couch a few days after his passing, and found myself in the front row, wearing my false moustache and blonde fright wig, dark glasses, jacket and tie, a huge wooden cross hung around my neck, like the old-school rapper Flavor Fav's alarm clock. So not really myself at all.

No, I did not sign the guestbook. I did not stay long, did not need to. I waited only long just enough, sitting through hymns and songs, a few tributes, to see the main attraction, Jane Couch herself, co-conspirator and widow, to admire her big hair and clown-lady makeup, smile something of a Cheshire Cat smile or grin, and then watch her, standing at the microphone in her pleasingly tight-fitting lady-ruffle suit, fake hair gleaming and crazy make-up melting, weeping of course. And then to think, almost effortlessly and ever so briefly my singular homicidal thought, perhaps even only the thought of the thought really, a small, smooth pebble skimmed gently across the still surface of my cerebellum-lake, and before I was even done with it, the pebble-lake-skip composition, to see her clutch her chest and fall, as if only fainting from grief or excitement or relief, but never, I knew immediately, to take to the stage or screen again, never to profess faith healing and to solicit donations ever again, not to jump or leap or weep or exclaim, not for her criminal enterprise.

I stood quickly, calmly, but not to join those rushing to attend, pointlessly, to their stricken Jane. Cries and gasps and weeping and hallelujahs erupted, and appeals to Him ensued. "She's not…dead?" those in the chapel kept asking, saying, as if people as her did not die, this despite their assembly that afternoon in their Heaven-on-Earth to note the passing of her hubby.

I easily, quickly, made myself lost among a dozen other distraught followers too horrified to stay there, too scared of death, of all things, embarrassed perhaps, and so I was easy to be unnoticed in the departure, despite looking like Andy Warhol, finding my rental car, secured for this kind of public occasion, left unlocked, key in the ignition as I had planned, and was gone before the ambulance and police arrived.

It was still early evening, so I drove the few blocks over to Il Fornaio for an early dinner, the chefs that month visiting by way of their rotating menu the culinary environs of Sicily, and featuring pasta con le sarde: fresh sardines, sautéed in extra-virgin olive oil, deglazed with white wine, dressed with golden raisins, pine nuts, almonds and chopped fennel, then tossed with pasta and garnished with toasted bread crumbs, which was both the most challenging and pleasing food I'd had lately. And a very, very nice glass of red wine.

And you know what I like best about the Il Fornaio in Newport Beach, besides the complimentary parking and the perfectly manicured if sterile olive trees and the tidy Bocci ball court and the excellent food? I really enjoy the view. On one side there's the wide San Diego Freeway, on the other, another LA Fitness. In the near distance are the familiar mountains. The sun cast its light generously, and I took off my sunglasses to allow it in. Dining on the evening's delicious regional specialty in the orange-hued golden-hour tableau, I observed the attractive athletes bouncing up and down on their stationary bicycles high up on the fourth floor of the gym. Like them, I could watch drivers traveling northbound to Long Beach and Los Angeles, and southbound to San Diego, envision their trip through the nearby Marine Base, past the recently decommissioned nuclear power plant, some perhaps continuing to navigate the world's busiest border crossing, then powering down Mexico Highway One as it becomes a two-lane artery through the desert of cirrios and boojum cactus and rocks to the high-end seaside resort and desalination plant and expensive hotels and discothèques of Cabo San Lucas, then across on the ferry to the Mexican mainland at Guaymas and perhaps continuing south on along the Pacific Coast and on into Central America, perhaps through and even into Ecuador passing, if not of course visible in any real sense at this point, only the endless construct of the mind, the faraway Galapagos Islands made famous by Charles Darwin and marine iguanas, where L. Ron Hubbard never ever visited, not even in his frenzied fevered erotic intergalactic time-and-space journey and guerilla warfare campaign against reality and democracy, his nautical fantasy journeys of fraud, theft, deceit and fevered scribblings, all of it so very far, and satisfyingly, from sardines and death.

I digress, once again. It's what I do now, a lot. In fact, I recommend it. Sure, I have that luxury, having made a killing — ha —on the stock market, lately rebounding as they say, stashing away money here and there, setting up through my lawyer a small retirement account for the limo driver, contributing anonymously to Planned Parenthood, and buying even more Laundromats.

That evening at my favorite upscale Italian restaurant, again sitting alone, I indulged in a special treat, my own Jane and Peter Couch Memorial Dessert of tiramisu and grappa, blowing out the small candle I'd asked the waiter to put on the cake.

"Birthday?" he asked, politely, if awkwardly, considering the scene, and likely wondering if, all alone tonight, I'd survived cancer or beat illness or was remembering a lost love.

"Rebirthday," I answered. "No need for you to sing, thanks."

And, indeed, all possible wicked irony and guile aside, I blew out that single thin candy cane-striped candle with a sincerity, a genuineness, I recognized happily, gratefully in myself, and slowly ate that delicious moist Italian dessert and tipped the curious and kind waiter, generously.

I stopped afterwards, on my drive home, to pick up a few items at the Whole Foods, now my regular and exclusive shopping spot. On my way out, at the checkout, with my half-pound of organic Jamaican Blue Mountain Coffee, a bottle of Green & Red, a week's worth of probiotics, fresh-squeezed organic high-pulp orange juice, wholesome seeds and nuts, wheatgrass for pressing in the morning, I spotted him, was surprised if delighted, the ridiculous televangelist Sonny Hymn himself, a sort of whack Pentacostalist if that mattered (it didn't), with his slick pouffy-sprayed gray hair bouffant and shit-eating grin, standing right there at the next cashier. He was passing his Visa card through the register scanner.

Hymn turned to look up, toward me, as I hoped he would, as I imagined he would, standing with my items behind him in line. Our eyes met. Or, rather, my eyes met his amazing hair first, and then I took in his golden rings and his Rolex, confirming his identity not just as Sonny Hymn, faith healer, organizer of "Miracle Crusades" himself but not even completely needing to recognize him, so clear and proud and confident, so obvious and transparent was his falsity and duplicity that he was visibly enveloped by it as if, yes, an aura, a massive string of those same Christmas lights as at Trinity TV heaven, an electric halo, the foggy micro-climate of bright and shining and pure total bullshit. Even with my experiences thus far, seeing this fake-o up-close and real was a startling if rewarding moment for me, transcendent I guess you could call it.

Then, yes, as before, almost reflexively, as I could not seem to help myself at this magical serendipitous opportunity, not mediate (not that I wanted to) the near-reflexive power of the fomentational anti-divine death-compeller: Chest. Clutch. Drop. And he was dead as a stone before he hit the floor of the Whole Foods and, once again, I watched as a small assembly of misguided if otherwise good people, Samaritans trained in CPR, employees on their way to fetch the store's defibrillator, customers dialing their cell phones for 9-1-1, did their useless collective best to participate in the reviving of the prophet, which was just not gonna happen, I knew. I concentrated on containing any further manifestations, disappearances, and slowly backed up as my easiest potential exit of the store was as a result of all the commotion blocked anyway. With my basket in hand, I strolled my way back through the long corridors of highest-quality organic produce and boxed goods, multi-grain cereals, fine cold-pressed nut and vegetable oils, fruit-juice sweetened cookies, imported olives and cheeses, frozen gluten-free pizza, wine, wine and more good wine — my favorite aisle — the small selection of hemp shoes, organic cotton tunics, ecologically smart bulrush plates, bamboo napkins, vitamins and more vitamins, cleansing formulas, hippie vests and sexy all-cotton maternity dresses, cook wares, non-plastic containers, gourmet knives, imported and local teas and coffees, all of it, and made my way around the back of this massive wonderland of good health, prosperity and positive living to find my way up front at the express check-out line (Ten Items or Less) back in the front but at the far other end of the huge bank of cashiers and far away from the paramedics now rushing in through the large glass front doors, then pulling a blanket over the limp corpus of Hymn (undisappeared, thankfully), and passed along my items, and accepted the somewhat distracted cashier's reflexive offer of cash money. For amount I chose "other" and went home with my groceries, a hundred bucks, looking forward to an assassin film that evening before bed and some further strategic planning regarding my next Overdue, and marveling as one does on these occasions at one's powers, if still trying to stay humble, needing to stay humble as this was not the kind of thing you could brag on or share and did not want it to get in the way of other, normal daily activities, say, caring for exotic tropical flowers and maintaining a strict if gratifying exercise routine, dating, and still getting my usual eight hours of restorative and dreamful sleep. Life was certainly busy!

And so, five of them were already gone, if you are keeping track (and I certainly was) all of natural causes, my powers both accurate and fatal if not always entirely controllable, it seems. Yet there had been no accidents since the overeager vanishing of the purpose-driven ex-minister, only serendipity, no witnesses or innocent bystanders hit, my targeted power to end life and create, correct, modify circumstance pretty impressive, really, and me as free as a lemon, the picture of health, in eight weeks a man transformed, physically and spiritually, a wealthy, contented, fulfilled, fully realized being now unchained from any and all of the annoying recriminations of my past life, in control of my subconscious and delighting in it, and ready, prepared, eager for a long future, and possibly even, yes, immortal.

I took the ostensibly chance encounter (who knew about chance anymore?) with the doomed Pastor Hymn as not recklessly, improbably good fortune, but an indication of my own now even further-reaching powers to assemble those circumstances of my fate, subconsciously or consciously, and my bigger, wider purchase on the super-duper, my growing claim on the elements of my new life, including the singular directive power of The Book, the complementary and parallel coordination of elements — disguise, plumeria, fitness, Laundromat, meditation — all assembled, reassembled to surround me as I needed them, a palimpsest beneath The Book, an interpretation, as if I were a magnet and all of existence were delicate metal shavings gathering around me, sticking to me, yet also camouflaging me too.

*   *   *

I judged myself ready at last. It was a judgment call. There was no one else to consult. My nursery was in full bloom, either creating its own temperate eco-climate or responding to its creation, hard to know but flowers blooming everywhere. The Town Car driver was eventually released from scrutiny, put under the care of a psychiatrist and said to be doing well with hypnotherapy and the support of people who cared for him, as well as a trust set up for him by a generous, caring citizen who wished not to be identified. The widowed wife of Reverend Ron had taken over her husband's ministry, a strategic error of hers I would soon need to correct, but just now I had other fish to fry. Despite this, the place was crashing down around her, with rumors of its possible sale to Mormons or Korean Methodists or, who knows, anybody though probably not Rastafarians.

It was time. Yes, soon I would be off to beautiful Hemet, California, a town nestled in the embrace of Mount San Jacinto, hopefully with author Lawrence Wright himself, National Book Award finalist. I would contact his publicist, and hope for a response from the intrepid journalist, likely eager to join me in infiltrating the compound, to witness and offer the official account or so I hoped, imagined, predicted, fabulated, contrived, organized as a future, details of how exactly not yet fully established.

Here, then, is what would occur next, as I saw it in my dream, constructed it in my plan, of what was most required and necessary to meet the expectations required, demanded of any serious reader of *Going Clear*, toward answering the call of author Wright, toward fully understanding the ramifications of fully embracing the impact of the insane prophet-fraud whose disciples had stolen, lied, perhaps murdered and driven mad so many.

I would make it occur. Soon I would stand outside the high gates of the Sea Org headquarters outside of Hemet, the so-called Gold Base, attempting to penetrate the mental force-field of resistance organized there, weak by comparison to my own, ignoring and then palpitating the armed security guards and dissembling the cameras and motion detectors and electrified fence and guard dogs which protect the complex of buildings, apartments, a swimming pool, tennis court, gym and more.

I'd spend real money on the costume this time, needing to do this one absolutely just right: a funny tie, a vintage navy officer's hat, double-breasted blue coat, pleated white pants, gold buttons on my sleeves, shoes shiny, polished black, ship-shape, perhaps with a fake bulbous nose and my hair dyed bright red.

I'd arrive at this international vortex of prevarication and exploitation wearing the iconic uniform of The Commodore himself, sea captain, admiral, the contrivance of the impossible, the bigger the lie the easier to embody. Epaulets and stripes on my cuffs, deck shoes, an officer's hat with an anchor on it, elaborate if completely meaningless insignias, perhaps golden braids across my shoulder, a medal or two, dark sunglasses and a big smile on my ruddy face. My blazer would sport the initials L.R.H. and, perhaps the reproduction of a small, if extremely smart tomato plant, just to keep me amused. The uniform makes the man, people. Think it, and become it! It would work for me, this time more powerfully even than before.

And so convincing and welcome would be my sudden appearance, so potent and urgent would be my auric self-projection and my accompanying resultant crypto-magnetic perception-elaboration thought-control equalimetric force-field, my heliopsycho-gramaphone, phrenolating cerebelumator, my prefrontal cosmonofundulating thinksomnomulatator, my handsome, sexually powerful and charismatic hero-visage, my now extremely large and long and thick penis (fully erect) and my very big, round and smart head under my cap, the molecules and atoms and cosmic rays and radiation and enzymes and even the very ozone in my vicinity itself so cosmologically super-charged with authentic and meaningful and life-changing particles of pure power that yes, they would all see me there outside the crippled fence and be glad for this, my promised return at last. They would rush out past the guards, gates flung open, Tom and Kirstie and Priscilla Presley and John and David, all to greet me, to welcome me back.

They had, after all, kept my private room, my esteemed lordly quarters ready these many years, decades, decorated and furnished with all my familiar personal things, books, pipe, reading glasses, waiting to welcome me back to the quarters waiting since my "death" in 1986. And even as that giant mighty gate to Gold Base Headquarters would open and they and the other proud Sea Org members lined up as I had taught them, as they had said all this time they were waiting to do and so now had no choice, offering me the comradely space-salute, on this the happiest day of their lives, they'd perhaps wonder why Lawrence Wright of all people was there with me. But they are movie stars, not perhaps big thinkers like me, figures of light or only faded flowers, dormant, waiting to bloom again, something like the vivid and fecund plumeria flower I now nurtured, and I'd wonder if perhaps they were in that way immortal, too, as L.R.H. himself had seen that they were after all, all of this as they rushed toward me, and their doomed destiny.

I, however, will have changed not a bit, and will hesitate only a moment to adjust my nifty silk cravat and click my heels before advancing, and believe you me, I will be focusing absolutely all of my powerful homicidal brain-rays on each and all of them, unexpecting, all at once, these chosen ones, who will clutch, simultaneously and fall, dropping where they once stood because I, your narrator, a.k.a. Winchester Remington Colt, Kurt von Rachen, René Lafayette, Joe Blitz and Legionnaire 148, will have believed it, and will have made it so, and thus become the very best and most final revelation and realization and, indeed, personification of all that I have promised.

But then if you accept, understand, believe any of this, then you will believe just anything, so that the closed-circuit electronic witness, a battery of multiple security cameras, images captured on tape, will be/should be relied on to affirm his (my) return, to prove the promise made and fulfilled, provoking then demanding then affirming his re-disappearance once again, this time as killer-outlaw-space avenger and I, of course, will walk away, off-camera, first thanking Lawrence Wright, and never revealing my true identity, still needing to know just everything, on a path to anonymous immortality, living a life, finally, with meaning. And to think, all of this the result, indeed, of just one semi-illiterate man reading just one single book.

NOT ENEMIES, BUT FRIENDS!

THE JOB OFFER ARRIVED, I testified, from the community college in late summer and, after looking up its location on MapQuest, I accepted a part-time teaching appointment (sabbatical replacement) here in Orange County, California, USA, a strange new world where I found myself (as they say, as if they had been lost) surrounded by students, other instructors, administrators, drivers, shoppers, believers, citizens of a nation which I'd never imagined, and which I was immediately so mad at myself for not imagining despite playing around with the MapQuest street map, the aerial map and the zoom function, even pulling around the topography with that nifty little white magician's glove, from the foothills over the valley and to the Pacific Ocean.

And, yes, I was even madder at my friends and ex-colleagues back home in Portland, Oregon, living at the confluence of the Willamette and the wide Columbia in full view of Mt. Hood and God himself, snow on top of both of them, but with their phony geographical-metaphorical fantasies dreamed up as some kind of answer to George W. Bush and to the war. They seemed to see, I told the judge (because he asked me) a different, better place somewhere in another country, further north, with a parliamentary system, a queen on its postage stamps and a red maple leaf on its flag. There is failure, I offered, and there is the failure of imagination, and there is both of them together.

Or was it, I wondered aloud for the judge during Pastor Bob's trial, that it was all just me? Was it that I really had only imagined and not comprehended? Maybe I had not seen, like so many people had not seen, and here it was now, fascism, not quite the real thing, but the shape of it over everything, a bit like a weak shadow but too weak to even really be a shadow, the weakest outline of a specter cast against the atmosphere on an overcast day?

The judge did not seem to mind my poetry or my English teacher long-windedness or even my politics, my tendency to soliloquy or mixed meteorological metaphors. He seemed to study my face and enjoy my tattoos and for sure to appreciate my breasts. I knew what I had said. I continued, smiling.

Or was it, I asked, exactly like that presumed but not actual Sinclair Lewis quote about fascism in America coming wrapped in a flag and carrying a cross, at which point the defense attorney objected loudly but the kind old judge rolled his eyes, and only turned to our heroine — me! — smiling, and asked if I could please limit my answers to those which dealt most directly with the question, please, Miss Holloway?

Except that, as even the newspapers pointed out, and as my own attorney reminded everyone there in the courtroom, Pastor Bob had in fact wrapped himself in an actual American flag and, yes, had been carrying a cross when he abducted my twenty-two beginning Composition students, although I had at the time mistaken his cross for a sword. Easy mistake.

I, Maggie Holloway, was the star witness. Judge Joseph Lawrence Penhall was the nice, round, avuncular old man jurist right out of Frank Capra. He liked me, I could tell (everybody could), but still he required me — admittedly, after the defense pretty much insisted — to explain my own bit of modestly criminal misbehavior in detail. The court reporter could not keep up as I am a fast talker. The audience was rowdy. People laughed. The place was packed. Judge Penhall banged his gavel every once in a while, admonishing those in the courtroom. Everybody, it seemed to me, was guilty of something. This was something of a relief to me.

Indeed, my own testimony, my volunteer ACLU lawyer told me, seemed for a minute or two there to threaten the case against the semi-famous mega-minister though everybody knew it really couldn't, shouldn't matter. After all, I was not on trial, she reminded me, unconvincingly, and did not actually even need a lawyer. Except that I was on trial, sort of. Yes, I conceded, sure, I said, looking right at the defense attorney. Okay, why not, it is true that somewhere during that first week of classes I had in fact sighed really loud and said "Don't blame me, I'm Canadian," or something like that, which sounded to me at the time I said it like the once-ubiquitous sarcastic Steve Martin comic refrain, "Well, excuuuuuse me."

Honestly, I was not even sure what it meant when I said it except that the phrase seemed to capture the comfortable absurdity of the moment and my own uncomfortable place in it and perhaps, I might also have imagined then, everyone's place. That's what I testified.

Maybe I thought I was sort of making fun of myself and all of us, I said under oath, and that we were all in on the joke. Clearly, I was wrong.

Someday I will read the actual trial transcripts and be pleased at what I said. I remember being cute and funny, but who knows?

Here the defense attorney asked why I would want to make fun of anybody at all, like that was a bad thing, and I admitted to the court that I'd probably made a mistake there too, confusing my role as a teacher with my role as something else, a person maybe. That's how I testified at Pastor Bob's trial, getting another big laugh from the kind old judge and the packed courtroom at the part about a teacher being a person, ha ha.

What came out of my mouth that particular morning in the classroom, I went on to explain, seemed to me to both echo and respond to the lies from Powell, Condi, Cheney, Bush, all of them, at the same time and, in my mind, to speak to the lack of consequences — you could, it seemed, say anything — and, most of all, to answer the foolishness of all those post-election "migrating to Canada" jokes traded among my former friends: the e-mails, empty threats, weary and stupid hypotheticals, the fatalistic politics of early middle-aged liberals in the City of Roses who, although they could not imagine anything but a two-party system, refused to go along to demonstrations or vigils and were afraid to host even a lousy Move On house party, were nonetheless threatening to pick up and move to a constitutional monarchy which probably wouldn't take them anyway.

It had sounded to me, I explained to the court, like a cartoon punch line, a potential new popular expression, spoken the way everybody in America had once said "Yadda, yadda, yadda" and "As if" and "Not so much" and asked sarcastically "Ya think?" and the other jargony, ironic, stupid TV sit-com sayings, catch phrases, jokes, idiomatic homegrown Americanisms which maybe meant something about something but when you listened to them closely, meant nothing at all or worse like, "Hey, dude, it's all good" when, no, actually, it was not all good, it was all fucked up, dude, which my students also called me, a woman and not a dude, until I asked them not to, please.

So that I had that first time shrugged and offered my own wry sociolinguistic neologism or neo-Maggie-ism or whatever it was, smiling, to my innocent (and, it turned out, no, not so innocent) students and thought, stupidly to myself, that they were with me, that we were, yes, all of us in this together, which, again, no, we were not.

To which the judge advised that I needed to please, Miss, watch my language.

This phrase was red meat to a writing instructor, but I knew what he meant and I let it go. I had certainly been watching my language. I had been watching other people's, and listening too. But not closely enough, no.

*　　*　　*

But I should first tell you, as I told the court, more about Rancho Valley Community College, where I worked part-time as an Adjunct Instructor of English, in a one-year replacement position for somebody researching a book. Contingent faculty, adjunct, part-timer I was called, as in contingent, meaning "dependent for existence on something not yet certain or happening by chance or without known cause." As in a contingency, a variety of event that may occur but that is not likely or intended, a possibility perhaps that somebody has to prepare for. Dictionary definition is my students' favorite rhetorical strategy, one which, along with Wikipedia, I of course discourage.

Lucky me, I am myself now a Wikipedia entry. It's not much about me, not really. Half of it is blue links to other people, places and things: Orange County, California. Pastor Bob. Kidnapping. Evangelical homosexual pastors. At the top are cautions about problems of neutrality, and a big exclamation point in a yellow warning triangle. My listing, it says, is "in dispute."

Before the kidnapping of most of my writing class, for which I was of course totally (Totally, dude!) unprepared — Is anybody prepared? It never came up in staff meetings — I'd been trying to model critical thinking, as the Ed School and professional pedagogy types who ran the RVCC English Department liked to call it. The unrelenting use of that phrase by my new colleagues — all presumably critical thinkers but also, interestingly, pro-war, anti-union, anti-gay, born-again Christian Republicans — caused me to see a vision of myself strutting down a long, lit-up catwalk — busy disco beat thump-thumping and mirror ball spinning — and then, as my weird dreamo-political vision opened up into an admittedly self-indulgent full-on reverie, to further see my colleagues prancing in front of and behind me in spangles and minis and leather and see-through undies.

Some show that was. Sexy stuff. First the fussy old closeted Speech teacher with the "Bush '04" sticker on his office door and then the lady department chair with her Christian fish symbol lapel pin and then the Economics instructor, who included in his course syllabus the photograph of himself, shaking hands with Ronald Reagan and then, me, Maggie Holloway, supermodel-er. We vamped and posed and teased together like contestants on *Project Runway*, the studio audience full of eager administrators, deans, coaches and the secretarial staff, students, the custodians, all assembled adoringly at our feet.

The story of that fanciful nightmare I naturally kept to myself, like so much I'd kept since arrival at the tiny two-year community college situated in the middle of what remained of the very last orange grove left in the county named after the fruit, along with my concern about the ancient dilapidated mobile home unit in which I taught, the broken clock on the wall, the forty-year old Rand McNally Map of the World hung next to it, and the locked metal storage cabinet in the corner of my classroom marked, ominously with a small tag that read "Property of Calvary Worship Center."

By the end of week two most students remaining in my early morning M-W-F Comp 100A class adjacent Campus Security, the faculty/staff parking lot, the handicapped space and "Reserved for Employee of the Month" spots (which provincial vista I observed from my podium next to the whiteboard and the scary cabinet) were having none of it. Not critical thinking, not the organization of an argument, not the reading assignments and, later, not the national poll about angels and, most especially, not my question about the cause of poverty, which was, to be fair, a trick question, wasn't it, one of those clumsily freighted rhetorical brain-teaser fake-outs which teachers like but students don't, not particularly?

But I am getting ahead of myself, as I did in my testimony. As I do, it seems, in life. I was up on the stand for a total of two days. I enjoyed it and didn't have anything else to do, not since my teaching was over. I was good at it, and Judge P. seemed really interested in my students, if mostly the details of where they were sitting, standing and when, and if in my estimation they could themselves be relied upon as witnesses. My testimony was all about corroborating the physical circumstances, of establishing where people were, as if we were blocking a play or choreographing a dance.

"No," I said, "they cannot be relied upon." I explained that my students were delusional, like the rest of the country. "But, still, they are often telling the truth."

He raised his eyebrows, but not in a hostile way. I elaborated. His eyes twinkled. The courtroom was full, air conditioned, with drop-down theater seats and a bailiff either standing next to the frantic court reporter or ushering people in and out, or scanning the crowd, ostensibly for disruptors, pro or con.

These kids seemed to think they all had a bright future, I told the judge, looking at the audience packed into the county courtroom downtown, most of them strangers to me. Maybe I should have been prepared for that, I said. I spoke into a tiny microphone under fluorescent lights and watched the Black lady court reporter's fingers bounce along below me. I looked at Henry Oh, sitting in the front row, who really did have a bright future.

Or at least, I said, these students of mine held in their imaginations a vague sense of a bright future. They anticipated a place for themselves in an institution, I told Uncle Judge, with a desk and a secretary and a computer and a parking space and an income.

When I asked them what their actual salaries might be in this presumed future corporate wonder-world, for a real, actual number, they said only, "A lot!" and were dismayed, really, I mean to say stricken, when I told them what most people earned, not to mention my own shitty take-home as adjunct faculty (no benefits) who picked up extra income tutoring rich Stanford-bound Indian and Korean and Taiwanese kids at Tutology on Saturday mornings, over in the mall with the PetSmart and the fabrics store and the paintball supplies warehouse.

"I like to call it 'Tautology,'" I told the judge, "just to amuse myself."

He laughed. I went through the roster for him, as I was instructed. There was Ali from Egypt, who insisted his name be pronounced not "Ah-lee" as I had on the first day of class, feeling pretty confident about my pronunciation, cultural-sensitivity wise, when I took roll. No, Ali had corrected me; it was pronounced "Al-eye," as in ally, as in opposite of Axis, which I kind of liked, actually. This ally, a twenty-year old chubster from Cairo with a wispy attempt at a beard, wore tight white t-shirts with a cigarette pack rolled up in his sleeve, blue jeans, sneakers and greased his hair back, all of which odd homage to American Graffiti or Grease was complicated, interestingly, by the colorful worry beads he played with. People assumed he was Muslim, he told us all, but he was Zoroastrian.

Sitting next to him was Ari (pronounced, thankfully,

"Ari") Cohen from Israel, who wore a bowl haircut with bangs, trimmed low on his forehead and covering his eyes, which caused poor Ari to always be looking up and out, sheepdog-style. I expected him to bark. But Ari was here to study, he'd told the class in his thick Hebrew accent on day one, then would return to Tel Aviv to perform his required state military service, he promised us sincerely, as, yes, a sharpshooter, where he'd presumably first get a real haircut and then a uniform and a rifle and no doubt be kidnapped immediately, held for prisoner exchange and be executed by Hamas.

There was Christian, who was indeed a Christian if not in fact an actual member of Pastor Bob's famous inter-denominational worship center down the road, and Garrett the Trekkie-Libertarian-gamer (no further religious affiliation) and Calvin, who was probably not a Calvinist but was Protestant he said confidently, and a cowboy, or at least dressed like one: boots, tight jeans, big belt buckle, hat and embroidered Western shirts.

There was Viktor from Tbilisi and Tori Nguyen and Tiffany Wong and Jesus Alvarez, all graduates of local high schools, if barely, or takers of the GED, the state's equivalency test: Russian Orthodox, Catholic, Catholic, Lutheran. Yes, Lutheran. Don't ask how I know this.

Okay, ask. The judge did. We two were putting on a good show. I was Johnny Carson and he was Ed McMahon.

Because they told me, I answered. We'd had that difficult discussion about belief, or not. As in "believe." Everyone enrolled in this class had a funny name and their faith in a god and a doubtful story, at least to me, but the kidnapping occurred at a moment in our nation's history, which is to say only a few months ago, when most stories seemed to me to be just plain lies anyway.

Or was it my own confusion about what I was hearing, seeing, reading, correcting and handing back with comments ("awk," "logic problem," "parallelism," "huh?") not to mention what was actually happening, and not their confusion or their remedialism at all — my confusion about the war, for instance, and the lying president — which did not matter? Maybe it was that so much did not matter finally. Maybe that is what caused me to somehow suggest or imply or leave the impression that I really was Canadian and was not making a joke. And maybe it was not really a joke but something worse than a joke, and which you and I could see now would be of course misunderstood because all the talking and the lying and even the listening was so otherwise unremarkable, except as against my students' sincerity.

*   *   *

Henry Oh was sincere and Juana Deompompa Dewey was sincere and my uniformed California Army National Guardsman was sincere, if each in their different and remarkable ways, beautiful and dumb. Private Charles Drew had not enrolled in college or, for that matter, enlisted in the military for the twice-a-month weekends which paid for his classes, in search of anything but sincere. Not facetious or ironic or paradoxical or dichotomous, each of these vocabulary words I'd written on the whiteboard and assigned the class to look up after it became clear in discussion of the *New York Times* article on angels that students did not know what they meant. Charles seemed to be there to learn how to read.

After week one, I reported my stubbornly high enrollment numbers to the born-again Department Chair of my wild daydream fashion show, mentioning to her that I had an illiterate student.

"He doesn't belong in my class," I said.

She sat behind her desk and advised me of both the department's responsibilities and of its limitations, and of the need to maintain high enrollments at least until after the census.

"Is he a behavior problem?" she asked me.

"Hardly," I said. "He's in the Army," I reminded her. Charles was in fact overly polite, obedient, and eager to follow orders when not asking to be excused to visit the men's room, where he bivouacked for what seemed like twenty or thirty minutes before returning to class, when he came back at all.

She looked over the writing sample I'd brought in, where he'd answered the essay prompt about the Lincoln Inaugural speech by writing my name, his name, the date and what I took to be his rank and serial number.

"It's not like he's a prisoner of war," I offered this woman wearing a golden ichthus pinned to her jacket.

"Students often have trouble with interpretation, don't they?" she asked. She must have seen me noticing the little fishy lapel pin. She seemed to want me to make a sarcastic remark, or maybe, suddenly, to confess to her my own personal devotion to her Jesus, or so I speculated.

"Interpretation?" I answered instead. "No," I said, trying to make sure she saw that the Private's page was otherwise blank. Her office was decorated in plaques and photographs and clear Lucite statues in the shapes of books and eagles and crosses and, indeed, a plaster of Paris Christ with an open cavity in his chest into which you could look and see a bloody red heart. But no actual books.

Everything else about this school, this county, I could almost accommodate, but no books in the English department chair's office struck me as a poorly-chosen detail you'd include only in a bad short story — a joke, an anecdote which, ultimately, the reader or listener just would not accept, but which I was being asked to accept in what passed for Real Life here.

I tried again. "You misunderstand. He can't actually read. He's illiterate. He writes his name but only pretends to know what I'm talking about. His sentences, when he writes them at all, don't make sense. He asks permission to go to the bathroom and he stays there for half an hour. It's possible he has a learning disability, or a bladder disability."

"Well," said the Chair, sitting at her desk among her trophies and perhaps reconsidering my hiring, "he was placed in your class, which means he took our assessment test. This is public education. We are not allowed to turn students away."

"But he can't read," I said. "Don't we do something, tell somebody? Shouldn't we call his commander or somebody?"

"You can't be serious," she said.

But I was serious, and I made what they call a mental note to get the name of his commanding officer — I remember thinking that ridiculous phrase, "commanding officer," as if I knew what it meant — but, of course, I misplaced that note.

*   *   *

And there were, finally, the three Kellies, each of them blonde, cute and skinny. They drove the boys in the class crazy while all three girls failed the course. There was tall Kellyrae Gray, the basketball player, Kellie St. Pierre (volleyball) and Kelly Stevens (song squad, whatever that was). Kelly (I think) Stevens told me she was in school to better herself, which I asked more about because it seemed such a charmingly anachronistic phrase coming from a nineteen-year-old. Dickensian even.

I couldn't actually tell them apart, these three shining and smiling giantesses, so I created a seating chart with their names. But I never ended up using it because, helpfully, they sat together, so I just looked in their direction and answered whoever spoke using her, their, everybody's first name.

"Better yourself, Kelly?" I asked.   I offered that self-improvement was indeed an admirable goal, which sounded to me like Bronte or Dickens, like both of us play-acting at being characters in *Great Expectations* or *Jane Eyre*.

But this Kelly corrected me. She was in college because, she explained, it was going to make her prosperous. Prosperous! She wore her hair in a straight-up pony tail. Bending over her book or paper, her enormous Scrunchie wiggled at me like a hydrangea blossom in a gentle breeze.

"Going to college makes you rich," she said, like some

People's Republic of China prosperity slogan meets middle-of-the-night television infomercial.

Naturally, I addressed her immediate problem first, which was Point of View.

"Not 'you,'" I offered. "Please avoid Second Person. Either 'people' or 'me.' And," I said, tackling the substantive part of her declaration, "I think you might mean that, typically, people with college or university degrees have higher earning power or seem to wind up at higher economic status, right?"

"I mean me, I guess," she said, rolling her eyes at the grammar lesson. Then, slowly, this Kelly, stretching out the sentence, pausing between each word and rolling her eyes, said, "Going...to...college... makes...me... rich."

I was still confused. "You, personally? Only you? It sounds like somebody pays you," I offered, smiling along in the direction of my gentle joke. "To be here, I mean?"

"No, but my parents gave me a car," she said, smiling. "A Mini. And we have our own place, me and Kellyrae, cuz they pay the rent, and they pay for my cell and I get an allowance, too. So, yeah, I guess they do. Basically."

"So going to college really does make you, personally, rich," I said, sort of delighted at how things had turned out, irony having been trumped once again by reality. "You, in particular!"

"Yes," she said.

"Well, it's nice work if you can get it," I laughed. And almost everybody in the classroom laughed too, except Kelly Stevens herself. Some students seemed to be laughing with her and some at her, but it all sounded like pretty much the same laughter and it was hard for me to tell.

And now, months later, we are all of us wealthy and prosperous too, except for PFC Drew. Even Juana Deompompa Dewey from Manila, who wasn't abducted, was not taken away in the church van for the half-day field trip with the rogue pastor, what Henry and I call the "mini-Rapture," but whose own lawyer argued was so traumatized that she got a Tier Three settlement payout. She can't disclose the amount but I happen to know that the money bought her and Sergeant Sarge or Sergeant Butch or whatever his real name is a townhouse near the college, and a beach house in Mamburao, right on the sand. Semper Fi!

Charles Drew couldn't read, but you can. You can review my deposition. Anybody can, and the trial transcripts too, and my answers to the nice old judge, all of it part of what is called the public record. But I was there, and I remember. The two questions I asked in the classroom were, exactly, "Do people actually believe in angels?" and "Well, then, what causes poverty?" Go look it up yourself, or read the article online. There's a link on my Wikipedia page.

These two questions led to the first visit by the minister and then, pretty much directly to his second visit, the felonious hostage-taking at nobody knew when, exactly, in the morning, on a Friday in the early part of the century anyway.

Part of this confusion was my fault, for not wearing a wristwatch, or so I was made to believe. I had joked about the busted wall clock in the classroom during the first week, after taking roll and distributing the reading list, syllabus and sign-up sheet.

"At least it's right twice a day," I'd said, laughing to myself and looking for assent from the class.

"Right?" I asked, "twice a day?" in another effort to establish a tone which might inform a realistic teacher-student relationship, one of generosity and collaboration in the pursuit of, yes, critical thinking and scholarship but with room enough for some easy cornball humor of the we're-all-in-this-together variety. Then I pointed at that giant faded world map, with its embarrassingly prominent, to me at least, "Union of Socialist Soviet Republics" instead of "Russia" and "Georgia," and the Canadian "Northwest Territories" instead of "Nunavut," and I said, "At least this still works," smiling.

None of the students laughed here either, except Henry, quietly, to himself. I was probably already in love with Henry then, who appeared on my class roster as "Oh, Henry," like the candy bar or the name of the convicted Texas embezzler and famous short story writer of minor classics including "The Gift of the Magi," that treacly ironic tale of misplaced personal sacrifice and poor communication, not unlike this one.

My jokes were old and jolly, weren't they, democratic, I might have thought to myself, in their reach for empathy? But, no, the students didn't get them, didn't even seem to recognize them as jokes.

But I wonder why they didn't know enough to at least laugh anyway. Why didn't they know to pretend, to play along with the recitation by their teacher of dumb jokes that you could deduce if you tried just a little — even if you didn't understand them — were, respectively, a reliable and jolly old chestnut and a bit of easy existential humor. If only you thought for a minute about what the teacher was offering, and why.

And what about my gestures and facial expressions, huh, and the tone of my voice, which the students did not seem to understand or recognize either? Maybe this was what "Canadian" meant to them, to their parents and teachers, I thought later, to the citizens of this brave new county. Maybe. But still I wondered: if you saw the shapes made by someone's hands in the air and that expression on somebody's face wouldn't you divine that it meant somebody was asking you to try on some empathy? Wouldn't you laugh or nod or something, pretend, anything, please, well, wouldn't you? And in doing so wouldn't you then understand that if you just did that, performed this act, an act of faith maybe, you might just get it somehow, or perhaps know what it felt like to get it even if, in fact, you didn't quite, not yet?

But I wonder now if anyone could have known what they made of me on that very first day, or later that week, when we read the First Lincoln Inaugural together and talked about it before they wrote a first draft of their summary, quotation, citation and analysis paragraphs and, no, Charles Drew did not.

Certainly not me, not until the trial when, along with details from the police report, victim and witness testimony and depositions, the prosecution revealed to the judge and jury the existence of the surveillance file (in reality, a loose-leaf Pea-chee folder — "evidence"!) which it turned out the three Kellies had begun assembling on me from the very beginning, and then delivered to the pastor at the mega-church.

*   *   *

I occasionally have lunch with Juana Deompompo Dewey, the young Filipina mail-order bride married to her seventy-year old retired U.S. Marine sergeant named either "Sarge" or "Butch," or "Bulldog," depending. He introduced himself, variously, using all of them, as if he were an entire regiment and not a single old limping ex-troop with a gut and suspenders and a blue disabled parking pass hung on his rearview. He suffered from too many easy identities, had been a Sergeant, wore a butch haircut and looked like a bulldog. Now he was retired. These were his life's variables, and he used them. He had duty. He had a pension. He had a lot of free time. He had a wife, and a slave too. Neat-o. I believe now that he thought she might run away. So he chaperoned Juana to the classroom, then hobbled back to wait for her in his Town Car out in the parking lot — the part left for parking and not for temporary classrooms — for fifty minutes, drinking coffee from Dunkin' Donuts and listening to Rush Limbaugh, loud, with the windows down, until class was done and he could drive her home to make him a real breakfast.

She wore jumpsuits to class, smaller, tighter versions of the gray old-guy ones also worn by Mr. Dewey. Together the two of them looked like mechanics or inmates or some kind of very small toxic clean-up squad in HAZMAT uniforms. Juana was lovely, with dark black hair the color of a cormorant's feathers, purple in places in the light. She seemed to speak for the class when she responded to nearly all of my questions, slightly hurt, that she "did not like to argue."

The rest of the students chimed in with their assent except for, on that Monday of week three, my own wonderful, handsome, smart if still scarily shy Henry Oh, who explained, helpfully, that argument meant debate and using evidence to persuade. About him I wondered, first, if he was gay or, if not, if he had a girlfriend and, second, why he was in this pretty much remedial writing class at all except that — as I liked to remind myself and my students — all education was in its way remedial education, at least to a point, wasn't it, so that they should not let that get them down?

Here Charles Drew, my Army Reservist dressed in full camouflage and boots, white t-shirt underneath, raised his hand and shouted at me, and plenty loud, "Ma'am! What does 'remedial' mean again, ma'am?" in that rifle-shot staccato command-and-obey lingo beloved of our proud armed forces. This threw me, the way he kept doing this respectful if frightening military barking at me in the classroom, oblivious, it seemed, of where he was, and especially startling since the rest of the students either whined or mumbled, forcing me to ask them to repeat themselves, when — if — they spoke at all.

"Remedial?" I asked the class. "Definition? Anyone?"

I once again pretended to survey the room, all the while using my keen peripheral vision to gaze upon my lovely young Henry Chung-Ho Oh, sturdy shoulders, six-foot five, a Korean god-boy-man wearing his big black plastic-rimmed Superman eyeglasses and giant retro-style "Joe College" sweatshirt, his strong body crammed into a tiny desk. He stared at the top of it and spoke to it, not to me. He didn't gaze back, wouldn't or couldn't, it turned out. Not yet.

Henry adored me even then, and has since admitted it, but did not speak directly to the teacher when reliably answering questions or elaborating to the class, which I suspected he could have taught except for his Big Problem, which I soon discovered was a variety of pathological shyness we have since overcome together through a regimen of, yes, political re-education and sexual therapy, all thanks, it turns out, to crazy Pastor Bob, defendant, defrocked minister, and star of a popular video clip on You Tube where, ignoring the famous British atheist-scientist interviewing him, he leans instead into the camera with his big, faggy head and says, grinning, "I think I know what you did last night," a line from a teen-scream flick, and pretends to misunderstand the implied comparison of his followers, saying he doesn't know anything about the Nuremberg rallies. Go look it up yourself sometime.

I watched Henry Oh closely, aiming my super-duper lover's gaze at him, flooding him with my eros-aura-vision, enveloping him in a warm sexual force-field until I thought I risked levitating him or wetting my panties. I made sure that the other students didn't see me. I joked around with him. Once I grinned and called him "Hank."

Class was like that. I'd ask a question. Nobody would answer. I'd stand there, silent. Nothing.

"How about you, Mr. Oh?" I would finally ask. And, reluctantly, Henry would turn around, push the specs up the bridge of his nose like Clark Kent from Seoul, and address the class in a near-whisper from his usual place in the front of the room.

PFC Drew left the room, to go to the toilet once again. The three Kellies took their careful notes. It was the opposite of the Nuremberg rallies I guess, or at least quieter, and smaller.

*   *   *

After three weeks it was fun, if too easy, the inside joke-within-a-joke which I seemed to be sharing with everybody whether they knew it or not, or maybe only playing on myself. I told the judge that I knew better but, still, to accommodate the surprising pleasure of it, to dress up my ruse in an appropriate costume, I found myself book-marking the Environment Canada Weather Office page on my computer at home, and listening to the CBC's *As it Happens* weeknights at ten on the local public radio station. I cut out photographs of Lake Victoria and the Sunshine Coast and stuck them on my fridge, carried around a *Maclean's* like I was actually reading it (I wasn't; it's terrible, if you want to know, *Newsweek* with a head cold) and even bought a red maple leaf sticker flag for my clunker of an old Honda, the way I'd seen Americans in Europe, not to mention Canadians, display flag patches sewn onto their rucksacks. This was hollow and silly behavior, and I knew it, which is maybe exactly why I did it.

If anybody had challenged me, a real Canadian say, I would have either laughed it off and stopped immediately or collapsed into grief, self-loathing and despair at my foolishness and poor judgment, including moving here in the first place, but of course nobody did ask, not about anything. In fact, the more people I met in my new home the more quickly, more easily, I began introducing myself as Canadian and saying "Don't blame me!" and still no one laughed or even asked me what I didn't want to be blamed for, or challenged me on my nationality. I mean, you could just look at me and see I'd never even been to Canada. It became a sociological experiment for me, but with no hypothesis, no control group, no cause and effect or conclusion, no single-blind. Or so I told the judge, who always seemed more interested than he should have, maybe because he liked talking to a smart, pretty young woman or because he was concerned that my assumed citizenship gambit really could somehow compromise the otherwise open-and-shut criminal case against Pastor Robert the Homo.

That's briefly what the defense hoped for, helpfully sharing with the newspapers and the all-news radio and the local TV news that Maggie Holloway, age 31 of Tustin, part-time English instructor, had routinely represented herself as a foreign national when she was not in fact from Canada at all, not one bit, which made this a lie and not a fib and her a liar, ladies and gentleman, he argued, and perhaps even a, yes, national security threat. Portland, Oregon, where I was born, was certainly much closer to Canada than Orange County, California or so the smarmy defense attorney pointed out, but still, it wasn't Canada, was it Mizz Holloway?

"No," I'd had to admit on the stand, "Orange County is not Canada," which, like my earlier answer about teachers, also got quite a big laugh in the courtroom and made the bailiff smile, and forced the defense attorney to reconsider the direction of his cross-examination, which is maybe why he never brought up the part about me sleeping with my student, Henry, assuming that he knew.

Henry himself, a witness and also a plaintiff, testified in his new full deep voice that it seemed to him as if the soon to be ex-leader of the mega-church, the mega-meth-eating, male prostitute-visiting (as in "he 'visited' a prostitute" like you "visit" your old auntie in the nursing home) evangelical preacher had been doing pretty much spontaneous outreach along with the pre-planned, well-organized, highly choreographed (and "totally gay," as the kids say) kidnapping that morning, trying to take everybody in the room with him, not just his flock as planned, as long as he was at it.

So that Pastor Bob's lawyer, distracted, and seeing an opportunity on another front, actually changed his tack about my own low-grade lying and argued, without shame or irony, that Henry's testimony "now proved beyond a doubt, members of the jury, that at least some of the charges could not, should not be considered, in fact, premeditated."

Weird details like that one seemed important during the trial at first, then not. This was the nature of the "search for justice," explained the judge, which turned out to be a fairly quantifiable thing, he said. The exact time of my question about the cause of poverty mattered, for instance, but not the question itself, he explained. Confirming when I had asked it of the class corroborated the time of the nutty minister's subsequent abduction after all (meditated upon beforehand or not), which nobody contested anyway. And what he actually said did not particularly matter either, unless this offense were going to be tried as a hate crime which, it seemed, it was not, and which mattered to me, plenty.

"But it was," I argued to the judge, "a religious hate crime. A crime committed by a religious person who was full of hatred, against those of other religions, or of no religion."

"Objection!" hollered the defense attorney.

"Overruled," said the friendly judge. Damn, he really liked me. He seemed to bend over his big polished desk, glancing again at my breasts and, from the way he crooked his neck, perhaps smelling the air for my perfume.

"The witness is biased," responded the defense attorney. I was starting to like him too, despite it all, and to understand that futility was his job. We had the same job. We were both good at it, but neither of us were not going to get any awards.

"And," he added, "she is unreliable." But the judge only smiled and again said "Overruled" and waved him away and called me "Miss Holloway." Sometimes he said it like I was his equal, his peer, both of us sitting there in the hall of justice, and sometimes he said it like he was my elementary school principal speaking over the P.A. and I had to go to the office, and sometimes like I was the *Playboy* Playmate of the Month.

Judge Penhall instructed me to go over once again the discussion I'd led about "belief," which he put in air quotations, which now everybody it seemed to me was doing during the trial, all the time, as if taking my Henry's lead. This seemed right to me. It seemed natural and appropriate that so many Americans had taken to raising their elbows and wrists and holding up two pairs of fingers, crooked, like bunny ears, near their own ears. Have you ever watched somebody do that, the way they are suddenly revealed as innocent and honest, and the way that time hesitates for a moment in front of them as they lift up all of the power of English-language punctuation to protect us all, you and me, as if against the take-off of bomb-dropping planes and the men who sell them? Or how you see them like the airport runway operator instructing the taxiing of a 707, with his headphones on? The mid-airness of human communication is revealed there, fleeting and ephemeral and suddenly the quoter is as close to honest as they can be, even if they are actually lying, maybe especially if they are lying. There is as far as I know no hand sign for any other punctuation, not comma or period or exclamation point or colon. Why is that? And shouldn't there be?

Judge P. was especially interested in the discussion where I'd asked students if religious people weren't also atheists because, intellectually, they could easily enough not believe in God, like non-believers do. They'd all disagreed, of course, I told the court, my faithful students saying that they did believe in God. I asked them whose god, and they admitted theirs, and only theirs. I realized that there was nobody else who was ever going to let me tell this story, not ever, not the way I wanted to, and not in front of a couple of hundred people, with reporters and some students and even a few colleagues. I went for it.

"So," I'd said to the class and the judge and the courtroom, "you can and do quite easily not believe in other people's gods, right?" And they agreed. My students, I mean. "I mean," I'd gone on, "you are by definition an atheist, a nonbeliever, about a Muslim god and a Jewish god and a Zoroastrian god — basically any and all gods other than your own — so that, intellectually, you are practically an atheist about a whole lot of God. In fact, most of the time, in most ways, you are mostly atheist. As regards all the possible beliefs in all the gods out there in godland, you don't believe in most of them, nearly all of them, right?"

And the judge certainly seemed pleased. He smiled and thanked me, and for a moment I thought maybe he'd add more charges for our side, but instead he asked me to remind him, please, what day exactly I'd asked that question. He liked my speeches, my monologues. I got the feeling he wanted to be a student in my class himself, or at least the principal. And so I consulted my roll book and lesson plan, and I told him "Monday," which date later in the trial the three blonde Kellies' journal corroborated, which seemed to make me both honest and guilty, which I was so getting used to.

*   *   *

"Why did you call me 'Instructor'?" I asked Henry this morning in bed. "Why not 'Instructor Holloway' or 'Instructor Maggie' or 'Maggie,' like I always asked everybody?"

He only laughed through his huffing and puffing. It was early Sunday, and Henry was going at me from behind, his body damp from his post-run shower, the sheets getting stuck around us both as he twisted to get just the right angle and grip on his big round wifey. Henry had brought me my cup of organic Fair Trade Jamaican Blue Mountain dark roast with steamed milk and a maple oat scone from Whole Foods and both of the newspapers, too, but soon enough I had him out of the bath towel and back in bed with me instead of sitting out in the living room reviewing the LSAT and doing yet another self-test.

People are suspicious of wish fulfillment stories, of which you may have by now divined this is one, and "majorly," as the kids and everybody used to say once, incessantly, and not so long ago, maybe five years, at least as long as the war, before they started saying something else.

It is my position that they need to get over it, start wishing, and be ready, sisters and brothers, for fulfillment, "Ya think?"

And, yes, "Instructor" was at least better than being called "Ma'am," which was what my perpetually AWOL-in-the-men's room Reservist called me, and not facetiously, when he asked dumb questions (people, there are some, lots of them) or requested my permission to go the "latrine," even after I took him aside after class and reminded him that he didn't need to ask, and that we civilians called it a restroom, please, and could he please come right back this time?

Me, I would have been alright with facetious, in fact completely fine with it, with my still reasonably sexy if a bit soft grown-up woman body, magenta streaks in my hair, multiple piercings, vintage jewelry, thrift store skirts, "Ramones" t-shirts and leather jacket with the "He lied. They died." button so that, no, I was not at all uncomfortable with facetious or even sarcastic, welcomed them both, would have been grateful for more. More facetious, please. More sarcastic. I see now it's possible they made me what I am today: plump, rich, happy, pissed-off, aware of my enemies, despised by my enemies, and in love with Henry Oh, father of our unborn child.

And it is true that on Monday of week four I brought in photocopies of the article in the *Times* which reported on a poll of Americans of whom 78% said, when asked (somebody had asked, who knew why?), that they "believed in the literal existence of angels." Henry had made me so proud by turning to the class and, yes, raising his long arms and big hands way, way up over his head and using his helpful air quotation marks around the "said" and the "believed" and the "existence," broke down the problematic poll and its meaningfully meaningless results; also the premise, the language, the "social construction of reality," even speculating on the science of a poll based on a loaded question and a telephone sample survey of a thousand Americans, selected randomly, and, for the first time that quarter he turned back around and looked at me when he was done, right in the eyes, and I think now that he was maybe checking me out too, finally.

I picked up on Henry's helpful exegesis and reminded the class of the text of the famous Lincoln speech.

"So, did President Abraham Lincoln," I asked the class, "mean real angels when he said 'the better angels of our nature' in his inaugural?" It was an easy question. I was not being too hard, was I?

Nobody responded.

"And what," I continued, marching on, "would the world look like if people, not to mention presidents, really did 'believe' — whatever that means — in actual angels, in dead people reborn, phantoms, ghosts, fairies, specters living among us?"

Sure, it was a loaded question. But still no response. I avoided staring my love-stare directly at Henry, however eager I was to stare at him, at his black hair and his dark eyes, and instead took a deep breath. Perhaps I did not even notice Private Charles Drew, or maybe he had gone to the latrine again. It's the kind of thing you think about when you are called on to recollect, and discover that you cannot find something, someone. I soon gave up on the interrogatives, out of some kind of generosity or impatience, it is hard to say. It probably didn't matter. I decided to just give them the answer, as it were, if still decorated in the rhetorical bows and ribbons of the Socratic Method, critical thinking and then some.

"Wasn't Lincoln speaking about angels metaphorically?" I asked. "Isn't this figurative language? Or did President Abraham Lincoln believe in real angels? And what are angels? And yes, what does 'believe' mean, anyway?" There were italics in every one of my sentences, which I spoke like we had a bad phone connection.

Finally Ari Cohen from Israel raised his hand.

"The world would be like…" he paused as if searching for it from his seat, struggling to answer my earlier question as if the question were a literal one. I had rushed, apparently, though I doubted he would find it, not through his bangs.

"It would be like in that movie when the little boy sees dead people but the man, you know, what's his name…?"

"Bruce Willis!" said Juana.

"Yeah," said Ari. "Bruce Willis doesn't understand that

if the boy sees dead people then he must be one, right?"

At this, the class stirred, if only slightly. I was thrilled. I smiled, nodded. It's possible I looked like a bobble-head doll in the back of a car.

"Am I right?" asked Ari, standing up, as if he knew.

"You are so right," I said, and Ari beamed. A few students, at last sensing some kind of victory, looked his way and clapped, except, I see now, for the Christians. It seemed to me that Ari was offering for the first time, even if accidentally, a critique of his sort-of adopted country, of the war, of Bush, of Guantanamo and Abu Ghraib, of a nation of dead people seeing other dead people and not knowing it, not recognizing themselves, all of which I guess I offered in response.

I asked Ari to come up to the whiteboard and write his thesis.

"We'll all help him," I said. "It will be great! Won't it?" I offered him my bouquet of dry erase markers — black, green, red or blue — and he picked one and stood there ready to start writing, or at least just to stand there.

And maybe, it occurred to me, Ari was somehow wise to my own Canadian deception, hip to my second helping of irony, osmosistically, by accident or through dumb luck. And maybe we had blasted through it together and were having a genuine moment. I listened to the echo of the students clapping and I wondered for the first time after weeks of pretending to be somebody's cartoon Canadian if, now, at last, I'd been recognized by at least one person as a fake and a fraud, and I felt at that moment of maybe being caught, of being guilty, as successful a teacher, citizen, person as I'd felt since I arrived.

I smiled and nodded, my mind racing. I stepped backwards rhetorically, way back, one giant step, trying for the anthropological angle to distract them, and myself.

"Class," I said. "Ari is onto something big here." I went on. "Humans have historically practiced ancestor worship, so we locate meaning and value in the idea of angels, in representations of those people who came before us...dead people, right?"

I had plenty more to say, about civic responsibility and language and the Civil War and Iraq. But here I was interrupted by Juana, urgently raising her hand, on her face an expression, yet again, of dismay. Hopefulness bowed to confusion. This would not be good, but it was important, I knew, to let it happen. One step forward, two steps back, but we were at least walking.

"Bruce Willis is dead?" she asked.

*   *   *

And it was a few minutes after the beginning of the next class, on Wednesday of that week, I told the judge, that the closeted homosexual drug-snorting call-boy-hiring evangelical minister appeared in my classroom for the first time — trespassed, technically, since all non-students are required to check in at the Administration Office, not to mention get the instructor's permission — and asked those students who were members of his congregation to stand in a prayer circle and just ask the Lord to just redeem everybody and just praise Him and just give ourselves, me included, to Him while I walked, slowly, across the room over to the phone thinking I might try to get Campus Security on the line.

He'd first peered in from the deck outside my trailer through the small foot-square glass window in the classroom door, an oversized Alice in Wonderland looking down into a little room, an unfriendly giant peeking into the tiny diorama of a classroom or a small-world museum full of desks, a big hungry cartoon cat looking into a cartoon mouse hole. His face, vaguely familiar to me, seemed confusingly circumscribed, rearranged behind the thin wire of the window's safety glass. Behind the symmetrical arrangement of those lines it reminded me of a learn-to-draw grid, his nose in part of one square and eyes, ears nose similarly plotted, one of those magazine ads or instruction books which fooled you into believing it was easy to reproduce the bunny or the sailor.

He disappeared just long enough to step back and open the door. As he entered the classroom, I assumed this vaguely familiar-seeming man was a school administrator or a dean I had not yet met, though one who resembled, oddly, the famous mega-church minister just then the focus of allegations, reported in the papers and on television, by a male hooker named Jimmy. It was as if Pastor Bob might have had a brother or cousin about the same age who'd taken a different path, one of public education administrator at a small community college, except that he was gay.

This look-alike somebody or other had a wicked, prissy little smile and sideburns, an extremely butch if precise and too-perfect haircut, so gelled and ironic that I remember thinking that he was somebody Trey, my best friend in Portland, would like. To hate, I mean. This guy was, as Gay Trey would say, as homosexual as the day was long, and anybody could see that, especially a card-carrying, condom-carrying fag hag like me, but he was clearly hiding it, or trying to, and failing.

And, yes, I still carried that actual card in my little wallet, a gift from the one and only Mister Trey Anthony Jones (1971-2006), who I had known since high school, who had changed his name to Troy for a while and then back again to Trey, who had been doing fine on AZT and vitamin therapy and diet and living in Southwest Portland and working with what was left of Act Up. He was the only person with whom I'd really still been talking back home but then he was not, because we buried him, me and his mother and my former friends.

"The undersigned," read my card, "is, officially, a Fag Hag entitled to all the rights and privileges pertaining to..." and so on, campily, with the photo of the two of us, me and my now-dead friend taken in a photo booth at a Fred Myers taped on the back, mugging for the camera.

This other fellow wore brown slacks and a too-tight white dress shirt like some kind of homo-Mormon-Xerox machine repairman. He immediately took a seat next to Ali, clumsily fitting himself into the old-school style school desk, sliding in sideways and sitting at the same time, tucking his knees underneath.

I smiled at him, but he did not smile back at me. I might have been smiling about Trey, who would have said something wicked and perfect, in that way that you do sometimes without realizing the real target of your smileage.

Then tall Kellyrae Basketball motioned at him from across the room, with a close-to-her-chest twinkle-wave, and a shy smile. He acknowledged her with a slight nod. And then Kellie Volleyball. And then Kelly Song Leader with the British sports car and the full-time job as a student of betterment, who stood up and walked across the room and gave him a hug and then sat down next to him, even as I was talking, which should have clued me that something was up, that he was not a dean or an administrator.

*   *   *

My question about angels and belief was not such an ambitious one, or so I'd thought at the time, not in the U.S. of A. in the year 2007. Maybe I thought it was hardly a question at all. I thought wrong, again. Henry and I went over events of that day together on our first date, after I had been relieved of teaching duties and Pastor Bob was out on bail, in between the cuddling and the monkeying around and then the moist consummation on the fold-out sofa in my old studio apartment in Tustin.

Honestly, I couldn't shut Henry up after that, fine after so much quiet. One thing I've learned: Ordinary language accommodates a lot for a long time, and then it does not, and finding the moment when it doesn't is where life is either renewed (as then, for me and Henry and, more so, with the expectation of Little Baby Oh) or you realize that you really do have to shut up and move away to Canada, which is a real place, a sovereign nation with socialized medicine and not just a metaphor for whatever it means to a lot of silly, fatalistic Americans. I thought I knew that once, but I didn't, not really, did I? Let's say I didn't realize until it was brought to my attention that morning, witnessing the instant prayer circle he arranged in my classroom, the evangelical minister suddenly standing with half of my students surrounding him, while the other half, the Orthodox Christian, the Jew, the Zoroastrian, the Lutheran, the Roman Catholics and Henry Oh looked to me for some explanation for what was happening while Charles Drew was, as usual, in the latrine or had disappeared someplace, by now a place nearly of imagination, well beyond my ability to account for him or his circumstances, or my own or yours.

"Spirit intervention!" the strange man had announced, standing up and taking Kellie Song Leader's hand. And then he and Kellierae and the other two Kellies arranged themselves in a circle in the middle of the classroom, heads bowed, hands joined, while Ali Mohammad, Ari Cohen, Garrett Thomas, Calvin Cooley, Christian Sommers, Tori Nguyen, Tiffany Wong, Viktor Mjolsness and Juana and Henry and I watched. Until I finally said something.

"Excuse me?" I asked.

And, because I was so startled and confused and still (back then) a polite, reasonable, stupid person, I also asked, "Can I help you?" which was exactly dumb and wrong for so many reasons, and which embarrassed me at the time but struck me with some satisfaction later when I recounted that part to the nice judge and the jury, as being particularly polite, particularly calm and so, typically Canadian, as imagined by all those potential ex-pats I'd left behind.

No, I said on cross-examination by the defense attorney, I did not really mean that I wanted to help him, not at all. I had no help to offer, even had I wanted to. I was not offering it and he would not, of course, have desired my variety of help anyway, I said. I was offering clarity about the situation, trying to establish that something was wrong, that we were all in distress.

Pastor Bob ignored me and led the group in prayer. "Join us," he said. As if. Kelly Song Leader sort of flipped her head and smiled and said, "Yeah, join us."

Seeing their chance to at last get close to the pretty girls, in fact hold their hands, Garrett the Libertarian, Christian the Christian and Cowboy Calvin got up and joined the circle.

I reached for the campus emergency telephone on the wall, a phone I'd never used, with a tag that read "Call Extension 8 for Campus Security," which was only next door. I was not sure the phone even worked.

The phone rang and rang and rang. I could have left the classroom and run over to the Campus Police trailer, but it would have meant walking through that prayer circle, not to mention jumping ship on my other students, a couple of whom had gotten out of their desks and stood against the other wall.

The two Security guys employed by the school were more often than not out patrolling the campus in their souped-up Cushman cart with the siren on top, dressed in short pants and wearing sunglasses and matching doughboy hats.

After a while the phone switched over to a recording.

Then Captain Randy picked up his cell phone, interrupting the voice of Gwen the dispatcher.

"Help," I said. "Where are you?"

"I am in the field," he said. "Who is this?" I thought he meant that he was patrolling. But he really was out in the field, the big vacant lot next to the orange grove, which the Board of Trustees leased to a pumpkin patch in the fall and a Christmas tree guy in December.

The prayer group began singing, and loud. They had lovely voices. I had to shout at Randy.

"He just walked right into the classroom," I said. "He's maybe five-eleven, 160 pounds. Short hair. Slight build. I really don't know who the hell he is."

I couldn't hear over the singing, louder and louder, about the Lamb of God and the Blood of the Lord. By now they were swaying together, and I noticed Calvin had each of his arms wrapped around a Kelly, his hands moving toward their butts. Lucky dude, *dude!*

That half of the class which hadn't joined the bespoke revival meeting only watched. A couple of them yelled something at me, hard to hear over the racket. Finally I heard Tiffany Wong.

"Pastor Bob," she said. "It's Pastor Bob. Just tell them it's Pastor Bob."

I started to tell Captain Randy, but he interrupted.

"You mean our Pastor Bob, from Calvary?"

At the trial I explained how Pastor Bob quickly concluded the prayer and singing circle and left the room, and how the three

Kellies and the three smitten converts returned to their seats and sat still while I waited for Security to arrive to escort him the hell away, too late for that of course, because he was by then long gone.

*   *   *

Two days later, I looked at big, tall, gorgeous Henry for help once again. His eyes dropped quickly, as usual. He seemed to divine something in his desk's shiny imitation blonde wood-grain surface, perhaps his own reflection, perhaps some vision, I speculated, maybe even a pleasing future with me on top of him?

Beyond shyness or reluctance, his affinity for wood grain or fear, whatever it was, Henry the Beautiful Giant Korean's writing and class participation were excellent, and he was one of those students about whom I suspected a personal history of some complexity. And I did not doubt that Henry, whom I had now taken to thinking of as the Man of Steel (Christopher Reeve version) would find something whichever way he looked in life, wherever he looked, whatever he looked through perhaps with x-ray vision, and perhaps share it with me.

Meanwhile I wondered if the clueless Juana could sense my heartbreak at having to smile gently and, once again, decline to accept her predictably wrong answer and politely thank her for her effort, acknowledge her trying, speaking to her encouragingly after class and trying again.

"Finally, only one thing causes poverty," I said again. "What?"

Juana raised her hand. "No money," she said.

"Well," I began, trying to find a way to explain the illogic of defining something by providing an example of it. "No," I said, "not exactly. I mean the way only one thing causes divorce." When nobody said anything I said, "Marriage. Like that. So what causes poverty? What creates conditions which almost require it?"

Ali had an answer.

"No job," he said, playing with his beads.

Ari hollered another. "No money."

Some of the class turned to look at him, then at me, including Juana.

"Well, yes, lack of money, maybe due to unemployment or low wages," I said. "But those aren't really causes of poverty. Those are manifestations. Poverty means more than an immediate lack, right?"

I nodded along with myself, which I did a lot of in front of this class, hoping for another applause moment, agreeing with myself as if to show what was possible here, as if having the conversation, the discussion with someone like me, someone who was in fact exactly, actually, me, could prove that such a conversation was indeed possible. It was a conversation between two reasonable people though, of course, the complication was that it was still only me up there, going on as if none of Wednesday's class had ever happened.

I pointed at Tori Nguyen, still nodding to myself.

"Poor living conditions," she said. "Okay," I said, "closer."

But I reminded the class that since poor living conditions were indicators of poverty, she was still falling into circular reasoning, saying the poverty was, basically, caused by being poor.

"Class," I said, "it's not that hard."

But it was hard, wasn't it? To be fair. And I was perhaps asking for too much, especially at this moment, in this place, in this country, trying too hard, and failing.

"Dirty water?" asked somebody else.

"Folks, it's easier than all this," I said. "You're making it harder than it needs to be. If there are ten marbles and I own nine of them and Kelly owns one, then who's rich and who is poor?"

Juana raided her hand. "You are rich, Miss Maggie."

"Yes, now you've got it. But why?"

I felt almost sure that they understood the direction of this little game of arithmetic, the arc of inquiry and that if, in this movement toward reaching a threshold it would be so fine if it were Juana herself who stepped over it, triumphant. I felt confident about trying again, slowly, carefully, from the beginning.

"So, then, Juana," I asked, looking at her, "what can we say actually causes poverty?

Here Viktor from Tbilisi yelled out. At the top of his lungs he screamed, "Communism!"

I started over. I looked at Juana, then moved toward her. I opened my palm. I pointed to it, as if it were full of aggies. I pulled something out of it, between my thumb and forefinger. I held it in the air.

"Juana has one marble, and we agree that she is in something we will call poverty." I put it on her desk.

"I have nine marbles, and I am not in poverty," I said, hopefully.

I closed my palm and held my hand close to my chest.

"Let's agree on that, right?"

They seemed to be following me.

"So, let's think, class," I said. "What causes her to be poor? What is the one clear and obvious and completely objective thing which we can see, based on this evidence, which creates, causes, demands that she be in what we'll call poverty? There is only one answer."

Garrett raised his hand. "Why are we talking about this in a writing class?" he demanded.

"Because writing requires critical thinking," I said. "Logic."

"But this is math," he said. Some of them laughed. I ignored them.

And still nothing from Juana. Three Kellies scribbling. Ari staring up over his chin.

"Henry?" I asked once again, desperate now, and yet confident, eager, aroused.

The entire class turned to him, Tiffany and Ali and Ari and the three Kellies, Viktor and Tori and the rest. I'd come to depend too much on him, I knew, to rely on the shy man-boy who had always played along, but always came through, and I knew that it was wrong to demand this from him. But still.

I waited. At last, Henry turned around. He spoke to the class.

"Wealth," he said, quietly. "She wants you to say... wealth."

Then he stood up, nearly taking the desk with him. He

was even taller than I'd realized. His voice grew louder, but calmer too.

"She means that wealth causes poverty," he began. "If some people have wealth, it is because others don't. Wealth is finite, so that we measure it in relation to something, or else we don't. Measuring it is science, analysis." He paused. The room was quiet.

"Pretending it's infinite is the triumph of this horrible system, of delusion and exploitation and of capitalism and war, of organized religion, patriarchy and fantasies about believing in angels."

He really said that. All of it. And then he sat back down, and stared at his desk, and we all heard the rattling in the supply cabinet.

*   *   *

Pastor Bob had arrived on campus very early Friday morning. He had parked the church's white ten-passenger van with the big cross on the side next to Juana's retired Marine husband's handicapped spot, empty at 5:45 AM. He had sneaked into my classroom and waited. There he'd listened to me from inside the metal storage locker as long as he needed to and then leapt from it like Elijah or a jack-in-the-box wrapped up, yes, in his flag, carrying his Bible and his cross, and rescued at gunpoint (a handgun too, naturally, though unloaded), as he testified, "our children from that heretic and unbeliever."

I guessed at the time, but of course the authorities could

not take my word for it, as it was always a few minutes after two o'clock on the broken clock in the classroom, and I did not wear a watch and hadn't thought to ask students to pull out their cell phones.

That's what I told Captain Randy, campus security chief, who arrived in his own executive golf cart about five minutes after I picked up the classroom phone and dialed Extension 8, which I knew from the time before, with Pastor Bob and the Lost Children already out of the parking lot. And it's what I told the real police officer, dispatched by the city, who arrived in an Irvine P.D. cruiser to find me and the un-kidnapped, Juana and Henry, and those three who'd escaped —- Jesus, Tori, Tiffany —- who'd run away screaming somewhere in between the classroom and the parking, toward the cafeteria.

All were officially elevated to "eyewitnesses," had returned to the crime scene, and were waiting. But the cop got lost trying to find the ICFC — Interim Classroom Facilities Complex — which was what these mobile homes, modular units parked on the edge of the lot interimly for twenty years, had been called for that long.

Henry stood with me, waiting while law enforcement interviewed Juana and the ex-Marine. Juana, who was wrong not occasionally, not most of the time, but each and every time she answered anybody's questions, who would have failed my class despite never missing one, did not know precisely when Pastor Bob had stolen the kids either, but suggested that the cops ask her husband.

"Ask your husband?" the officer had repeated, confused.

And then I explained, and the cop interviewed Sergeant Dewey, USMC, who had observed Pastor Bob escort the kids into the white van at 8:15 AM he said, according to his dash clock.

That important detail was later corroborated by the playing of a tape of *The Rush Limbaugh Show* in court, where, from the stand, Bulldog confirmed the exact time as when one Shawna from El Centro called offering "Dittos" to Rush and complained about the Democrats not backing our boys, all too-familiar talk radio boilerplate and generic-seeming in its theme except that the witness had recalled Shawna's name and her re-mark exactly, and so confirmed the time. And what mattered again, it seemed — not what she actually said or what Rush said about anything and certainly not the war — was that she had been on the radio talking that morning so that the retired Ma-rine could tell the police, who could testify in court.

In its way, this was also the kind of corroboration I had been looking for, just somebody else, military or civilian, old or young, American or Canadian, believer or unbeliever, anybody, to confirm what I had myself seen and heard. I had hoped that we'd all get to listen to the radio show, or hear the transcripts read. I hoped somebody might put Rush or Shawna on the stand, but no.

*   *   *

Sarge, Juana, the department chair, these men and wom-en and young people seemed to me to not ever have been living in the same nation as I did, not the same country or state or county or city or school district as the one which, again, I'd imagined. They didn't embrace what seemed like the assumptions you'd think people might embrace, didn't gather around together like people in the same boat, or people sinking in the same boat might gather, might embrace, or even acknowledge, and say let's be up front and just get on with it, eh?

Yes, I had even begun saying "eh" like a Canadian though some people in this place were so oblivious that they seemed to think I was saying "a" as in the letter of the alphabet, which didn't make sense at all, but what did here, finally? I might have said "b" or "x" and wondered how they would have responded. Ma'am, why are you reciting the alphabet? But no, after all, Disneyland was the most frequently referenced locale here, the easiest and oldest operating metaphor for this place, tired yet un-killable.

Nobody seemed dare acknowledge to anybody else any of the ubiquitous oddness: the small black Styrofoam mousehead silhouette ornaments on the car aerials, the fourteen lane-wide freeway on which traffic never moved, the mega-store near campus called "Christian Discount Books," which meant either that you got a discount if you were a Christian or that the books were on sale, or both. ("Welcome, friend. Would you like the Christian discount?") The tiny, lopsidedly big-boobed women in their giant white four-wheel drive full-sized pickup trucks or Lincoln Navigators with three televisions inside, and, yes, the American flags, decals, bumper stickers, license plate frames everywhere, displayed as if these people needed to remind themselves that they were Americans, and to remind or coerce the rest of us.

This was, I testified in court, also part of what inspired my change of citizenship to kanuck: I was tired, exhausted of being reminded. Pretending to be Canadian — it could have been Swazilandian or Icelandic — had cheered me, and soon after joking around in class I'd told a student in office hours, for which I was not even paid, and during which I ate my homemade lunch to make me feel better about doing work for free. Then somehow I'd told the whole class again, and then colleagues.

That metal supply closet was locked during the school week, used on weekends when the college, a public higher education institution paid for by taxpayers, rented out its trailer to the famous mega-church for youth Bible Study meetings on Sunday nights, presumably for the overflow teen congregation that couldn't fit into its massive complex. Only a few hours before my class met on Mondays there had likely been praying and singing and possibly the gibberish of speaking in tongues and just giving oneself up to the Lord. I'd wondered for weeks about the contents of that locked closet, which stood there, like the Ark of the Covenant.

By now my teaching was, I admit, pretty much all modeling and newspaper articles. I typically launched into digressive extemporaneous asides inspired by the need to explain another vocabulary world — oops, vocabulary word! — or how to read the newspaper, ending up in a discussion of Canada, public radio, irony, angels, the political economy of humor, in addition to whatever I had started out trying to define or answer or explain in the first place, which is to say that my pedagogy was increasingly *ex tempor,* a series of lessons in thinking and writing that were, I told myself, vital remedial education, civic literacy.

Who, if not me, would teach them this stuff? Nobody. So I determined to teach my students everything. "You must know everything!" I would announce. The clock didn't work, I had all the time in the world, and nobody in Administration ever came out to the trailers to check on me, students, instruction or who might be hiding with the angels.

*   *   *

And, lo, this time I was not afraid of Pastor Bob with his fascist props, his Bible and his cross, wrapped in Old Glory. Not at first. "Yes," I continued, as he sprang from the cabinet and motioned at the three Kellies, Garret, Calvin and Christian, "wealth causes poverty."

"Spirit intervention!" he hollered at them, for the second time in a week.

I walked over to the phone on the wall. I picked it up and dialed, and listened as it rang and rang and I kept on talking. "Marriage causes divorce. In the way that life causes death. Like that," I said. I was on a roll. I was staying calm, sort of.

"The point," I said, as I watched Pastor Bob and his students assemble into what I thought would be another prayer circle, "is to isolate the terms of the discussion, to begin with definitions, to establish cause and effect and a place from which to begin."

But then Pastor Bob took out the stupid little gun and aimed it at the rest of the class, at my kids, and now I was truly scared. I had never even seen a real gun. Juana stood next to me.

"Henry Oh?" asked Pastor Bob. "Are you joining us?"

At first Henry only sat there at his desk.

"Henry," said Pastor Bob. "Will you deny the power of the Lord Jesus, Henry Oh? Will you walk with me, away from this evil place?"

He pointed the weapon at Henry like we were at Columbine.

"Yes. And no," said Henry Oh, standing up and seeming to make as if to disarm Pastor Bob.

"Do you not believe in our God?" asked Pastor Bob. "Will you deny Him?"

"I do not believe," Henry answered. "I deny!"

But Pastor Bob did not shoot Henry there in the classroom, not with his unloaded pistol. He didn't shoot anybody. Instead, he moved closer to the door, pointing his flock outside. Juana and Henry and I watched him hustle the kids out onto the deck and into the parking lot, saw three of them break away and run toward the cafeteria, even as he loaded the rest into the van and drove away.

Captain Randy finally picked up.

"It's him again," I said, to the phone. "I mean it's me, Maggie Holloway. He came back, only this time he has a gun."

"Who?" asked Captain Randy.

"Who else?" I asked.

*　　*　　*

I might at that moment have finally understood exactly where I was, with a deep abyss on either side and a clear, narrow path in front of me, seeing clearly and willing at that moment to challenge, destroy, annihilate every privilege, prejudice, assumption, every angel, every other invisible foolishness, every advantage not to mention the sheer arrogance which had allowed the horrible stranger to enter the classroom, my classroom, in the first place, and now to remove from my stewardship, my responsibility, these enrolled human young people, innocent, remedial and defenseless.

Maybe making up the Canada story had been my response to the initial move here, the new job and surroundings, which I could now diagnose (self-diagnosis, and therefore deeply flawed) as some kind of self-defense mechanism. I liked their flag. Surely I had been unhappy. Surely I was grieving and lonely. The pretend national identity fixed that, made me less unhappy, gregarious even. My friends had embraced a variety of self-hating irony, beyond the simple hating of others, and stupid, easy humor. This seemed to require the humiliation of those who couldn't fight back or refused to hate themselves or didn't know better, along with a reluctance or inability to go along with any joke, pun or affect which required group participation, solidarity, a sympathetic worldview, being right or correct or together at least twice a day. Except for parroting some idiot phrase.

No, most of my students did not know where Canada was anyway, or that there even existed a Canadian Broadcasting Corporation, which I'd also mentioned in class. None knew about the nightly public radio station which aired *As It Happens*, not surprising perhaps, because they did not even recognize the local NPR station. As it turned out, they did not know public radio existed at all. None of them had radios, except in the car.

"Paid for with your taxes," I explained to them, sure that, here in the county of libertarianism and fiscal conservatism and organized selfishness they must, at least, have heard of taxes, at least have learned — been taught — to object to them.

The department chair assigned a new instructor to the class, which resumed without me one week later. I surrendered my roll book, lesson plans and the outstanding, ungraded paper set, their revised drafts on the Lincoln. I received an envelope from the district a few months later, delivered registered mail to my home. I'd taught less than half a semester, but inside were student evaluations of me or, rather, photocopies, dated a week after the kidnapping. On one side were Scan-Tron bubble forms and on the backs were comments they'd written. Somebody had compiled them, in no particular order, which I read through and felt pretty shitty about.

Teacher said there were no angels.

She is a nice teacher. She dressed funny. But she is nice.

She is from Canada, which is B.C, which means Before Christ.

She tell too much her own opinion in class. She doesn't like the Fox News.

This class is too much work, with no real pay-off.

I had biology and geology this quarter, and work at Dave and Buster's where I am Asst Mngr, and the teacher should of known that most American students have jobs and other obligations so this class should be way easier.

Pastor Bob is an asshole. Teacher rocks!

There was way too much reading this is a writting class not a reading class.

She thinks she's soooo hot. She's not that hot. She's weird. Freaky. Probably a liberal. Good teacher. She is fair.

I like her hair.

I would defiantly recommend her as a excellent teacher even though she can be kinda hard.

And, though I almost missed it, there was one more, the very final evaluation, on the bottom of the thin pile only by an accident of collection and photocopying and arrangement, a coda to the semester. It was written in funny, girly, curlicue handwriting which I could not identify.

We are not enemies, but friends. We must not be enemies. Though passion may have strained it must not break our bonds of affection. The mystic chords of memory, stretching from every battle-field and patriot grave to every living heart and hearthstone all over this broad land, will yet swell the chorus of the Union, when again touched, as surely they will be, by the better angels of our nature.

*   *   *

Henry told me all about Pastor Bob (always with the first name, these Hawaiian shirt-wearing men of the cloth — rayon, I think) and his mega-church that very first time I took him to bed, after I'd been put on administrative leave which, technically, meant he wasn't my student and I could fuck him silly. Since arriving in this country FOB at age nine my boy Henry had attended weekly the 6:30 AM Korean-language service at the mega-church with its very own off-ramp on the toll road — "Worship Center Drive" — next to the self-storage complex and the Home Depot, with his old parents, in between the even earlier in the morning Spanish-language service and the first English-language one in the main auditorium. A "dynamic" Korean-American preacher stood next to its founder Pastor Bob, and translated.

Henry talked freely about it now. He stood up straighter. He looked people in the eyes when he made love to them, by which I mean me. He shouted when he came. "Fuck," he cried, "Jesus!" And then he laughed, and we both laughed, and he wrapped his arms around me and pressed his chest against my back and we lay down together spooningly in the dampness.

He was over being a victim now, he said. Of kidnapping, he told me, during our first time together, of victimization. That's what the experience had taught him, and which, now, the sex had reinforced. Never again to be a victim.

He was a scholar now, a linguist, he said. And he was always, always talking to me and talking in air quotes, as if making up for lost words, as if needing to be extra clear about the difference between what he'd heard then and what he was saying right now. He walked around naked afterwards, talking and talking with his four fingers in the air around his head, higher and higher, sometimes looking like he was the Easter Bunny. This seemed to have been the problem of his former life, other people's problems really, a failure to distinguish between who was talking, to whom, and who was listening. Apparently the fingers helped.

"'Just', always 'just,'" he told me, the words in quotation. "And everything was always 'dynamic,'" he said. "It was also always 'on fire'," he says. "Or, 'just on fire'." This morning Henry advised me in his anti-sermonette that you can find what you want to hear in any tongue, and he meant it: Korean, Farsi, Latin, the movements of beautiful women in flowing gowns gesticulating for the deaf, and in Christian Rock lyrics too, of course. Why not? Henry Oh became ecumenical, then skeptical, which I say are good first steps to all-out atheism, god bless him. Some people call themselves anti-theists, I told Henry. Me, I like "naturalist," though it sounds a bit like nudism, a camp full of naked people playing badminton at a mountain retreat in a grassy meadow under the sun.

Understand that for most of my Henry's young life all of what he heard of the world was spoken, sung or prayed on Sunday mornings and at weekly Teen Nights, Fellowship Bingo and Saturday morning pancake prayer breakfasts at the megachurch. He practically lived there.

Henry was bilingual back then, he said. Tri-lingual, quadri-lingual. All that language, and still he couldn't bring himself to speak. Nonbelievers thought he might be retarded or gay.

"At home I spoke Korean," he told me this morning after I turned over onto my other side to face him. "At school I spoke standard written academic American English."

He grinned. We both recognized that phrase from class.

I must have said it a hundred and fifty times. Canada, by the way, has two official languages. And recognizes nine regional ones. Is that the good part, about Canada I mean, that they can talk in many tongues about seal-beating and strip-mining and ice hockey.

"I obeyed the Commandments. I respected my father and mother. I kept the Sabbath holy and I bore no false witness. I wore my Jesus Glasses all the time," Henry said. "So I could read and write and just praise His Holy Name, constantly."

I liked his cool old-style specs. Buddy Holly. He put them back on after the lovemaking. I kissed him on the mouth and then on the forehead, and I rearranged my big Crate and Barrel pillows and turned on *Weekend Edition* and waited for the Puzzle Master while I drank my still-warm, still-perfect coffee. And then I sat up and start sorting through the newspapers. Henry sat on the divan and got dressed again, redressed you might say, which we say a lot around here actually.

*   *   *

We live well. We sleep on, eat breakfast on, and make love on the adjustable bed advertised on public radio, which is good for my pregnant lady lower back. On any other, normal Sunday I would have put on my robe and moved to the living room, to the six-foot deep four-thousand dollar sofa we bought at Pottery Barn. We receive three daily papers including the *New York Times* and do just great on the settlement. This is even more fun than it sounds because, apparently, it can last. We plan to travel after the baby, to Canada of course, British Columbia, maybe even live abroad. Meantime, I coach Henry and we work on his application materials and personal statement and I read the drafts of his essay, and I go to Vinyasa yoga, which is gentle yoga, and read one of my dozen or so books on pregnancy and childbirth, mostly, *What to Expect When You are Expecting*.

But this morning was different.

"In church they speak something else altogether," Henry warned me. "You'll see. A different language, but all the same words, over and over again." He stood at the bathroom mirror, gluing on the fake moustache he'd brought home from the year-round costume shop in the strip mall.

"But they always said the same thing every week. Why? Why was it the same thing every week?"

We both knew why, but it helped to be reminded. There was a lot of interrogative around our place. It was always Twenty Questions, if mostly rhetorical.

"Yes or no only," I reminded Henry.

"Is it to reinforce their limited worldview?

"Yes?" I said.

"Right."

"Is it to change the meaning of questions?

"Again, yes," I said.

Then Henry pulled a wig out of an oversized Costume Cabaret bag, a big red curly nightmare of a thing. I put it on and looked like Orphan Annie. I opened my eyes too wide and while Henry was talking, I saw the notice in the paper, lying there open on the bed, and the photograph too, the official portrait, in that now regular column in the *Los Angeles Times*, "Other Military Deaths."

My heart dropped, and I thought for a moment that the weight of it might crush the baby, which I didn't really believe but could not help myself from thinking, the way you do when the total responsibility for another person and for language and your whole sense of yourself means you could, maybe, crush them just from standing too close to them. I stood up, got out of bed, Henry's semen seeping from me, looking for a towel and trying to recall where I might find a pair of scissors.

I listened to Henry ask his questions, normally something I enjoy. I always enjoyed answering "Yes." I put on my slippers. I listened for a "Yes" answer. I reached over and picked up the paper.

"It was rote learning," Henry said. "Rote living."

"Form of a question," I said, "but yes."

"A requirement of any kind of cult or sect?"

"Yes," I mumbled.

"What?"

"Yes!" I said. "Yes!"

And, guess what? You can answer the same questions over and over again, and you will, if you are lucky or observant, find that your answers at least will become more and more precise, especially when they are always the same word. It's just the way that you can fold a crease in newsprint over and over again, maybe six or eight times, until the gentlest pressure will tear that paper perfectly, which is a beautiful thing made out of elaboration and repetition and care, and which looks like a nervous habit or fun if maybe the father of your child is not paying attention and you just keep agreeing, affirming.

And so I quickly folded the clipping into itself until it became a smaller and smaller packet, a sachet, or one of those fortune-telling games some girls made in elementary school, and I hid it in the big wig so as not to distract or disappoint Henry (I told myself) and I showered and got dressed and off we went as planned, the two of us, to the Mega-House of the Lord, with the news hidden up there.

Besides his law school application essay and cover letter, Henry was also writing his big-time scholarly essay, just for me. A love letter he called it, albeit an academic one written in, of course, standard written academic American English, with foot-notes and a colon in the title. An expository love letter, with a thesis and a Works Cited page.

Henry says the paper will explore the meaning of the reductive grammar and syntax of evangelicals, fundamentalists, born-againers, literalists, postmillenial dispensationalists, call them what you want, the Worship Center crowd. He tells me it attempts to analyze the ritualistic and repetitive use of that single and singular word, "just," in their prayers, sermons, songs, conversations. As in "We just praise you, Lord" and "Lord, we just bring all our praises to you" and "Jesus just wants you to just let Him in." and, above all, "Just say your holy name, Lord."

"Attempts to analyze" is typical Henry.

And there was, after all, nothing preventing us from get-ting into the Prius this morning, driving a couple of miles, park-ing in the massive church lot and entering the Worship Center, no stipulation in the settlement against it, no restraining order, for the ten AM "English-language contemporary" service, with an American Sign Language interpreter standing next to the pulpit. This was still America, after all. Sort of.

We were there to do field research, to count from a pew right up in front. Henry wanted to be accurate, just (ha, ha) to be sure that his recollections about the overwhelming reiteration of a singular adjective or whatever part of speech it is (okay, I know, it's an adverb) were accurate.

I wanted to believe him but I was skeptical about how he could explain or argue a whole impulse, behavior, ritual through studying the phenomenon of people repeating a single word, apparently without, he promised, even realizing it. Not a mantra, exactly. More like the opposite of a mantra, meant to distract rather than focus the devotee, like saying "like" or "um" or "you know."

But he was right, my Henry, who looked like a taller, thinner Charlie Chan with his funny droopy moustache and me next to him looking like the famous poor little rich girl, except pregnant as a house, and apparently made so by the famous Chinese movie detective played by a Swede. In fact, Number One Son seemed to be kicking a bit that morning. I rested my hands on my tummy and felt relieved, and left smudges on my white blouse, my fingertips black from newsprint ink.

We found a place on a long pew near an exit (just in case) and, yes, it was the second word the interim pastor spoke and Henry looked over at me and nodded at the note pad in my big lap for me to make a hatch mark like we'd agreed. I did, but lost track after maybe the first fast fifty "justs" with the congregation not even ten minutes into the service. Did these people even listen to themselves? They said "just" more than they said "Amen" or "Jesus," which was of course also part of Henry's thesis, this constant and annoying reductivism, this failure to communicate, this stuttering confession of resignation or whatever it was.

And I was not even counting the lyrics of the songs sung as a congregation, or the hymns or whatever they were called, performed by the choir or by the band, "Gideon's Big Trumpets," a not-bad twelve-person jazz fusion ensemble wearing matching fake tuxedo t-shirts. They choreographed their stage moves like they were James Brown's backup band except that they were all white boys I recognized from Rancho Valley's marching band.

The Worship Center itself looked like a casino, a game show studio or indoor sporting venue, with a big video screen in the center, a sort of mosh pit for dancing and jumping around in front of the stage, and comfortable movie theater chairs in the back with small screens set in the seatback in front, like on Jet Blue.

I looked around for some of the other students from the class, for the Kellies who spied on me. I looked for my former department chair, who basically fired me, and for the Economics teacher who organized the attack ad in the local newspaper. I wanted to ask them all about Pastor Bob, which was mean and wicked and vengeful of me.

I did that kind of thing now, for myself and Henry and for the babe on the way. It's fun, and I've come to feel that it is the right thing to do, especially with the baby hearing everything I say, according to *What to Expect*: voices, music, Republicans.

Lately I walked right up to drivers in parking lots and I asked them politely. I signaled to them and they rolled down their windows, maybe thinking they could somehow aid an obviously pregnant woman in distress who, they flattered themselves into thinking, they might help. I smiled. I looked straight at them.

"I was wondering..." I asked. I smiled again. I reminded myself to ask using that annoying up-lilting interrogative voice so many of my female students used, even when they were not actually asking a question.

"What it is going to take for you to finally remove that 'W' sticker from your bumper?" I asked. They went a little blank, then summoned up the weak, polite smile of somebody who's just helped a sick relative vomit. Or I'd get a sigh, exhausted and "Oh, please. Give me a break."

Sometimes, I got called "bitch."

To be fair — not that I believe in fairness anymore, not since I believe in fulfillment instead — I did occasionally get a guy who nodded and said, "You're right, ma'am," (I love that pregnant lady "ma'am") and said he opposed the war now and promised me he would take off the sticker the minute he got home.

I believed him. Another angry person, betrayed, but now redeemed, though without the nice check for recompense like me. Sometimes maybe just meant justice.

*   *   *

Of course, Henry and I knew all about Pastor Bob. So did the congregants. He rested in seclusion somewhere in Arizona with an electronic monitor on his ankle, completing his de-homosexualization therapy and treatment for substance abuse. He had been officially reprimanded by the church's Council of Ministers, Restorers and Overseers.

Really, that's what it was called. He'd been promised one final year's salary ($150,000 per anum, which is a big joke compared to what Henry and I make!), and been restored to the bosom of his loving and forgiving wife and children, if also exiled from his former congregation because of the "distraction" his continued presence would present. He'd been convicted and sentenced.

Jimmy the male hooker had gone public, I had not been offered further teaching by the district (okay, partly because I was suing them), Henry my former student and I were living together and expecting (what a great fucking word that is, expecting!) all in the space of only months.

I didn't spot anybody I knew. Then the music was over and the sermon was on, broadcast on the big screen, the new guy talking about Pastor Bob.

"An obstacle," said Pastor Bill, the interim minister, "to the anointing of unity. The gates of hell," he promised the congregants this morning, "shall not prevail here, not in this house of godliness," which I watched the signer interpret and which despite Henry's explanation later, in the car, I knew I still would never understand, and did not want to.

It went on for nearly an hour.

Justs? We counted. Two hundred and thirty-eight.

Walking out into the parking lot afterwards I had to admit to Henry that I'd come along to the service mostly just to see the collection plate part, for myself, which was also mean, not that I felt bad about it. I make a point of trying not to feel bad.

"I wanted to see these folks actually take out their checks and their cash," I said, still wearing my fright wig as we got to the car, even as Henry gently tore the ridiculous moustache from above his lip, "and put it in the plate. I wanted to see it with my own eyes. It was bounteous, Brother Oh."

The Prius was hidden between two SUVs. We got in. It has an onboard GPS, with the Thomas Guide programmed in. I like to watch our progress, little green blips, as we follow the route devised by people we've never met, who had our best interests in mind regarding fuel economy and speed.

"Doesn't somebody in the Old Testament hit a rock or something and water comes out?" I asked. "It was like that. We hit us a rock, Honey," I hollered. "Hallelujah!"

My boy Henry knows his scripture. Fifteen years of Bible study, Sunday school, prayer group and Vacation Bible School, too.

"Moses," he reminded me. "That was Moses. Interestingly, he was supposed to speak to the rock, but he hit it instead. Weird. His brother Aaron had a speech impediment. Did you know that?"

He smiled. The Prius purred. We made our way out of the parking lot.

Henry said "interestingly" a lot lately. He quoted Numbers as we turned onto the boulevard: "'He lifted up his hand, and with his rod he smote the rock twice: and the water came out abundantly,'" said Henry, lifting his hands. "'And the congregation drank, and their beasts also.'"

"Whoa, careful with the quotation marks," I said. "Hands on the wheel, pal."

"Don't worry, Mags," he said. "I am not going to smote anybody."

We drove past the entrance to a new development, two giant fake Roman pillars out front of a big lawn. A small Mexican teenager jumped up and down on the sidewalk, holding a large Styrofoam arrow above his head. I waved to him.

"Next time you might try something more New Testament, sweetheart," Henry said. "Try 'Everyone who drinks this water will be thirsty again, but whoever drinks the water I give him will never thirst. Indeed, the water I give him will become in him a spring of water welling up to eternal life.'" The Mexican kid waved back.

"Wicked shit," I said. "Eternal, indeed. No, we won't go thirsty, you and me. Almost eternal anyway, if we've invested wisely."

I loved it when he did the quoting, though, honestly, a little went a long way. Sometimes he did it again, a second time, in Hangungmal. Henry has a lot to work through, and we think the gestalt helps. Besides, everybody should try saying things in more than one language. Or at least try listening. Bush lied. Bush mintio. Bush hatte gelogen. Bush 눕다, 묻혀 있다.

I reached out to him, across the car. "Eternal life, maybe

not quite," I said, thinking of the news secreted in my wig. "But law school for you, a down payment on a house, and a stay-at-home mommy, wife, lover and, when I get around to it, bestselling author of a tell-all memoir."

Indeed, justice had flowed like a river for sure, amen, praise be. Criminal and civil suits, one settlement bigger than the other. And of course, Henry had gotten his own check. We were a two-earner family, except that neither of us ever went to work. I liked to call it a trust fund, if built on other people's trust. Amazing that after the payouts there was a church left at all, but the congregation's faith was strong and it had twenty-five thousand members and this was a wealthy county and they were insured, it turned out, for this kind of thing, at least to a point.

They'd still had to take out a second on the Worship Center but this morning the sanctuary had been full and the wallets and purses brought out. It seemed there was no end to the fleecing of the devoted sheep. What, I often asked myself, causes wealth?

"Turn around," I said. "I think I want that sign. I want that arrow."

*   *   *

Back home, after church, over my second cup of coffee with steamed organic milk, with a soft-boiled egg and heirloom tomatoes and crusty sourdough and prenatal vitamins, having answered all of the radio puzzler's clues correctly again for a second time, and lying comfortably on the monster couch in the living room, I read the rest of the paper with my wig on, or pretended to read while figuring out why PFC Drew had appeared, just when I'd forgotten him. The "Model Home" arrow-shaped sign was hung on the wall, a hundred bucks having easily persuaded the kid to give it to us and, I hope, quit the job. What a story he would have to tell his boss. I thought that I might start buying foam board arrows from all the poor kids I saw dancing and hopping and jumping and twirling on street corners, at least till the baby arrived, passing out money like John D. Rockefeller, except real money not just nickels and dimes.

I heard Henry's voice doing something funny. I looked up from the "Week in Review."

"Peek-a-boo," he said, and I assumed he was rehearsing for the baby, practicing his goo-goo "Who-does-Daddy-love?" baby talk, but I saw that he was staring through the near-perfect square hole I'd left in the newspaper, on that page I'd torn with my fingers, the place where Charles Drew had been, and which I'd been not thinking about, not much, no not much.

From under my Orphan Annie curly-top I pulled out that square of newspaper, and I unfolded it and looked at it again, at the obituary and the photograph and the creases I'd put across his young face. Maybe I still somehow hoped it wasn't him, that somehow being stuck under my wig might have changed things, but of course it was him, right there. Roadside bomb, age 24, Private Charles Mason Hamilton Drew III, with his thin lips and hat too small for his big head.

"Number four thousand, nine hundred and ninety-nine," I read out loud, and handed the obituary to Henry.

"Today?" he asked. "Just now?"

"I couldn't show you before," I said. "I couldn't talk about it."

"He was in Iraq," Henry said. "That's where he was all the time."

"I know," I said. "Even when he wasn't. He was always there."

"I'm sorry," said Henry. "I'm so sorry." And he took me in his arms like a grown man and somebody's father too.

"You're sorry?" I asked. "You didn't do anything. I'm the one who's sorry."

"I'm sorry for you," he said.

And for a little while, right there I mean, perhaps for five minutes, I allowed myself to be held and be sorry and stay quiet and feel nothing at all, not even the baby, mostly because it was all I could think to do. Or not do. I was at a loss. As if Loss were a place and you could be there, or maybe look around and suddenly realize you had been there all along.

*   *   *

Or, maybe, instead, when Henry got out of the car to put the nifty sign in the back I took off my wig and pulled out the clipping and balled up my origami and threw it out the window and watched it drift away in the wind. Charles Drew was dead, and not even a landmark death anyway, if you were counting deaths. And nobody was, except me. His murder would change not a thing, the poor big dumb innocent loser.

And, no, I hadn't done anything to stop it, not me, big loudmouth Maggie. I'd only been Canadian, which, sure, turned out to be fun and profitable and not so wrong, not really. And was more than a lot of Americans bothered to do. But still. This boy, he was gone, gone, gone now forever, maybe because I never did tell anybody, not the Department of Defense or the Army Reserve or his commanding officer that he couldn't read, which might have got him kicked out, maybe, discharged for being illiterate.

Who was I kidding? None of them could read, not really. They must have all known anyway. And, besides, even though I might be a bad liar and a lousy teacher and even seduced my student, I am not, finally, a litterbug.

*　　*　　*

Soon there was a baby shower, without Henry's parents, who did not speak to us because, well, of all of it, which was fine I guess: my being non-Korean, my being Henry's former teacher and ten years older, us being infamous now, him being doomed to a hell of everlasting damnation. Like that.

Still, I was pretty sure they would come around in time, when they heard the actual pitter-patter of little half-breed Oh feet. We were not registered anywhere, because we are so fabulously rich and just buy whatever we want anyway.

Henry called his parents, wrote, emailed. They said they were ashamed, and were moving back to Korea, which nobody believed. What did he tell them?

He said that he was not ashamed, not of anything, and that we were staying here and that he was going to law school and when they changed their minds they were welcome to come visit him, his rich white Canadian-American wife and their grandchild, all without God.

I love that phrase, "All without God."

There is, of course, no God here and there is little evidence of Canada either, at least not that I can see as I drive around buying arrows, or thinking about it. Lesson, students? There is probably no God in Canada either, thank God.

I invited everybody from the composition class that I could find to the baby shower. There is Facebook. You can find people. I called Juana. We are not enemies, but we are not friends either.

There were actual real angels at the expecting party, but they were dressed in black robes, a small group of old ladies from the local retirement home I join in peace vigils out on the big intersection on Friday afternoons with our signs and our anti-war banner. We look like the Supreme Court, except not. My bulging tummy is obscured by the million dead courtesy Bush and his crowd, but I still stand out.

People honk, flash us the peace sign. Men pull over and give us the finger. The old ladies love it when I trundle over to the open car window. Nothing frightens an asshole like that more than a pregnant woman, and off they go.

Juana and Sarge came to the party. Judge Penhall sent a card and a gift of the most beautiful pink outfits.

No balloons, I told everyone, because we want to save

the marine mammals. Sarge laughed. He thinks I mean him, the big fatso. He'd explain to his child bride later, both the ecology and the self-deprecating joke. I played a lot of music on the beat box, mostly early Dylan. I have a homemade mix I like. I love it when Young Bob introduces his version of that old folk song he's redone by saying that he's been all around this country but he never found Fennario. The name of that song, as the name of the baby, is "Pretty Peggy-Oh."

Henry and I plan to stay living here in this sad country, and in this reactionary county, if you call that living, with the Minutemen Militia and the Minutemen Women's Auxiliary (I shit you not) and the Tea Party harassing Mexican day laborers in front of Home Depot, and the corrupt sheriff and the lady dentist who filed a case in the Supreme Court of the United States of America alleging that the new president is not really a U.S. citizen, that he was born in Africa and is a Muslim, and should not be president. It all makes you feel kind of proud, the way it puts this place on the map.

At this baby shower, in the public park around the corner, Henry and some of my new Women in Black and Yoga Mommy friends pulled together three picnic tables and arranged lovely place settings. My mother was visiting from Eugene, with her oxygen tank on wheels and her eyes full of tears at my tremendous good luck. There was a cake baked with organic whole wheat flour and fancy dark chocolate frosting, with fruit inside. The foothills were golden and the air was warm. I just love this place.

I pretended that my dead father was there, too, as were

Gay Trey and Private Charles Drew.

I've been around this whole country, and now, it seems, I live here permanently, own a home, pay taxes, sort my recycling, surveil the church of my choice, stand on street corners with old ladies. Yet I've never actually found the place anybody imagined, not here, not anywhere. It's possible I made it all up, imagined it myself, created it.

Pretty soon Henry will be practicing public interest law and I will be a PTA mom. It's all quickly become as real, or unreal, as God or the war or Canada or the dead Guardsman, or at least as reliably confusing anyway. So, confusion, and imagination, too! It's all good, as the kids say, despite everything, though what do they know?

ACKNOWLEDGMENTS

Thanks, friends!

Lisa Alvarez, Gustavo Arellano, Wayne Clayton

Jonathan Cohen, Leslie Daniels, Kedric Francis

Federico Garcia, Ben George, Don Girard

Rhoda Huffey, Brett Hall Jones, Louis B. Jones

Dawna Kemper, Jim Krusoe, Michelle Latiolais

Diane Lefer, Bob Myers, Ryan Ridge,

Beth Riley, Tina Richards, Sally Shore,

Honora St. Clair, Linda Sullivan, Oscar Villalon,

Monona Wali, Ming-Yea Wei